ALEXANDER WILSON was a writer, spy and secret service officer. He served in the First World War before moving to India to teach as a Professor of English Literature and eventually became Principal of Islamia College at the University of Punjab in Lahore. He began writing spy novels whilst in India and he enjoyed great success in the 1930s with reviews in the *Telegraph*, *Observer* and the *Times Literary Supplement* amongst others. Wilson also worked as an intelligence agent and his characters are based on his own fascinating and largely unknown career in the Secret Intelligence Service. He passed away in 1963.

_a&b_

Wallace Intervenes

ALEXANDER WILSON

Allison & Busby Limited
12 Fitzroy Mews
London W1T 6DW
allisonandbusby.com

First published in 1939.
This edition published by Allison & Busby in 2016.

A CIP catalogue record for this book is available from
the British Library.

10 9 8 7 6 5 4 3 2 1

ISBN 978-0-7490-1840-5

Typeset in 10.5/15.5 pt Adobe Garamond Pro by
Allison & Busby Ltd.

The paper used for this Allison & Busby publication
has been produced from trees that have been legally sourced
from well-managed and credibly certified forests.

Printed and bound by
CPI Group (UK) Ltd, Croydon, CR0 4YY

CONTENTS

CHAPTER ONE

Foster Gets His Chance

A young man sat moodily in the comfortable depths of an easy chair of dark green leather, and gazed round him, from time to time, with an air of complete boredom. A newspaper and a couple of magazines lay on the floor at his feet, a tankard half-full of beer was on a table at his elbow. The large room, of which he was the only occupant, had the appearance of a flat in a West End Club. Sporting prints and pictures adorned the walls, which were distempered dark green, a colour which predominated, for the carpet, as well as the numerous armchairs, were also of that shade. At one end was a great bookcase packed tight with volumes; at the other a buffet. Several writing tables were placed at various intervals against the two remaining walls, in one of which was a large fireplace, now hidden by a screen, while each easy chair possessed as companion a small round table complete with ashtrays and matches. Undeniably a man's room, it was snug and restful. There was one peculiarity about it, however; it possessed no windows, being lighted day and night by several powerful though softly shaded electric globes. It was in fact underground, the basement of the drab building in Whitehall which, although so uninteresting to look at, is the home and headquarters of the British Secret Service. The rest room, generally known as the messroom, is reserved, as a rule, for the senior members of the department, but no objection is raised to its use by the half-dozen or so young fellows eager to make good in the exacting profession to which they have been appointed. Their selection, after the most exhaustive investigation into their antecedents and accomplishments, was considered all that was necessary to permit them the entry by the men whom Sir Leonard Wallace called his experts. They possessed their own room, but it was a small, not over-comfortable flat at the top of the building, and refreshments could not be obtained there.

Bernard Foster was one of the juniors engaged in the process of winning his spurs. The son of a famous soldier, he had passed from Shrewsbury School to Sandhurst, thence to the Guards. An extraordinary aptitude for languages, a daredevil temperament, and a spirit of adventure, however, had gained the interest of the Chief of the Secret Service, who had served under Foster's father while in the Army, and knew the son well. Bernard was presented with an opportunity of which he eagerly availed himself. Yet for eighteen months now he had been occupied in minor and routine matters. He knew he was being carefully observed all the time, his ability and disposition judged from a fresh angle – Sir Leonard Wallace took no chances with his assistants; he did not put them in charge of any important undertakings until he was certain that mentally, physically and morally they were suitable for the big things. So much depends on the Secret Service man. He must learn absolutely that his own honour, his life, count for nothing.

He must be prepared to face desperate odds, danger, death, with the realisation that there is no reward except the abstract one which goes with success in the service of the country he loves. Failure and exposure invariably mean complete obliteration; he can expect no help from the authorities; no help can be accorded him. Governments cannot recognise secret agents. A little carelessness, a lack of forethought, an impulsive word or action, may cause disaster. Where the welfare and honour of Great Britain is likely to be intimately concerned, Sir Leonard, of necessity, is extremely careful in his choice of the man or men to act. In consequence there is bound to be a hard and uninteresting period of probation before a young officer can expect to be delegated to the important roles with their difficult, perilous but highly adventurous aura.

Foster realised this; nevertheless, he longed for the time to come when he would be adjudged fit to take his place in the great game with men like Shannon, Cousins, Carter, Cartwright, and Hill, who, with Maddison and, of course, Major Brien, the deputy chief, formed Sir Leonard Wallace's little band of cracks. He had begun to fear that he was somehow not quite fulfilling expectations of him. Only that morning Willingdon, who had been appointed to the Intelligence Department at practically the same time as he, had been chosen for a mission of great importance. It was true that Willingdon had graduated to the Secret Service from the special Branch of New Scotland Yard, and had proved his capabilities on more than one occasion, but there were others. Downing, Cunningham and Reynolds had all been entrusted with work of a more exacting nature than any Foster had been instructed to undertake. It was no wonder he felt a trifle moody, therefore, when the thought would persist that he had failed in some manner to win the entire confidence of his chief.

He drained his tankard, and, rising to his feet, stood stretching himself. Bernard Foster was about the last person a casual observer would have imagined to be connected with the Intelligence Service. A little over six feet in height, he was lean with the healthy leanness of the physically fit athlete. A perfectly cut grey lounge suit rather suggested than hid the rippling muscles beneath. He had been a brilliant hurdler at school and Sandhurst had broken the records at the Royal Military College for the hundred yards and pole-vault and had equalled that of the two-twenty. In addition he was a very fine cricketer. Fair-haired and pale, he possessed a pair of sleepy blue eyes that gave him an air of bland innocence, an almost priceless asset in a man of his calling. A small, fair moustache adorning his upper lip helped to add to his ingenuous appearance, while a monocle which he frequently wore caused him to look thoroughly and completely guileless.

He was wondering what he should do to kill the time that was hanging so heavily on his hands, when a voice behind caused him to swing round. Confronting him was a small man with an extraordinarily wrinkled face and the figure of a boy. Everybody at headquarters was exceedingly fond of Gerald Cousins, perhaps Sir Leonard's most brilliant assistant. Foster almost went to the extent of hero-worship. He had learnt a great deal from the little man, who was always ready to place the benefit of his experience at the disposal of those keen enough to profit from it. The clouds left Foster's face immediately, a broad, cheerful smile replacing the gloom which had previously reigned there.

'By Jove! I'm glad to see you,' he exclaimed involuntarily. 'I've been feeling as blue as Oxford after the boat race.'

'Ah!' ejaculated Cousins; 'a joke methinks.' He placed his head on one side rather in the manner of a bird, and studied the young man towering above him. 'What's making you feel blue?'

'I'm eating out my heart for a job of work worthwhile. I have an uneasy feeling that the chief doesn't think I'm good enough or something. It's eighteen months since I joined the staff, and I've only been given jobs that any fool could have done.'

'There are some things,' returned Cousins, his eyes twinkling, 'which only fools could do. But cheer up, my lad. Haven't you learnt yet that the chief nurses those of whom he expects the most? At any rate, your time has come. I am just down from a conference with Sir Leonard and Major Brien, and my instructions are to send you up in ten minutes' time.'

Foster's eyes were no longer sleepy-looking. Open now to their widest extent, they positively blazed with excitement.

'What is it?' he demanded. 'What am I expected to do?'

'You'll be told by the chief. What have you been drinking – beer? Something light in the way of wine appeals to me most this sunny June morning. Where is Gibbons?'

'I don't know. He went out after drawing my beer for me. But, Jerry, can't you give me a hint? I'm in a state of – of—'

'Electrification,' supplied the other. 'I can see that. Never mind, you have only seven minutes, thirty-three seconds to wait. Gibbons!' he shouted.

A deep voice responded and, in a few seconds, a broad-shouldered, grey-haired man, whose luxuriant moustache and bushy eyebrows still remained their natural brown, hurried into the room carrying several bottles in his arms. He was an ex-sergeant of Artillery who, with a retired policeman, both of exemplary characters, looked after the fitful comfort of the men of the Secret Service.

'I've been getting up some wine, sir,' he explained apologetically.

'You must have known I was coming,' commented Cousins. '"Come, let us drink the Vintner's good health. 'Tis the cask, not the coffer, that holds the true wealth." How about forsaking beer for a glass of Moselle, Foster?'

The ex-guardsman shook his head.

'I want nothing more just now, thanks,' he responded. Cousins' face creased into a broad smile until every wrinkle seemed to contain a happy little grin of its own.

'"There is a tide in the affairs of man,"' he quoted, '"which taken at the flood leads on to fortune." Go to it Foster, and good fortune go with you.'

Feeling a sense of thrill throughout his whole being, Foster ascended to the floor whereon was situated the office of Sir Leonard Wallace. He stood for some moments outside the door attempting to gain complete control of himself, for the summons and Cousins' remark that his time had come had filled him with such exultation that he was rather afraid he might make a fool of himself in his delight. However, nothing was more unlikely. The Secret Service training teaches a man to hide completely his feelings if necessary, and Foster had learnt his lesson very well. There was no sound from within the room, which was hardly to be wondered at, as it was soundproof. He knocked loudly. Almost at once the door was opened by Major Brien, who greeted him with a friendly by smile, and bade him enter. Sir Leonard Wallace sat at his desk, his favourite briar held firmly between his strong white teeth. His steel-grey eyes bored deeply into those of Foster as that young man approached. Apparently satisfied with his scrutiny, Sir Leonard nodded his head slightly, and smiled.

'Cousins has told you that I have decided to give you a job of very great importance?' he stated rather than asked.

'Not exactly, sir,' was the reply. 'He told me you wished to see me, and certainly gave me to understand that the time I have been longing for has come at last.'

'You are keen to show us what you can really do?'

'Keen sir!' repeated Foster. 'I have thought of nothing else since I joined the service.'

'Very well, your chance has come. Sit down.'

Foster sat in the chair indicated, but declined the cigarette offered him. He was far too interested and inwardly excited to bother about smoking. Brien drew an armchair up to the other side of the great desk; threw himself into it. The manner of the two, particularly that of Sir Leonard, might have greatly disappointed a man who had not had Foster's opportunities of observing them. There was no indication in the demeanour of Wallace that he was concerned with anything but the most casual and unimportant matter. His unruffled, easy-going, unexcitable temperament, his air of complete nonchalance, had at one time deceived Foster as it had done so many others, but he had learnt, like those who worked with the chief, to recognise the dynamic driving force behind the calm manner, the brilliant brain, the working of which was cloaked by that lazy, attractive smile. Sir Leonard tapped out the ashes of his pipe into a handy ashtray, sat back in his chair, and regarded Foster.

'You get on very well with the ladies, don't you?' he asked surprisingly.

The young man started. Despite his efforts, his pale face coloured a trifle.

'I – I suppose I do, sir,' he returned slowly, 'but I have never really considered the question.'

'Well, I have,' commented the chief dryly. 'I have noticed that you attract them. Don't think you have been spied upon for any ulterior purpose. It is all part of the observation it is necessary to make of men who join the service, in order that I shall have full knowledge of them and how they are likely to fit in. You get along very well with young girls. I am wondering if you are likely to appear as attractive to a lady, who, though young and handsome, is also a widow and an experienced woman of the world. But that will be up to you, Foster. You will have to go out of your way to make yourself attractive to her, though that does not matter so much as the necessity for you to appear utterly infatuated with her. Ever been in love?'

'Several times, sir.'

Wallace and Brien laughed.

'Then you'll know how to appear in love again,' observed the former, 'but for goodness' sake don't let the real thing worm its way in. The lady in question is decidedly handsome, as I have already mentioned; in fact,' he glanced at Brien, 'she's reputed to be beautiful, isn't she?'

His second-in-command nodded.

'I believe so,' he replied. 'I haven't seen her, but she is certainly spoken of as one of the most beautiful women in Germany.'

'Who is she, sir?' ventured Foster.

'The Baroness von Reudath,' Sir Leonard told him. 'Now listen carefully to me, Foster. I have been watching your work and weighing you up for a long time, and am quite satisfied that you have the making of a very good Secret Service man in you. Quite candidly, though, I did not anticipate starting you off on independent work with an affair of such great importance. It happens, however, that the German secret police are very much on the *qui vive* these days. Every man who enters Germany is compelled to undergo a rigid scrutiny and investigation into his antecedents. Under the circumstances, Major Brien and I came to the conclusion that we would be taking a greater risk in entrusting the present project to one of the experienced, tried men than to you. Germany's espionage department is excellent. It is quite likely men like Shannon, Cousins, Carter, and perhaps Hill and Cartwright, who have been forced into the unwanted limelight on occasions, are known. They can all disguise themselves well enough to defy detection, I know, and their credentials can be made entirely fool-proof. Still there is always the unexpected element to contend with, no matter what precautions may be taken. Something unforeseen may arise which would cause betrayal. Once that had happened our plans would be ruined. It would become next to impossible for any of our agents to get a footing in the household with which we are concerned. You know quite well the drastic measures concerning everything and everybody the Gestapo is apt to take once it smells a rat.'

Wallace paused, and Foster smiled slightly. He was quite *au fait* with events in Germany and the methods of the secret police.

'Now in your case,' resumed the chief, 'no possibility can arise of your connection with us being either suspected or discovered. It was because I anticipated that such a necessity as this might occur that I have kept you wrapped in cotton wool for so long, so to speak. Mind you, as I previously stated, I did not foresee that an affair of such great importance would be your first big job, but there it is. I rely on you, and it is up to you to make good. On my suggestion you resigned your commission in the Guards like many another wealthy young man. You have earned the name of an idle man about Town, go to all the functions, and generally comport yourself as hundreds of others. No one, I am presuming, suspects your connection with this department?'

His grey eyes bored deeply into those of the man he questioned. Foster shook his head at once.

'Not a soul, sir,' he declared firmly, 'not even my mother and my sister. The guv'nor knew, of course. It was through him, I believe, that I came to your notice.'

'Not exactly,' smiled Wallace. 'I had been observing you for some time before he spoke. However, to resume: Whether His Excellency, The Supreme Marshal of State, von Strom, is himself in love with Baroness von Reudath or is merely very friendly with her, I do not know. It is certain, however, that they are on excellent terms, and that she is very much in his confidence. A report received yesterday from Gottfried in Berlin indicates that the Chancellor himself is also known to place some of his problems before her.' Sir Leonard smiled slightly. 'It is not necessary for me to explain how Gottfried obtained his information. I will tell you this much, though; the baroness possesses two companions. One is an English girl who was born and has lived most of her life in Germany – her name is Rosemary Meredith – the other is a German, Dora Reinwald. Miss Meredith happened to be at school with the baroness in Hanover. The war more or less ruined her father, and she was forced to seek her own livelihood when she grew old enough. Gottfried knew her well. It was partially through him and partially through Baroness von Reudath's own affection for her that she obtained the post she now holds. You will gather that she is one of us. You must have nothing to do with her; that is, if you succeed in becoming on intimate enough calling terms with the baroness. Any communication between you may only cause harm to overtake one or both. You will work entirely separately – she has her orders, you are now receiving yours. Of course I don't mean ignore her altogether. Simply behave towards her in the casual manner usual when meeting the paid companion of a friend.

'Baroness von Reudath arrives in London tomorrow. She will be entertained a great deal by the many friends she has here during her stay of a week or ten days. The day after tomorrow Lady Ashington gives a reception at which she will be present. You will receive a card, and Mrs Manvers-Buller, who has known the baroness almost as long as she has known you, will present you to her. With you it will be a case of love at first sight. For the rest of the baroness' stay in this country you will never be very far from her, but don't overdo it. If you gain her interest in you, then go wherever she goes until you have succeeded in becoming thoroughly intimate with her and – in her confidence. If she will have nothing to do with you, we must try other means of finding out what I want to know or else rely entirely on Rosemary Meredith. Presuming that you will succeed in becoming very friendly with the baroness, you will eventually go with her or follow her to Berlin. There you will get in touch with Gottfried, who will convey any future orders to you. As he is the Berlin manager of *Lalére et Cie*, what more natural than that you should go to him to purchase perfumes for your inamorata? Whatever you learn from the baroness concerning the three things I shall presently enumerate, no matter how trivial it may seem, and even though reported as a rumour, don't fail to inform Gottfried. But be very careful how you obtain your information. Sophie von Reudath is an exceedingly clever as well as a beautiful woman, and, if you once raise her suspicions against you, you will be done. If she speaks to you of these things, show little or no interest, appear to have one thought in your mind only and that your infatuation for her. Circumstances must guide you in your method of obtaining your facts without causing distrust. She may possibly talk of them to you, though it's most unlikely; you may overhear or see something, however, that will tell you a lot. In any case your job will require infinite patience, tact, and ingenuity. I recognise that I am staking a lot on giving a young, inexperienced man like you such a task, but you are the right type for the part I have cast you to play. It is certain your connection with the Secret Service is unknown and unsuspected; above all, I fancy I have discovered in you certain qualities which should prove of great value under the present circumstances. You have your chance, Foster; take it!'

The young man swallowed convulsively. He had never anticipated anything like this, and for a moment he found himself bereft of words. Eventually, however, he succeeded in murmuring huskily:

'Thank you, sir. I won't let you down.' His blue eyes met the grey ones of his chief with a look full of confidence.

'I am sure you won't,' smiled Wallace. 'Remember: if you are in any difficulties in Berlin, go and purchase perfume at the Lalére agency in the Unter den Linden and consult Gottfried. But never, under any circumstances, go to him if you feel you are in danger or suspected. No doubt of the bona fides of Gottfried or Lalére and Company must be raised. To all seeming, throughout the world, Lalére's is merely a famous and popular perfume firm. In Berlin Gottfried is one of the Prussians of the old school – a strong, fanatical devotee of the cult of *Deutschland über alles*. Nothing must occur to weaken or endanger his position in Germany. You must lose your life rather than imperil Lalére's. Understand that perfectly?'

'Yes, sir,' replied Foster firmly and at once.

'You will not be entirely alone. Once you are established in your friendship with the baroness, I will take steps to see that someone is nearby to help you in the event of trouble. But that someone will not be Gottfried. Now all that remains is to tell you what it is I hope you will succeed in learning from or through the baroness. The Marshal has formed and carefully drawn up secret military plans. It is believed that the final scheme was discussed and agreed upon at a private meeting in the residence of the baroness. The Chancellor and the Minister for Propaganda were the only others present. It is not known if the baroness actually took part in the discussion. I am anxious – very anxious – to know what those secret military plans are. The second item concerns a very deadly gas which is reported to have been invented by a German scientist named Hans Mohrenwitz, the third is a wireless ray invented by another scientist named Joachim Bräu, which is said to have the effect of putting aircraft out of action. I want details of the gas and the ray, every item of information concerning them you can gather, in fact. You may think I am setting you a herculean task, Foster, but I am only asking you to find out what the baroness knows. If she knows nothing, we must go elsewhere. That's all – for the present.' He held out his hand, which Foster gripped with great warmth. 'Good luck, Bernard,' was said in a tone of deep sincerity. Major Brien also shook hands and wished the young man good luck. Foster turned towards the door, with an unaccustomed though very happy lump in his throat. He had almost reached it when Sir Leonard called: 'You're twenty-six, aren't you?'

'Yes, sir,' replied the ex-guardsman.

'So is she,' murmured Wallace. 'What a delightful age for a romance!'

CHAPTER TWO

The Baroness von Reudath

Foster duly received his card for Lady Ashington's reception, and proceeded to the house in Belgrave Square wondering what the immediate future held in store for him. He was not blind to the fact that the path he would have to tread might prove to be one of desperate peril. Hitherto he had not been engaged on any enterprise overshadowed by much danger. Now, alone, unaided, he was expected to carry out a task that would quite likely involve him in trouble not only with the German secret police but with the Marshal of State himself. He certainly had been given his chance – a glorious chance – and he intended grasping it with both hands. Nevertheless, it must be confessed that he felt a trifle worried. Ever since he left school he had been thrown constantly in the society of girls, most of them his sister's friends. He had got on very well with them; had more than once imagined himself in love, only to find out that there was a disease that frequently gripped young men called infatuation.

This fact was pointed out to him by the girls themselves, who being very modern in their ideas, were extremely sensible. Now he was asked to become infatuated, or at least pretend to be infatuated, with an experienced, worldly-wise woman. The questions that bothered him were: Could he do it, and gain her interest and sympathy? Could he succeed without her seeing through the deception? He recognised the wisdom of Sir Leonard in selecting him for the part. He knew himself to be good-looking and attractive to members of the opposite sex – there was no nonsensical or mock modesty in the composition of Foster – in addition his circle of friends was acquainted with his amorous affairs, and would, therefore, not be surprised at another. It would be rather distasteful to make love to a woman with the purpose of worming important secrets from her, but a Secret Service man cannot regard his feelings or those of others when duty bids otherwise. Unpleasant functions make part of the price one has to pay for serving one's country in such a capacity. The disturbing thought occurred to him that he might find the young baroness distinctly attractive and, despite all his efforts to the contrary, actually fall in love with her. He had no illusions on the score that he was impressionable. To betray the woman one loved seemed a desperately low-down thing to do. He resolved to be on his guard from the very first, and avoid falling in love with her if he possibly could. But what difference would that make? It was his business to get her to fall in love with him, or at least become fond of him, wasn't it? As low-down to disclose the secrets of a woman who had conceived an affection for one, and therefore trusted one, as to betray the woman one loved; more so in fact. Such reflections caused a little frown to appear on his ingenuous face; he shrugged his shoulders rather painfully. Perhaps for the first time he was realising something of the unsavoury side of Secret Service life. His instincts rebelled against accomplishing anything by underhanded means, but it never occurred to him to attempt to back out; he would go through with his job to the bitter end no matter what it cost him personally. As a Secret Service man he had no right to personal feelings, and perhaps he comforted himself with the thought that nothing can be underhand that is performed in the service of country.

He arrived at Lady Ashington's stately home to find himself in the midst of some very famous people. His host and hostess greeted him charmingly, saying a few words to him before turning to welcome other guests, and leaving him free to wander about at will. He found several acquaintances, and entered into conversation with them, but all the time his eyes were searching, trying to catch a glimpse of the woman with whom he was to become infatuated. He saw no one quite resembling the description he had been given, and he did not mention her to any of his friends. Sooner or later, he knew, Mrs Manvers-Buller would arrive and pilot him to the baroness. She had appeared once from out of the throng, had smiled and nodded, but had passed on, which suggested that the baroness had not yet come or the time was not ripe for the introduction. Foster was a little intrigued by the position occupied by Mrs Manvers-Buller in the affair. He knew that she was a great friend of Sir Leonard and Lady Wallace, but he did not know that she had more than once been of much assistance to the Chief of the Secret Service; that she was, in fact, a kind of honorary member of the department. A great traveller, with an intimate knowledge of and acquaintance with some of the greatest diplomats in the world, she had, on occasion, passed on most valuable information to Wallace acquired during her peregrinations abroad. She possessed a tremendous, almost fanatical devotion to Great Britain and the Crown. If she had not occupied her very important position in society, and was not more useful to him as she was, it is likely that Sir Leonard would have offered her permanent employment in the Secret Service. He had known her since she was a girl at school with his sister. She had married the Honourable James Manvers-Buller, a man considerably older than herself, and it was through him that she had obtained her flair for diplomacy and international intrigue. He had been the first secretary of the embassy in Paris when he had died, just as he was about to be appointed to a higher post.

Foster saw Lady Wallace sitting with an elderly peer, and approached to pay his respects, not of course as one of her husband's young men, but as a friend of the family. She kept him in conversation for some time, her beauty sending a thrill through his receptive heart. He had known her for many years, but time made no difference. Whenever he saw her, the same feeling of worship possessed him. He was not unique in that respect. The charm and beauty of Lady Wallace makes slaves of all who know her. It is a tribute to her sterling character that women worship her with the same sincerity as do men. Sir Leonard is wont to declare that the greatest puzzle of his life is, and always will be, what she saw in him to cause her to love and marry him, but then the man who thinks least of Sir Leonard Wallace is notably Sir Leonard Wallace himself. Foster stayed talking to her as long as he dared, only tearing himself away when the baleful looks of the elderly peer told him that the latter considered him *de trop*. He departed in search of refreshment with some cronies of his, and it was while at the buffet that Mrs Manvers-Buller came to him. She chose the moment well. Surrounding him were nearly a dozen young men and girls, most of them engaged in twitting him about the air of boredom he had thought fit to adopt. Into the circle stepped Mrs Manvers-Buller, a small, bright-eyed, vivacious woman, leaning on the arm of an attendant cavalier.

'Did I hear someone say that our Bernard is bored?' she demanded.

A regular chorus gave an answer in the affirmative, and Foster grinned sheepishly.

'I never feel very happy at these affairs,' he confessed.

'Well, shall I show you how?' she asked. She turned to the man at her side, one of the under-secretaries of the government, spoken of as a cabinet minister of the near future. 'It would only be a kindness on our part to bring happiness into his young life. Don't you agree, Bunny?'

Several of the girls standing by laughed. The fact that Mrs Manvers-Buller addressed an important Member of Parliament as 'Bunny' struck them as amusing. The under-secretary did not view it in the same light. There was no doubt but that he felt his importance, and considered it undignified to be called by such a name, particularly before a crowd of young, irresponsible people.

'Why did you call Mr Erskine "Bunny"?' asked one smiling girl.

'He used to twitch his ears delightfully when he was a schoolboy,' explained Mrs Manvers-Buller. 'The performance thrilled my young heart, and I christened him Bunny. Won't you give a demonstration, Michael?' She turned to the frowning MP.

'Were you not talking of – er – bringing happiness into the life of Foster?' he asked hastily, amid further laughter.

'Oh, so I was,' cried the little woman. She slipped her disengaged arm into that of Foster. 'Come along, Bernard,' she commanded, 'we'll introduce you to Sophie von Reudath. She'll be a change from these bright, unsophisticated young things.'

'He'll fall in love with her,' jeered one of Foster's companions.

'So much the better,' pronounced Mrs Manvers Buller. 'Sophie likes to be loved – I think it's time she found another husband.'

'Oh, I say,' protested Foster. 'Isn't this rather like leading a lamb to the slaughter?'

'You won't consider it slaughter when you see her,' was the response.

As they crossed the crowded room, the under-secretary leant down until his lips were very close to Mrs Manvers-Buller's ear.

'Do you think this is – er – judicious?' he whispered. 'Foster is rather impressionable, and the baroness is known to be a very warm friend of the—'

'Bunny,' interrupted the little woman, 'you have an evil mind.'

They found the Baroness von Reudath holding a little court in an alcove. Sitting on either side of her were two cabinet ministers, another stood close by; various other important people, men and women, stood or sat in the vicinity. Foster started to draw back, but Mrs Manvers-Buller had no intention of letting him go. She was a privileged person, and into the circle she stepped, to be greeted by the baroness with a little cry of delight.

'My friend,' exclaimed the latter in perfect English which had hardly any trace of a foreign accent, 'I thought you had deserted me.'

'Why this relief to see me, Sophie?' demanded the outspoken little woman. 'Have these intriguing statesmen, knowing you are *persona grata* with the powers that be in Germany, been attempting to pump you?'

'Pump me! What is that?' asked the baroness.

Laughing protests came from the ministers. They felt no sense of resentment against Mrs Manvers-Buller. Everybody liked her; apart from which it was generally recognised that she was a very valuable little lady. In addition, they felt that perhaps it had been a trifle unsporting to get the baroness to talk about conditions in Germany, especially when she was visiting England on a holiday. Foster studied the Baroness von Reudath with a great deal of interest. At first sight of her he had had difficulty in suppressing a gasp of sheer admiration. She was certainly beautiful; more beautiful that he had imagined. Her corn-coloured hair was brushed back from a high, flawless forehead, and caught up artistically at the nape of her neck. She was no stranger to the use of cosmetics, but obviously applied them sparingly. Delicately pencilled eyebrows surmounted a pair of frank blue eyes framed by long, dark lashes. Her nose was small and well-shaped, her mouth could not have been better conceived by an artist, her ears, from each of which hung a valuable pearl, were shell-like in their daintiness. She possessed a pure, creamy complexion. Altogether a woman any man might be proud to— Foster pulled himself up abruptly. There he was – thinking of her already as something to be loved, forgetting that she was the confidante of perhaps the most dangerous man in Europe, a woman who was probably the holder of secrets that might at any time mean war. There was something else besides beauty in her face. The broad forehead, the determined little chin, the almost arrogant tilt of her head proclaimed intelligence, strength, character. Altogether a glamorous personality. Foster began to fear that he was already more than half in love with her. He felt that he liked best about her the frankness of her eyes. She was as straight as a die, he thought, the last person in the world to betray any secret that had been confided to her care. He reflected that his task had suddenly assumed gigantic proportions, and for more reasons than one.

Mrs Manvers-Buller shooed away the statesmen as though

they were so many sheep, declaring that Baroness von Reudath did not want to be bothered by a lot of hoary-headed old sinners, when young men were longing to enter the realms of beauty and romance with her. They went meekly, one or two chuckling, one or two sighing, perhaps regretting their lost youth.

'Really, Elsa, you are too terrible,' declared the baroness, her eyes twinkling merrily, 'you make one feel hot and cold all over.'

'I am glad you feel something,' retorted her friend with mock severity. 'You should be ashamed of yourself casting your spell on the venerable *seigneurs* who fondly imagine they are ruling England.'

'But if they do not rule,' laughed the baroness, 'who does?'

'The newspapers, my dear. But let me present to you a very bored young man who declared that he is never happy at an affair like this.'

The Baroness von Reudath had already cast approving eyes on the tall, well-set-up figure of Bernard Foster, whose faultless evening attire showed off his lean, athletic form to perfection. The introductions were effected.

'If you are not happy why do you come?' queried the baroness.

'God knows,' remarked Mrs Manvers-Buller, answering for him. 'The young men, far more than the girls, obey the dictates of society like a litter of puppies running after their mother. If you ask them why, they will make some fatuous remark about its being the thing to do. They turn up in top hats, stiff collars, and morning coats to attend the Eton and Harrow cricket match even in the hottest weather. I say attend, because nobody goes there to see the play – they'd be fools, if they did, for there isn't any worth talking about. If it were the fashion to bathe naked in the Serpentine in the middle of winter, they would do it, simply because it would be the thing to do.'

Sophie von Reudath's laughter rang out in a silvery peal, while Erskine and Foster eyed each other with somewhat embarrassed looks.

'Really, Elsa,' began the former, 'you do—'

'Now don't you pretend to be a prude, Bunny,' interrupted the little lady. 'I heard that you joined a nudist colony last summer.'

''Pon my soul! This is too much,' cried the scandalised under-secretary. 'Who libelled me so grossly?'

'Nobody, my Bunny. Really, you're too serious to live. Take me somewhere where there is champagne with ice tinkling musically in the glass.'

They wandered away together and, before long, Foster found himself alone with Sophie von Reudath. She made room for him on the lounge by her side.

'Tell me about yourself, Mr Foster,' she begged. 'Are you also a Member of the Parliament?'

'Good Lord, no,' he returned with more force than politeness 'I beg your pardon,' he added hastily. 'I did not mean to be so vehement, but I can imagine few things more futile than being a Member of Parliament.'

'Oh, but why?' she asked. 'Surely an ambitious man would have his hopes centred on a position in the Cabinet, and what could be greater than to be one of those governing your country?'

'Few can attain to such heights,' he told her, 'and fewer still succeed in arriving before their best days are over, and they are half-senile, doddering old men.'

She laughed.

'Your sentiments,' she declared, 'are very much like those of Elsa.'

'Well, it's the truth,' he persisted. 'Young, energetic, enterprising men are kept back to a ludicrous extent in this country. The old hang on to their jobs like grim death, and are terrified lest a younger man gets a foot into the nest they have made so comfortable for themselves. It is not only the case in Parliament. The same thing applies in the big firms, even in sport.'

'You sound as though you are bitter about these gentlemen.'

'It is because old men who are long past their best hold the reins in this country,' he went on, 'that we have become such an unenterprising nation.'

'I wonder if Britain is really so unenterprising,' she mused.

'Of course it is. You belong to a nation that is far more enterprising and go-ahead. I sometimes think you Germans must smile at our futility.'

'I am not a German, my friend!'

He turned and looked at her, surprise showing in his face. She noticed that, for once in a way, his eyes had lost their customary sleepy look; decided that he was far more alert that she had supposed, and liked him the better for it.

'Not a German!' he repeated. 'Why I thought—'

'My husband was a German,' she told him. 'I am an Austrian – a Viennese. But you have not told me yet what profession is yours.'

'I am a gentleman of leisure,' he replied with a half-ashamed grin. 'I was in the Guards, but resigned my commission. There is not much fun in soldiering in peacetime.'

'You would like a war?' she asked quietly.

'Heaven forbid!' he cried earnestly. 'I hope there will never be another war.'

'My feelings are exactly as yours in that matter,' she declared. 'Another war would be too terrible to contemplate.'

For some minutes she spoke lightly with several people who had strolled up, while Foster rose and stood impatiently waiting for them to go. His impatience was not assumed. He wanted to have her to himself in order that he could gradually allow her to see that he was becoming infatuated with her. His desire to be alone with her was not altogether from a sense of his duty. She fascinated him; he found her a very charming companion. It seemed, however, that his wishes were doomed to disappointment. No sooner did one person or party wander away than another approached. At last, when they were again alone for a few seconds, very daringly he suggested that they should seek a place free from interruption.

'I have never met anyone quite like you, Baroness,' he explained hastily, 'and I should very much like to be able to talk to you without others constantly butting in. It's horribly selfish of me, I know, and please tell me if you think I have stopped with you long enough.'

While he was speaking her eyebrows rose slightly, and he feared for a horrible moment that he had offended her. Then she smiled gloriously, and rose.

'You shall find a quiet spot,' she agreed, 'but I cannot give up too much time to you, Mr Foster. I have a duty to my host and hostess which I must not neglect. Where shall we go?'

Rather surprised that she had acquiesced but decidedly elated, he led her out into the gardens, which had been decorated with innumerable little coloured electric lights and in which cane chairs and tables had been placed. Many of the guests had sought relief out there from the heat of the crowded rooms, but Foster found two chairs and a little table in a secluded position in the midst of a clump of rhododendrons. The early June moon looked placidly down from a clear sky, like a benevolent deity keeping watch and ward over puny mankind. The baroness sank into her chair, with a little sigh of pleasure; accepted a cigarette from her companion.

'It is delightful out here,' she decided; then, after a short pause; 'So you have no profession. That is a great pity, Mr Foster.'

'I suppose you think I am a waster,' he murmured ruefully.

'No; I do not think that. It would be foolish of me if I did. It does not require great perception to know that you have much character and many good qualities. But like many of the young men of these times you regard life from a wrong angle. You are too quiescent – I think that is the word I need. A little while ago you spoke of the men who continue to hold the power in their hands, and keep younger and more energetic men out. You like others, resent it. Yet you take no steps to alter these things.'

'What steps could we take short of staging something like a revolution?'

'It would need no revolution to force the men in power to recognise you and your rights. Supposing that all the men in this country below the age of fifty, no matter what profession is theirs, united together and demanded recognition, what would the result be? Why, my friend, the government would no longer remain in the hands of those who have grown old and weary, the army and navy would not be controlled by officers who lack energy and enterprise because age had taken its toll of them; the courts would not be presided over by judges and magistrates whose minds were no longer alert. The same thing would apply to all other professions and trades. The young would hold all predominant posts. I do not mean the too young. A man is at his best from the age of thirty until fifty – perhaps to fifty-five. After that he should be content to retire, and make way for a younger personality. After all, when one has worked hard for thirty years, one deserves to enjoy leisure. It is in my mind that there would be little unemployment if fifty-five were universally considered the retiring age. There would be no necessity for what you call the dole. The money put aside for that would be paid out in pensions to those who had worked hard and deserved it. I feel that you young men who grumble are to be blamed. You would only have to assert yourselves in unity to obtain your rights. It is not fair to scoff at the lack of enterprise in those who hold the power, when you yourselves are so much unenterprising as to permit them to do so.'

'I suppose you are right, Baroness,' agreed Foster, thinking at the same time that he, at least, was a member of a service – perhaps the most enterprising and successful in the world – which was entirely controlled and in the hands of comparatively young men. The oldest member of the staff was Maddison, then about forty-six. Sir Leonard Wallace himself, he knew, had recently only reached his thirty-eighth birthday. Perhaps, however, it was unfair to think of the Secret Service as a shining example of youthful enterprise, when it was a profession in which only youngish men could be expected to succeed. The hazardous nature of its demands, the strain, the difficulties could only be faced and endured by men physically and mentally in perfect condition. Foster felt a little bit ashamed at having given the baroness the impression that he had no profession. The more he learnt to know her, the more he hated deceiving her. He wondered what she would think if she discovered the truth. 'But in your own country,' he went on, 'there are many men holding important positions who are well over the age of fifty-five.'

'If you are referring to Germany,' she returned a trifle coldly, 'I wish you to remember that it is not my country.'

'But—' he commenced, and paused for a moment abashed. He

wondered why she persisted in her assertion that she was not a German. 'You do not consider,' he queried presently, 'that your marriage to a gentleman of German nationality made you of that race?'

She shrugged her dainty shoulders.

'According to law – yes, but not otherwise. I am an Austrian, and very proud of it, Mr Foster, even though my poor country has been divided up and impoverished until it is almost obliterated. The heart of Austria still beats fervently and firmly, and you must not think, like so many people, that Austria and Germany are names very nearly synonymous. But to resume our discussion, you say there are many men holding important positions in Germany who are over fifty-five years of age. You are incorrect to say many. It is certain that there are fewer than in this country. Those who govern are nearly all young men.'

'What about the President?' he asked.

'Ah!' she exclaimed, and he could see the gleam of her little white teeth, as she smiled. 'He is little but a figurehead. A great man – that was. He is content now to leave all to a younger and more virile man.'

'The Chancellor is a great friend of yours, is he not?' asked Foster greatly daring.

She was silent for a while.

'Yes,' she murmured at length 'he and I are very good friends. He is an Austrian also,' she added, as though in explanation.

'But not, I think,' he remarked quietly, 'as fervent an Austrian as Baroness von Reudath.'

'Perhaps not,' she agreed. 'He could hardly be expected to be under the circumstances.'

They were silent for some moments.

'I wonder,' ventured Foster at length, 'why you have been so kind to a dull nonentity, as to sit out here with him, when there are so many interesting men and women present only too anxious to claim your attention.'

'I do not consider you a nonentity at all Mr Foster,' she replied, adding frankly: 'I like you, otherwise I would not have come here with you. Perhaps also I am a little tired of talking politics and entering into the tortuous paths of diplomatic conversation. You see I am not trying to hide from you the fact, which is well known, that I have been concerned in political affairs in Germany. It would be a useless evasion, would it not? I am well aware that at the reception tonight are many who would like me to talk of Germany in the hope of learning something from me. Out here with you I am free from that, at peace, and in very pleasant company.'

'It is nice of you to say that,' he murmured.

'It is nice of you,' she corrected gently, 'to spend your time with me when, I am sure, there are many charming girls anxious for your society.'

'There are none here half as charming or as beautiful as you, Baroness,' he whispered.

She laughed softly.

'S'sh! Do not pay me such compliments – I like sincerity in my friends. Compliments without sincerity are very cheap, Mr Foster.'

'What I said was sincere – nothing could be more so, Baroness,' he assured her earnestly. 'I meant every word.'

'So . . .' She was silent for a moment, and he thought to hear a little sigh. 'I believe you,' she murmured presently. 'Thank you, my friend. Now we must return to the house. I am afraid we have already stayed away from the others too long.' They rose, and she took his arm. 'I had almost forgotten I am young also,' she confided. 'You have made me remember.'

'I am glad,' he told her with simple sincerity. 'Presently I shall be separated from you by more important people. Before I am forced to take leave of you, may I make a request, Baroness?'

'Of course. What is it?'

'I badly want to call on you. May I?'

She turned her face towards him and, in the moonlight and the illumination cast by the little lamps, he saw that she was smiling gloriously.

'I shall not forgive you, if you do not,' she vowed. 'As perhaps you know, I am staying at the Carlton. I shall expect you tomorrow at four, Mr Foster.'

CHAPTER THREE

Amid The Rhododendrons

'How did you get on with the baroness?' asked Mrs Manvers-Buller, a little later.

'Splendidly,' Foster assured her.

'I'm so glad. Be as kind as you can to her, Bernard. She's a dear girl. Your job is not too pleasant, is it?'

He stared at her with incredulous eyes.

'Then you know?' he gasped.

'Of course I know.' She smiled at him. 'I know a very great deal. Perhaps that is why I am so anxious that Sophie should not be hurt.'

'I won't hurt her, Elsa, if I can possibly help it.'

She patted his hand affectionately.

'I know you won't. I can't understand what she sees in that von Strom. He certainly seems to have blinded Sophie pretty effectively. One of these days, though, Bernard, everybody's eyes will be opened at once; then our friend the Marshal will fall with a bump that will shake Germany from end to end.'

'Elsa,' came in plaintive tones from Major Protheroe, 'need you stand flirting with that young fellow before my very eyes, when I am longing to take you into the garden.'

'I haven't said yet that I want to go with you into the garden,' she retorted.

Nevertheless she went. Foster was left on his own. Instead of rejoining the circle of his own intimate friends, he also wandered out once again on to the lawn. He felt he wanted to be alone, to think. Unconsciously his steps took him in the direction of the remote clump of rhododendrons where he and the baroness had sought seclusion. There seemed no one in that part of the gardens, and he was about to make his way to the chair he had previously occupied, there to sit, smoke, and think in peace, when the murmur of voices caught his ears. He pulled up abruptly, rather surprised that the sequestered little spot was occupied after all. He decided that he had almost interrupted a lover's tête-à-tête, and was glad that the soft, springy turf had silenced his footsteps. He was about to creep quietly away, when he caught a name, followed by a phrase in German. For a moment he stood irresolute; then approached closer to the rhododendron bushes on the side behind the chairs and stood listening. The phrase in German coupled with the name of Mrs Manvers-Buller had decided him. He knew that the baroness was in the house; had seen her taking refreshments with a crowd of other people just before he had emerged. Who else but she would be likely to talk German, and why was the name of Mrs Manvers-Buller mentioned? He disliked eavesdropping, but this seemed to be a case of necessity. It would be easy enough to retreat once he had ascertained that he was listening to a harmless conversation. There followed a silence so prolonged that he began to wonder if the occupants of the chairs had moved away or had heard him, and were keeping quiet on purpose. Suddenly, however, someone laughed.

'Why are you amused?' asked a woman's voice in German.

'I was thinking,' came in the deeper tones of a man speaking the same language, 'of the indignation of the little Sophie, if she knew that her movements were being watched by you and me. His Excellency does not like this tour of hers at all. He was particularly against her coming to England.'

'And you really think Frau Manvers-Buller is likely to be a bad companion for our Sophie?'

'My dear, it is known that the lady is the great friend of Herr Wallace, and we all know of the position he holds in this country. Who is to say that she does not act for the British Secret Service? It is no secret that the baroness and the Supreme Marshal are extremely friendly, and that he goes to her, and sometimes confides in her, perhaps under the force of his passion for her, for it is believed that he loves her deeply. Frau Manvers-Buller may quite well attempt to obtain from the baroness the secrets that have been confided to her.'

'Then she will fail,' replied the woman. 'No secret that is ever imparted to Sophie will be revealed without permission. She is staunch, and you know it. I hate this unpleasant task of following her about, and periodically searching her belongings. It is one thing to be of the espionage service, but quite another to be forced to spy on a very sweet woman simply because she *might* divulge something which His Excellency wishes to be kept secret. You and I know that it is nothing of any great importance we also know that this Frau Manvers-Buller has been friendly with Sophie since she was a child. Why then should she be suspected simply because Sophie has come to England, and because she happens to be friendly with the Chief of the British Secret Service? It is all a great waste of time, Carl.'

'Perhaps you are right. Nevertheless, His Excellency has given the orders, and it is for us to obey.'

'A fine man he is to give orders for the woman he is supposed to love to be spied upon!' The contempt in the woman's tone was unmistakable.

'S'sh, Hanni! What sentiments are these? If you said that in Germany, you would be likely to get into serious trouble.'

'We are in England, not in Germany.'

'But you will be returning, and then—'

'And then you will report what I have said! Is that so?'

'Certainly not,' protested the man. 'You do me a great injustice. Do you not know how deeply I love you?'

'About as deeply as the Supreme Marshal loves Sophie, I suppose. You men, whether the highest or the lowest, are all the same. Women are fools to trust you. Sophie, no doubt, has great belief and trust in His Excellency. Yet he has her spied upon. I tell you, Carl, I am sick of the business, for I have become very fond of Sophie.'

'What harm is there in it so long as she does nothing to betray the confidence reposed in her? If she does, it will be our duty to act. In that case I feel sure you will be the first to do your duty.'

There was silence for a few moments.

'How did you come here?' asked the woman.

'From the mews at the back. It was easy.'

'Why did you come?'

'Because at such a function as this people are more likely to endeavour to worm from the baroness what is not hers to tell.'

'You could not trust me to keep watch on her?'

'My dear Hanni, two are always better than one. Also, I was not sure that you would be brought. It is not usual for a maid to accompany her mistress to receptions.'

'You know very well that I always do. She likes to have me at hand to attend to her in case of necessity. It has been so since her illness.'

'And why is it that I find you wandering in the garden?'

The woman gave vent to a sound of impatience.

'Have I not already told you that I followed her and the young man, and listened to their conversation here?'

Foster started.

'Yes; that is so,' agreed the man. 'It was entirely innocent, you say?'

'Entirely innocent, my suspicious Carl,' was the reply, delivered in mocking tones. 'I am beginning to believe you are anxious that the baroness should do something wrong.'

'By no means, Hanni. I would regret it very much if she committed any action inimical to Germany.'

'Well, she has not, and will not.'

'Who was he – the young man sitting here with Sophie?'

'My friend, how do I know? His name I did hear, but I have forgotten it. As I told you, Sophie was telling him that he and the young men of England should assert themselves and not grumble because the old men hold all the good positions. It was delightful to hear her advising him like a mother. But I do not think that one could ever be assertive. He is too unintelligent and sleeping-looking. One of those who live for pleasure and nothing else.'

This time Foster smiled broadly. It was rather refreshing to discover the opinion the German woman had conceived of him.

'I must go in,' he heard her say. 'Soon the guests will be departing. Next time, when the baroness goes to a reception or a party, Carl, I advise you to leave watching her to me. There was no sense in coming in here. What could you do?'

'Well, what are you doing?' grumbled the other.

'Sitting with a man,' retorted the woman tartly, 'who is keeping me from my duty both to my mistress and to His Excellency. Perhaps I shall have something to say when we return to Berlin about the foolishness of my comrade.'

'I am only doing what I conceive to be my duty.'

'Conceive it in a more sensible manner in the future. You will look rather ridiculous if you are caught here.'

'I will not be caught,' was the confident reply. 'I will sit here until the guests are gone, and all is silent; then I will quietly go away.'

Foster, however, had other ideas. The discovery that the baroness was being spied upon by orders of the very man who gave her his confidence had roused a feeling of utter contempt in him. Like the German woman, he was inclined to say, 'A fine lover indeed!' But was von Strom Sophie's lover? From the very depths of his heart Foster hoped that he was not. The very thought gave him a sense of dismay; he hated the idea of any man having anything but the purest relationship with the girl he had already learnt greatly to admire. Of one thing he was convinced: the Baroness von Reudath must have been the recipient of very important secrets of the German Supreme Marshal, despite what the people he had overheard had said, otherwise, why should it be necessary to spy on her? It appeared that Sophie, after all, possessed the information which it was Foster's duty to collect. More than ever now his task appeared distasteful to him. But it was his intention to put a stop, if he could, to the activities of the man who had so confidently stated that he would not be caught. He did not wish to appear himself in the affair, because of his future actions, but he knew Major Brien and Sir Leonard Wallace were present at the reception. He had caught sight of them once or twice. Perhaps he would be able to get hold of one of them, and tell him before the fellow moved from his retreat. Waiting until the German maid had gone, Foster crept quietly towards the house. He was fortunate. The guests were departing, but he came upon Major Brien talking to a friend in an alcove. A Secret Service man engaged on a mission does not openly speak to another he may meet who is not in the case with him. But there are methods by which they indicate that they wish to communicate with each other. Foster passed close by Major Brien softly whistling a certain tune. He took no notice of his superior, but walked on into a little room which he found vacant, and entered. There he waited. In less than two minutes Brien strolled in; closed the door behind him.

'Well?' he queried in a low tone.

Foster plunged quickly into a succinct account of the conversation he had overheard, concluding by repeating the man's statement that he would wait where he was until the way was clear.

'I thought,' went on the young man, 'that it might be a good idea, sir, if he is discovered and arrested for trespassing. It would then mean that the baroness would for the future be watched by one person only, and one who is more or less sympathetically disposed towards her.'

Brien shook his head slowly.

'As soon as the woman knew that her fellow spy had been apprehended,' he declared, 'she would inform her employer, and someone else would be sent to take his place. It is much wiser to allow this fellow to go free, unsuspecting that he is known; then, for the future, you will have the advantage of knowing him as well as the woman when you see him, and can be on your guard accordingly. You obtained a glimpse of him, of course?'

Foster's jaw dropped. He had been too full of the idea of having the fellow arrested for trespassing to think about endeavouring to see what he was like. He confessed his omission very apologetically. Brien frowned a trifle, but did not reprimand him.

'You'd better get back as quickly as you can,' he ordered, 'and do your best to repair the error. You may be in time. Be careful he does not see you or suspect your presence. Afterwards go to Sir Leonard's house and, if he is not there, wait for him.' Foster hurried away without another word. As the door closed behind him, Brien slowly shook his head as though stricken with a feeling of doubt. 'I wonder,' he murmured to himself, 'if his lack of experience is going to let him down on this job!'

Feeling a little dismayed and rather annoyed with himself for failing to see the matter from the same angle as had Major Brien, Foster returned to the gardens, and stealthily made his way in the direction of the clump of rhododendrons. He made up his mind then and there that, in the future, he would weigh up every possibility before taking action. He had been given a demonstration on how risky it was to act on impulse; wondered why it had not occurred to him that it would be a great advantage to know the spy, also that the fellow's arrest would only mean his being replaced by another whose identity was unlikely to be revealed to him. He reached the great clump of evergreen shrubs without making a sound, and positioned himself where he knew he was bound to see the German when he emerged. The moon had set, but the multitude of little electric lamps still remained alight, and would provide ample illumination to enable him to obtain a very fair view of the trespasser. Several minutes passed by, and he began to fear that the man had already gone. Gradually a feeling of despair began to take possession of him. What a fool he had been to lose an opportunity which, he now realised, would have meant so much to him in the future. He was young and inexperienced, and perhaps may be forgiven for almost permitting a groan to escape from his lips at the thought that he had blundered right at the beginning of his first big job as a Secret Service agent. It was fortunate that he suppressed it.

Nearly a quarter of an hour had passed, and he was quite certain in his own mind that the German had gone, when suddenly, without warning, a man stepped into the open, glanced cautiously about him, and went hurriedly but with stealthy tread towards the mews at the rear. A great wave of relief surged through Foster, as his eyes eagerly took in an indelible, though perhaps somewhat blurred, portrait of the fellow who had been sent to watch the Baroness von Reudath. He was of medium height, rather stockily built. A soft hat was drawn low over his forehead, but, as he had looked up towards the house, Foster had glimpsed a clean-shaven, hawklike face, with large gleaming eyes and flashing teeth. Above all, a scar ran from the lobe of his left ear to the point of his chin. The Secret Service man was satisfied that he would recognise the German again anywhere. As he knew his first name was Carl and would also recognise his voice, he now felt no fears for the future.

It was a much happier young man who returned to the house than he who had left it. All the guests were gone, and only a few servants were about. They viewed Foster's appearance with a good deal of surprise, but, yawning prodigiously and murmuring to the butler that he must have fallen asleep in the garden, the Secret Service agent departed, found his car, and drove to Sir Leonard Wallace's residence in Piccadilly. He was shown at once to the cosy study which the chief designated as his den. There he found both Sir Leonard and Major Brien awaiting him. They greeted him with friendly smiles, and he was told to mix himself a drink, and sit down.

'Did you succeed in obtaining a view of the fellow?' asked Wallace.

'Yes, sir,' replied Foster.

He proceeded to give a description of the German, but was cut short.

'I also saw him and the woman,' explained Sir Leonard. He smiled at the look of surprise on the young man's face. 'I watched you and the baroness go to that delightfully secluded spot among the rhododendrons,' he went on, 'and witnessed the arrival of the woman. When you and the baroness returned to the house, I followed the maid. Close to it she met the man who had apparently been in hiding there. He accosted her, and they returned to the arbour. I had the satisfaction of listening to their conversation from the beginning. As the woman repeated your discussion with the baroness practically word for word, I was able to assure myself that nothing was said of a nature dangerous either for you or for Sophie von Reudath.'

Foster felt rather puny somehow as he listened with wide-open eyes – and ears – to the chief's recital.

'Did you know I was there, sir?' he asked.

'I saw you arrive,' nodded Wallace, and again the young man felt very small. It had never occurred to him that another person might have been listening to the conversation he had overheard.

'Don't look so dismayed!' smiled Sir Leonard. 'I took good care that nobody would see me. If you had searched you would not have discovered me. You have done very well, Foster; very well indeed. All I wish to urge upon you is not to act on impulse in the future. "Look before you leap" is a pretty good maxim for a young Secret Service man.'

Foster felt grateful for the kindly words. Nevertheless, he still considered that he had made rather a bad mess of things that night. If the chief and Major Brien had not been present at the reception he was rather of the opinion that he would have made a complete muddle of the whole affair. Sir Leonard realised how he was feeling, but added nothing further by way of comfort. He was well satisfied that his junior would be all the better for the chastening effects that a little harmless blunder or two would have upon him. Better for him to make a small error at the commencement of his career, when he was under supervision and could benefit from it, than a tragic mistake later on when he was working entirely on his own.

'We have been discussing,' resumed Wallace, 'whether it would be wise to inform the baroness that her actions are being spied upon. On the whole I am inclined to refrain from giving her warning. Knowledge of that sort might quite well render her so indignant that a breach might take place between her and von Strom. In that event she herself would probably suffer severely and, at the same time, we should not be able to obtain all the information we desire from her, for though it is plain she must know a good deal, I don't think she is aware of everything – yet. Keeping her in the dark about the man and woman spying on her means that an extra duty devolves on you, Foster. Not only must you do your utmost to discover what she knows, but you must protect her from these people, and prevent any suspicions rising in their minds against her. I was delighted to find that you got on so very well with her.' He smiled. 'Not a difficult matter to become infatuated with a woman like that, is it, Foster?'

'It would be difficult not to, sir,' returned the young man frankly, adding a little diffidently: 'I believe she is absolutely straight, sir, and not at all the kind to betray a secret confided to her.'

'I agree with you, absolutely.' nodded Sir Leonard. 'I took the opportunity of studying her, and am quite convinced that mentally and morally she is as beautiful as she is physically. That renders your job a hundred times more difficult – and more distasteful, too, I've no doubt. But it is your job, and you must allow no other considerations but that fact to creep into your mind. I believe you are calling on her tomorrow?'

'Yes, sir. At four o'clock. She suggested the time herself.'

'Excellent. She obviously likes you, which is the main thing. Next week she goes to Budapest. When she informs you, beg her to allow you to accompany her. By then you must appear hopelessly in love with her. We'll hope she will have fallen in love with you.'

Foster looked down at the carpet rather miserably.

'It – it seems so horribly low-down, sir,' he murmured.

Sir Leonard rose and patted him on the shoulder.

'It is,' he agreed, 'but it's all part of the price you and I, and all of us, have to pay for the privilege of serving our country. You don't want to back out, do you?'

'Back out!' exclaimed Foster, looking up hastily. 'Never!'

'Of course you don't. I have a feeling that when the show is over you won't find that it has been so distasteful after all.'

'You mean—'

'I mean nothing – just yet. Now run along, and don't lose sight of the fact that you have two spies to keep your eye on and prevent from suspecting either the baroness or yourself.'

'What about Mrs Manvers-Buller?' queried Brien. 'Didn't those people speak of her as a dangerous woman?'

'The man certainly did.'

'In that case, she had better be warned, hadn't she?'

Sir Leonard smiled broadly.

'Leave her to me, Bill,' he suggested. 'I'll take care of her, while the baroness is in London anyway. Later on she'll have someone else to take care of her – though she's perfectly capable of taking care of herself.'

'What do you mean by someone else taking care of her?' demanded Brien.

'Haven't you heard? This evening she accepted the hand and heart of Major Protheroe of the Horse Guards.'

'Good Lord!' exclaimed Foster involuntarily.

'Bully for her!' cried Brien with enthusiastic cordiality.

CHAPTER FOUR

Tête-À-Tête with the Baroness

Promptly at four on the following afternoon, Foster presented himself at the Carlton Hotel and asked for the Baroness von Reudath. He was shown up to her suite; found her awaiting him in a drawing room that was a mass of blooms. Standing in the midst of all those beautiful flowers, wearing a frock of some clinging material that showed off her slender form to perfection, the young Englishman decided that she looked more wonderful than ever. His eyes frankly shone with admiration, and the colour stole softly into her cheeks. She greeted him with outstretched hands, over which he bowed almost reverently.

'You see, my friend,' she declared, 'I am alone. I have kept one hour entirely for you.'

'I don't know what I have done to deserve such an honour,' he murmured, 'but I very much appreciate it. It is charming of you.'

'In you I know I have found a real friend,' she told him seriously, 'and genuine friends are very, very precious in this world. I have so many acquaintances, so many people who pretend they are friends, but who, I know, are not. I need someone very badly upon whom I can rely, Mr Foster.'

'You can always rely upon me, Baroness,' he assured her. He felt guilty, as he spoke, but, though it was his duty to learn from her the secrets she possessed, and impart them to his government, he, nevertheless, was quite determined that he would prove a very true friend to her in all other ways. That reflection did not go far towards salving his conscience, but it was, at least, soothing. 'I feel very proud and gratified,' he added, 'that you have singled me out as a friend, especially after such short acquaintance.'

She sank into a chair, and invited him to take another close to her own.

'Perhaps I am a very good judge of character,' she remarked, 'perhaps it is that Elsa told me so much about you.'

'Told you so much – about me!' he gasped. He was startled, apprehensive for a moment that Mrs Manvers-Buller had given him away. Then he laughed. Such an idea was, of course, absurd. 'I hope she told you nothing to my discredit,' he added in an effort to cover his momentary confusion.

She eyed him questioningly for a second or two; then she, too, laughed.

'I do not believe there is anything to your discredit in your life,' she pronounced, 'unless it is that you are not proud that you are susceptible to feminine attraction.'

'Did Elsa tell you that?' he demanded.

The baroness nodded, smiling a trifle mockingly at him the while.

'It is surely nothing of which to be ashamed. I think there must be something wrong about a man who is not impressionable. It is in our natures, is it not? But I know that one day to you will come the real thing; then you will love with all your soul, and for always. How you will love!' she added almost in a whisper. Then again she laughed up at him. 'How foolish you will think me! We will have tea.'

She rang a bell and, almost immediately, a waiter wheeled a little trolley into the room with the tea things. They spoke of casual matters until they were alone again; then she reverted to her first topic.

'I was wrong to give you the impression, Mr Foster, that I was entirely without friends. I have three, and they are very dear to me, but they are women. Elsa is one – unfortunately I do not see much of her these days – then there are two charming girls, Rosemary Meredith and Dora Reinwald, who act as my companions. Rosemary was at school with me, Dora I have known nearly all my life. I know they would do anything for me. But as I say, they are women. There are so many things a woman cannot do. I have no real man friend, one in whom I can put absolute trust. That is why,' she added candidly, 'I am glad that in you I have, at last, found one. You see, I know it, without asking you. One does know these things. Is that my woman's instinct, I wonder!'

'Your instinct has not played you false,' he murmured, 'but you talk as though you are in danger, or, at least, in trouble. Is it so?'

She laughed almost harshly.

'I am in deadly danger,' she declared, looking him full in the eyes. 'Sometimes I am afraid, but not often. I am not quite sure what it is I fear.'

At once he had moved his chair closer to hers.

'Tell me what it is,' he urged earnestly, 'and I swear to you, Baroness, I will do my utmost to protect you.'

She leant across and gently took his hand in hers.

'There are things,' she told him, 'of which I cannot speak – at least not yet. Perhaps someday I will tell you. I am happy to receive your assurance that you will protect me if the necessity arises. I fear that I am only a very cowardly woman after all, and I had thought that I was different from the rest. It is very comforting to know that I have now a protector in the real sense. Since my husband died, there has been no man to whom I could turn for advice and assistance. I am afraid poor Kurt was not of much use. He was thirty years older than I, and rather self-centred. Ours was not exactly a love match, but he was my husband. Since his death, there has been no man in my life at all.'

A wave of sheer relief and delight flowed through Foster. No man in her life at all! Then his fears were groundless – the fears that had entered his heart as a result of the conversation he had overheard the night before. The Supreme Marshal of State might be in love with her, but he was not her lover. It did not enter his head to doubt, for a moment, her words. She might be a very clever woman, experienced in international intrigue, and playing a part in the political world, but she was frank and honest. Of that he was absolutely certain. She could have no possible object in asking for his friendship, except the very natural one of a woman in trouble desiring the support and protection of a man on whom she felt she could rely.

'I cannot tell you,' he proclaimed, 'how glad I am that you have chosen me as your friend. You will never regret it, Baroness – at least, I hope you will not,' he added as an afterthought, his profession and his duty flashing into his mind with uncomfortable emphasis at that moment.

'Regret it!' she echoed. 'Of course I shall not. I confided in Elsa how badly I needed a friend. I am indebted to her for bringing you to me.'

Inwardly Foster felt inclined to curse Elsa, but decided at once that his feelings were unjustified. Surely he could be a real friend to the baroness and, at the same time, do the job that had been set him. Would he, after all, be betraying her, if he learnt from her the secrets she possessed and imparted them to his chief? In that way he would perhaps be helping to prevent another ghastly war, and she herself had declared to him that she was against war, asserting that another would be too terrible to contemplate. Foster suddenly felt that he was beginning to see daylight. It was conceivable that the plans of the Supreme Marshal had been told to her; that she had declared herself against them and, though too staunch to divulge them, was now in danger, because the man who was reported to be her lover feared that she might. That would explain why she was being watched. The reflection made him feel a great deal happier in his mind; he was perhaps not such a Judas after all. He decided to attempt to find out, if he could, what relationship, if any, actually existed between her and the Supreme Marshal.

'You have a friend – a man friend,' he remarked quietly, 'who is also extremely powerful. Have you forgotten him?'

She eyed him questioningly, her brows meeting together in a little frown.

'To whom do you refer?' she asked.

'The Supreme Marshal of State! Did you not admit that he was a friend of yours?'

He was astonished at the expression which, for a moment, transformed her face. It was gone almost as soon as it had come, but he was watching her closely. It suggested hatred, naked, uncompromising. What had caused it he was unable to decide at that moment, and whether it was directed against von Strom or himself. He could not conceive any reason why she should hate him, unless, by some means, she had discovered the part he was playing; neither could he imagine why she should hate the man who, though he might not be her lover, was certainly on intimate terms with her. The look made him think deeply. He wondered if again he had been implusive by accepting her at his own valuation of her. Suddenly she laughed, with all the silvery cadence which was able to thrill him so deeply with its music, but he was now on his guard more, and thought he detected a strained note in it.

'He is not a friend of the kind I need – like you, my friend,' she told him. 'Perhaps you also have believed the tales which have been told about him and me.'

'What tales?' he asked innocently.

'I know it has been said by evil-minded people that we are lovers; that I am his mistress.' Suddenly tears sprang to her beautiful eyes. 'It is untrue,' she cried vehemently, 'utterly untrue. Never was anything more wicked concocted in the minds of jealous people. I have not cared much before that such things have been stated, but I cannot bear that you should believe them. You do not, do you?'

She looked at him imploringly, all at once very much of a young, appealing girl. He marvelled at the mood which could so quickly transform her. His frank, open smile did a lot in helping her to recover full control of herself.

'I am inclined,' he chided, 'to feel insulted at your asking such a question of me, Baroness. Of course I do not believe such tales. I would never believe anything like that of you unless—' he hesitated.

'Unless what?' she demanded quickly.

'Unless you assured me they were true yourself.'

'You would believe me?'

He nodded.

'Yes; I would believe you, because I do not think you would ever tell me an untruth.'

The clouds cleared entirely away; she smiled at him now quite merrily.

'You are very trusting, are you not?'

'I trust you,' he responded earnestly.

Her pale, creamy complexion became suddenly suffused with colour.

'Oh, dear!' she cried. 'You and I have become all at once very intimate in our conversation. How surprised other people would be who knew that yesterday you and I met for the first time.'

'That is the value of friendship – a real, genuine friendship,' he reminded her.

'You are right. It is because of our friendship also that I did not wish you to think evil of me. The opinions of others I do not mind, but the good opinion of the very dear friend I have found means so much to me.'

'Thank you, Baroness,' he murmured gently.

'To you, I cannot be "Baroness",' she proclaimed. 'It would be ridiculous. You shall call me Sophie, and I will call you Bernard.'

'How did you know my name?' he queried curiously.

'Ah!' she laughed. 'How do I know so many things about you? A little bird with the name of Elsa whispered to me so much, Bernard.'

'The Elsa bird seems to have been very busy,' he grunted.

She helped herself to a cigarette, and pushed the large silver box towards him.

'I think I already owe a great deal to her. Yet what is the use?' she suddenly cried in vehement tones. 'It is wonderful to have your friendship, to know that I can depend upon your protection. But what use can it be to me?'

'Why not?' he asked in profound surprise.

'I am only in this country for a few days. Next week I go to Budapest, afterwards to Berlin again. How can your friendship help me when I am no longer in London.'

'I shall no longer be in London myself,' he told her quietly. 'Wherever you go, I will follow. I shall always be at hand – at least, while danger threatens you.'

Her eyes opened wide. In them he was certain he recognised dawning hope.

'Do you really mean that?' she asked.

'I certainly do, Sophie.'

There was a little caressing note in his pronunciation of her name for the first time. She noticed it, and again the colour stole into her cheeks.

'But this is too good – too wonderful of you!' she exclaimed. Once more, however, her manner changed. She shook her head peremptorily. 'It cannot be,' she declared almost sharply. 'You must not come.'

'Why not?'

'Because you would be endangered. No, Bernard, you must keep away.'

He laughed.

'Do you think,' he asked, 'that I would stay back, because I might otherwise go into danger? Can't you think that I would account any danger that might threaten me through you as nothing, so long as I were at hand to protect you?'

She regarded him for a moment, a look of tenderness in her eyes.

'Why do you feel like that about me?' she asked softly.

He looked down at the carpet under his feet; felt his own face grow hot and flushed.

'Please do not ask me, Sophie,' he murmured. 'I might say something foolish.'

For several moments there was a profound silence in the room. The tick of the clock on the mantelpiece seemed to grow incredibly loud. He looked up to find her eyes fixed on him with such a look of tender yearning in them that he was startled. He half rose; then threw himself back in his chair.

'To think,' he heard her say gently, 'that twenty-four hours ago you and I did not know each other. It seems impossible.'

'It is impossible,' he retorted, and was astonished to find how husky his voice had become. 'I believe you and I, Sophie, have been friends since the beginning of time. We have only just discovered it, that's all.'

'What a very nice thought! I think perhaps you are right.' The determination returned to her manner and voice. 'Nevertheless,' she persisted, 'you must not go with me to Berlin.'

'That's a pity,' he returned easily. 'I should much have preferred to travel with you. However, if you forbid it, I shall have to follow.'

'You are determined?'

'Absolutely.'

'You are a much more resolute person that I first imagined,' she declared with a little smile.

'And you,' he retorted, 'are far less of the cold, experienced woman of the world.'

'I am glad you have found that out about me. And now,

Bernard, much as it distresses me, I must send you away. I have many engagements. Perhaps tomorrow—'

'Tomorrow,' he declared, as he rose, 'whether you have engagements or not, I will call at eleven in the morning, and kidnap you. I will drive you out of London, and we shall spend a day in the country.'

'Oh,' she sighed, 'how delightful that will be!'

'You won't mind being kidnapped?'

'I shall love it.'

He departed, without seeing anything of her maid or of the two companions. He wondered if the former had been listening to the conversation. If so, she had heard nothing of any particular significance, unless she considered that the decidedly sentimental turn that the conversation had taken, and Foster's avowed determination to accompany Sophie to Berlin and act as her friend and protector, would interest her employer. The young man smiled grimly as he reflected that it would probably interest him very much indeed. Well, let it. He felt he knew how to look after Sophie and himself as well. He would have been convinced that there was nothing at all of the cold, experienced woman of the world about the baroness had he seen her just after he left. She stood for some moments gently stroking the hand on which he had imprinted a kiss, her eyes, in which was the softest light imaginable, gazing into vacancy. At length she stirred, went into her bedroom, threw herself on the bed. 'Sophie,' she murmured, to herself, 'what a little fool you are!' Her maid entered quietly to find her lying there weeping gently, and stole out again, her woman's heart torn between affection and duty. Duty, that cold, unfeeling monster, won. Thus the conversation between Foster and the baroness was reported to the fellow called Carl, who relayed it to

Berlin. The recipient of it, a man who had an iron grip on all Germany, promptly went into a towering rage, and began to hatch in his mind a scheme which eventually had dire consequences to more than one person.

Foster duly called for the baroness next morning, and found her awaiting him. He drove her into the beautiful byways of Surrey and Sussex, and she was enchanted. They had a simple but marvellously cooked luncheon at an old inn, tea at a charming farmhouse. When eventually they returned to the Carlton, to find to their amusement that a stream of callers had been enquiring for the baroness, she declared that she had never been happier or had had a more delightful time in her life.

Thereafter Foster took her somewhere almost every day during the remainder of her stay in London. In consequence, he became decidedly unpopular with the people who felt they had a right to a certain amount of her society. However, they were forced to be content with meeting her at the receptions, balls, and at homes which she could not avoid. Foster seldom attended these. He disliked formalities of that kind; besides which, he knew he could not expect to have Sophie to himself at them, and matters had now reached such a pass that he hated being one of a crowd round her. He and she spoke no more of the danger which she had hinted was threatening her. She volunteered no information concerning it, while he made no effort to question her. Her remark that there were some things of which she could not yet speak, but perhaps someday would tell him, had caused him to hope that voluntarily she might give him the information which it was his business to obtain. He was a trifle puzzled by her. During their trips together she spoke often of Austria, and it was not difficult to gather that she possessed a deep, abiding love for the country of her birth. This caused him all the more to wonder why she continued to reside in Berlin, since her husband was dead, and, above all, associate with von Strom and the German Chancellor, who, although of Austrian descent himself, was believed to have no particular affection for that country. It was quite well known that his ambition was to unite Austria and Germany, and make of them one large nation. Baron von Reudath had, shortly before his death, been very friendly with the Supreme Marshal. It was because of that that Sophie had been whirled into international politics, her shrewd common sense and keen judgement having, thereafter, proved of great value to von Strom; so much so that he had come to place immense reliance in her and discuss his problems with her.

The knowledge of this caused Foster to feel thoroughly amazed as he observed her keen enjoyment of their trips together. It was not a pose. She took an almost child-like pleasure in the outings. They certainly did her an immense amount of good. Two years previously, he learnt, she had had a bad accident, which had caused her heart to be severely strained. For a time her life had been despaired of, but a great physician in Vienna had pulled her through. He announced, however, that she would have to be careful, and would be more or less an invalid for the rest of her life. His prognostications had happily not been fulfilled. Gradually she had become stronger, though subject, from time to time, to fainting fits, especially when in a crowd. It was for that reason that she invariably took her maid, who was a trained nurse among other things – one of which Foster knew, and she did not, was membership of the German Espionage Department – to receptions, balls and theatres with her. She had come to London partially to consult a famous specialist in order to obtain a final opinion on the condition of her heart. Her doctor in Vienna had told her that she was now quite cured, a specialist in Paris had agreed with him. She pinned all her hopes on the diagnosis of the famous man in Wimpole Street. Foster and her maid Hanni accompanied her on the eventful visit, waiting anxiously in an anteroom. She came to them at last, her eyes sparkling, her cheeks glowing.

'It is true – there is no doubt!' she cried joyfully. 'He was very careful, very thorough, and he says I am in perfect health – my heart is now as sound as a bell. How I love your English idioms, Bernard.' She threw her arms round the maid's neck. 'How relieved you will be, my Hanni,' she laughed. 'No more need you accompany me to the receptions and fetes which must have bored you so much. I will not faint again – that is certain.'

'It a long time is since you did zat,' remarked Hanni in laboured English.

'I know, but there was always the doubt. You will be glad to be relieved of that irksome duty – yes?'

'Never am I tired of mine duty doing.'

'Noble Hanni,' applauded Sophie.

Foster felt he could apply another and far more deserved, as well as descriptive, adjective to the woman's name, but for obvious reasons refrained. He told Sophie with simple sincerity of his great delight at the doctor's verdict. She took his arm happily.

'Come!' she bade him. 'We will go and celebrate.'

Foster met the two companions, of course, and liked them both. It was not long before he found that they were entirely devoted to the baroness. Once, when he looked up from some snapshots the latter was showing him, he found Rosemary's gaze fixed on him. In her eyes he read sorrow and compunction; guessed that she found the task set her by the department she served as distasteful as he was doing. He wished he could have talked the matter over with her, but that was forbidden. He had been instructed to hold nothing but the most casual intercourse with her. She and Dora Reinwald presented a great contrast. Rosemary had beautifully waved brown hair, grey eyes, a slightly *retroussé* nose, and naturally scarlet lips that were most attractive in their shapeliness. She was, as a rule, vivacious, merry, and bright. Dora was of the pure Hebrew type. She had black hair parted in the middle and drawn back from her tiny ears. Her face was pale and serene, oval in shape, and perfect in every feature. Her eyes were large and dark containing in their depths that suggestion of remoteness which is so typical of her race. In her figure and all her movements she was amazingly graceful. Knowing of the unpopularity of Jews in Germany, Foster wondered how it was that Sophie retained in her service, apparently without question, a girl who was so obviously Hebrew. The three women were great friends – not once did her attitude towards the other two suggest that the baroness was mistress, they her paid companions, and Foster liked her all the better for it.

Without going near headquarters the Secret Service man daily reported to either Sir Leonard or Major Brien. There was never anything of much importance to tell them, but the chief insisted on his carrying out the routine. He was certainly interested in the baroness' announcement to Foster that she was in danger, though she apparently did not know exactly what it was she feared. Her statement that perhaps she would one day tell the young man of certain things she could not at present divulge also interested Sir Leonard, and set that astute mind of his very busily to work. Taking care, as he had been warned, to neglect nothing, however trivial it may have appeared to him, Foster did not forget to mention the look of hatred that had momentarily flashed across the face of the baroness, when he had reminded her of her admission that Germany's Marshal of State was her friend. This item of information caused a smile to spread over the chief's face.

'I think you can go ahead with your job, Foster,' he had declared, 'without your conscience worrying you any longer.'

Foster pondered over the remark without being able to understand the significance of it. He would have liked to have asked what Sir Leonard had meant, but could not bring himself to put the question. For one thing, it is not quite usual for junior agents to question the Chief of the Secret Service, for another, he rather feared that the answer might give him an unpleasant jolt, might in fact hurt. He could no longer disguise from himself the fact that he was deeply, irrevocably in love with Sophie. Here was no case of infatuation; it was undoubtedly, irresistibly, painfully the real thing. He was afraid that Sir Leonard's remark might mean that she was not worth consideration, for some reason or other and, though he would never believe it, even from the chief, he felt he could not bear to hear it. He had done exactly what he had been warned not to do – fallen in love with her. Whatever suffering would accrue from that fact was his own responsibility entirely. But how could a fellow help falling in love, especially with a wonderful, altogether charming woman like Sophie von Reudath?

Sir Leonard meditated on the inevitable with mixed feelings. Although Foster did not know it, his association with the baroness was carefully watched, and it was not long before Wallace was quite certain that his junior was actually and hopelessly in love. He was not surprised, or annoyed, neither was he gratified. The situation bade fair to present too many complications for him to feel much pleasure in it. A man pretending to be in love is quite a different proposition from a man really in love.

'It has its compensations,' he remarked to Major Brien,

philosophically. 'We certainly have one thing for which to be greatly thankful.'

'What is that?'

'The fact that she is also in love with him.'

'Do you really think she is?'

'Absolutely. She has surprisingly fallen a victim to his sex appeal, or whatever it is one falls a victim to, considering that she is generally considered to be an experienced worldly-wise woman.' He sent for Cousins. When that little man appeared: 'You and I will be taking a trip to the continent soon, Cousins,' he announced, 'and, for obvious reasons, will have to be disguised.'

'What as, sir?' queried the grotesquely wrinkled Secret Service man.

'That I have not quite decided. We shall probably change a good deal. It is always safest to appear as a native of the country one is in on occasions like this. As we shall be going to Germany, and it is almost certain that her very efficient secret police will be looking for us, or for someone from this department, we cannot afford to take risks.'

CHAPTER FIVE

Hungarian Nights

During the last two or three days of the Baroness von Reudath's visit to London, she made several attempts to dissuade Foster from accompanying her to Budapest, thence to Berlin.

'Why,' she would ask, 'should the danger which is threatening me also be allowed to fall on you?'

'For a very obvious reason,' was his answer, but he would not declare that reason, though all the time he longed to tell her it was because he loved her.

It is certain, however, that Sophie knew very well what he meant. Her remark, on one occasion, that that obvious reason was the very one which most caused her to wish he would stay in London was significant. At all events, she, of course, failed entirely to persuade him to let her go alone. His refusal, it must be confessed, gave her a great deal of frank pleasure even though she was honestly worried at the thought of leading him into peril. She declined to give him any indication of the direction in which danger lay and of what it consisted, despite several attempts on his part to find out.

'It is best that you should know nothing at all,' she told him; 'at least not until I am certain the danger really exists and is imminently menacing us. It will be time enough to tell you everything then.'

'It may be too late,' he warned her.

How prophetic words can sometimes be! He remembered his remark afterwards. So did she, at probably the most terrible moment of her life.

It was a glorious morning when they left London. Quite a large crowd collected to bid the baroness farewell at Victoria, and there were many significant smiles and whispers when it was seen that Foster was accompanying her.

Two attachés at the German embassy regarded the young Englishman with haughty, disapproving stares – much to his secret amusement.

Crossing over on the boat Foster caught sight of the man Carl sitting on a seat near the stern between two elderly ladies. He saw him again on the train. For a member of the German Espionage Department he did not seem particularly astute, but Foster reflected that the man had no reason to fear that he was known or suspected. The Englishman also remembered with a grin the opinion of him expressed by the maid, Hanni, which shows that one can never judge by appearances. In any case he considered Carl a fool. A man like that would not last in the British Secret Service a day. Sir Leonard Wallace would not tolerate carelessness. One of his invariable rules was that no matter whether an agent was certain or not that his identity was unknown to a party he was watching he must not expose himself under any consideration whatever, unless, of course, he was in disguise.

The journey to Budapest was almost a dream of delight to Foster. There is nothing, as a rule, either dreamlike or particularly delightful about train travelling even in the luxury expresses of the Continent, but he felt thoroughly happy. Except at night he spent practically the whole of the time with Sophie and perhaps during the trip they learnt to know each other completely. It is certain that, on several occasions, he was on the point of revealing to her the secret of his heart which really was no secret at all, at least to others, but then there is a trite, though very true, saying that lookers-on see most of the game. Rosemary Meredith and Dora Reinwald certainly did. With infinite tact they effaced themselves, and little was seen of them. The woman, Hanni, also took care to appear only on rare occasions to discover if her mistress had need of her.

A suite of rooms had been engaged for the baroness and her companions at the Hungaria Hotel in Budapest. Foster obtained a bedroom on the floor above which faced upon the Danube and the hills of Buda immediately beyond. It was an amazing apartment, very large and furnished luxuriously in the finest Empire style. Napoleon, it was apparent, had left his influence on the Hungarian mind. The high double doors ornamented with gilt relief, the walls covered with silken panels, the enormous chandelier hanging from the centre of the ceiling, the mahogany furniture upholstered in green brocade, the heavily draped windows, magnificent mirror, and deeply panelled, floriated ceiling gave the young Englishman the feeling that he was lodged in a palace. He had never been in Budapest before, and he decided he was going to enjoy the experience immensely.

Before dressing for dinner he and Sophie walked for a while on the Corso. There is something of the colour of the East about

Hungary, even the language was totally different from any of the European tongues Foster knew. The people interested him. There was something strong, vigorous and animated about them. They showed nothing of the bitterness of a race that had been tyrannised and oppressed for centuries; were eloquent in their cheerful vitality of the power of humanity to survive terrible disasters. Sophie knew Budapest, in fact the whole of Hungary, well, loved the people and the country almost as much as she loved her own. After dinner she suggested a visit to the Dunapalata roof restaurant. There they were escorted to a table in an advantageous position, from where they had a perfect view of the Danube, looking dark and fascinating far below. The declining moon threw into vivid relief the hills and castle of Buda, tinging them with an air of mysterious beauty wholly enchanting. The orchestra played a fast Viennese waltz and Foster became absorbed in watching the rapid whirling of the dancing couples. All the men and women were exceptionally well-groomed. Several officers, most of them in sky blue uniforms, danced with girls who could only be described as beautiful. The Englishman felt he had never seen so many pretty faces in one place at the same time before. Sophie loved dancing, but had perforce been compelled to give it up on account of her heart trouble. Now that she had been declared by three specialists perfectly fit, she was eager to commence again. Foster was no less keen to dance with her, though he had been rather diffident at suggesting it. He found that she danced divinely, became anxious lest she should think him an indifferent exponent of the art of Terpsichore. Such is the timidity and humbleness of love. As a matter of fact he was an excellent performer, and Sophie was quick to tell him so, a compliment which pleased him immensely. Thereafter they danced until well in the early hours of the morning. It is a tribute to his self-control that he did not tell her of his love for her as they danced that night. Her head reached just above his shoulder, and her lovely fair hair, shining dazzlingly under the brilliant light, fascinated him, the faint, attractive scene of it threatened to intoxicate his senses. The feel of her lithe body sent thrill upon thrill through him, causing him to long to clasp her tight to him. Although dancing with her was a sheer delight, it yet had its tortures, albeit even they were very sweet. On the way back to the hotel she was silent for so long that he questioned her about it.

'I think happiness makes me quiet,' she murmured in reply. 'Perhaps I am afraid that if I talk I will break the spell. Intrigues and politics seem very, very far away tonight, Bernard.'

'Why do you concern yourself with matters like that?' he asked impulsively. 'You were made for happiness and – and—' he paused in confusion.

'Were you going to say love?' she questioned softly.

'Yes,' he replied huskily. 'You were made to love and be loved. There is nothing of love in international politics, Sophie.'

'You are right,' she agreed in a low, bitter voice. 'Nothing but heartache and humiliation. For me there can be no thought of love until my task is finished.'

It was the first time she had gone so far as to tell him that she was engaged in an actual occupation. He started slightly. What task could it be to which she referred? Was she actively employed with the Supreme Marshal on a scheme possibly calculated to put Germany in an unassailable position of power? Gently he asked her to tell him what she meant.

'Not now,' she whispered. 'I think, though, that before very long I shall tell you all. There is just one link to a chain that I wish to find, afterwards you will help me to connect the whole chain together.'

'You are talking in riddles,' he complained, feeling indeed extremely puzzled.

'I am sorry, Bernard, but I do not wish to involve you. If you insist on coming to Berlin with me, it is best for you to know nothing at all. It will be easier then for you to avoid danger, or for me to keep danger from you.'

'But Sophie, I—' he began vehemently.

She gently placed her hand on his lips.

'S'sh I . . .' she murmured. 'I know the necessity of this. You do not. When the time comes I will tell you everything, never fear, and you shall help me. Afterwards, perhaps together, we will come back here to enjoy ourselves without any shadows to spoil our happiness, or go to my own beautiful Vienna. What do you think, my dear friend?'

'I shall be happy with you wherever it may he,' he whispered, 'but as your love for Vienna is so great, Sophie, let us go there by all means.'

After five glorious days in Budapest they drove over the Margaret Bridge to the isle of St Margaret's in the Danube. There they sat in the rose garden at Floris's, consuming tea and iced cakes, and taking delight in the laughter and light chatter round them. The garden was crowded with people, most of the women being dressed in chiffons and large hats, which gave them an appearance of gaiety eminently suitable to their prevailing characteristics. Foster felt thoroughly content. It was an idyllic spot in which to lounge with the woman who had taken such complete possession of him. But his contentment and hers were doomed to be rudely shattered. They both caught sight at the same time of Dora Reinwald approaching them. In her pale, usually serene face was an expression that told them she was the bearer of unpleasant news.

'Dora!' exclaimed the baroness, suddenly turning pale. 'What can she want with me? What is it?' she demanded in German as the girl reached their table. 'Why have you come here?'

'I thought it would be better,' replied Dora. She possessed a deep contralto voice, which contrasted attractively with the delightful silvery tones of the baroness. 'A courier has arrived from Berlin. I decided that you would rather be prepared to meet him than confront him without warning.'

Sophie's blue eyes opened wide. She was obviously very much startled. Watching her, Foster decided she was also momentarily stricken with fear, and again wondered of what she was frightened. He took good care to appear as though he did not understand.

'God in Heaven!' muttered the baroness in a voice that could hardly be heard. 'What can this mean?'

'He has a letter for you from His Excellency,' the girl told her. 'He says it is urgent. I pretended I did not know where you were, but told him you would be back for lunch. He has reserved a room at the Waitzner-Gasse, but announced that he would wait at the Hungaria for your return, as his orders were to place the document in your hands at the earliest possible moment.'

Sophie had fully recovered herself by the time Dora had finished speaking. She even smiled.

'It was sweet of you to come and warn me, dear,' she remarked gratefully. 'Where is Rosemary?'

'On this island, I think, at the Strand Bath with some English people.'

'Try and find her, will you? Warn her not to tell this courier where I am in case she goes soon back to the hotel and meets him. I want to have time to think. Perhaps Herr Foster and I will not return until this evening. If we do not, Dora, and the courier grows alarmed, inform him that I must have gone for some excursion, but must certainly return in order to dress for dinner.'

'Very well, Baroness.'

The girl hurried away, and Foster resumed the seat from which he had risen at her approach.

'Is there anything wrong?' he enquired innocently.

Sophie's face seemed suddenly to have become haggard. The beauty remained there, but she looked older.

'Forgive me for talking in German, my friend,' she begged. 'But it is my own language and it was natural to use it since Dora addressed me in it. I forgot you did not understand. A courier has arrived from Berlin with a letter for me.'

'Is there anything unpleasant in that? If it is none of my business, please say so, but you looked startled, and I—'

'I was startled. I think it means that I must leave for Berlin almost at once.'

'You mean, cut short your stay here?'

She nodded slowly.

'Yes. The happiness your companionship has given me has, I believe, abruptly been ended.'

'But surely,' he cried in dismay, 'our companionship can continue in Berlin?'

'In Berlin, my Bernard,' she murmured sadly, 'I will not be any longer my own mistress. All the time I will be at the – what is it you say in English? Ah! I know – at the beck and call of others.'

'But—'

'You are full of "buts",' she interrupted with an attempt at gaiety. 'Is it not your great Shakespeare who says, "But me no buts!"? I may be wrong. Perhaps His Excellency does not bid me return. I think, however, that it is so. What a pity that a time so delightful is to be so soon cut short!'

'Must you go?' demanded Foster. 'What right has he to order your return?'

'It will not be exactly an order, Bernard, but it will amount to the same thing. If I dared, I would not go.'

He regarded her with troubled eyes.

'I don't understand. Why is it you dare not refuse?'

'Because there is something I must know. If I knew that thing now, Berlin would never see me again.'

CHAPTER SIX

Summoned to Berlin

They lunched at the Dunapalata, afterwards going for a long drive by the banks of the Danube. On their return they swam together in the pool of the Gallert Hotel, later taking tea on one of the terraces. It was exactly six when they entered the Hungaria Hotel. They were hardly inside the lounge when a man rose from a chair made his way towards them. He was tall, military-looking, his grey lounge suit fitted him to perfection, but he gave the impression that he was more used to uniform than to civilian clothes. Handsome up to a point, Foster thought his lips a little too thin, his light blue eyes set rather too close together. His moustache and hair were blonde, the latter trimmed very close to his head. As he stopped two or three yards away, clicked his heels together, and gave the jerky little bow typical of the Prussian, Sophie seemed to become aware of him for the first time. She gave a little cry of genuine-sounding pleasure.

'Major Wilhelm! This is a delightful surprise. What are you doing in Hungary?'

'I am the bearer of a letter for you, Baroness,' he informed her.

'A letter! From His Excellency, do you mean?'

'Yes, Baroness.'

'That is nice. But why could he not send it by post? Is it very important?'

'Extremely important. I was told to deliver it into your hands without the slightest delay. I arrived this morning, and have awaited your return very anxiously ever since. No one seemed to know where you had gone, though your companions expected you back to lunch.'

'We decided to have a day out – my friend and I,' she explained laughingly. 'I did not know, you see, Major Wilhelm, that I was to receive a visit from you. You are staying at this hotel?'

'No, Baroness; I have reserved at the Waitzner-Gasse.'

'Oh! But you will give us the pleasure of your company at dinner?'

'I shall be delighted.'

'Good! Now please give me this important letter.'

'Your pardon, Baroness. If you will do me the honour of inviting me to your private suite, I will there hand it to you. There are certain matters which I am to convey to you by word of mouth, and this crowded lounge is hardly the place for confidences.'

'How mysterious you are,' she laughed. 'Very well; you shall come with me to my drawing room.'

Foster had moved a little aside during this conversation. The unperturbed, gay manner of the baroness had provoked his admiration, knowing, as he did, how much the coming of the courier had upset her. He did not fail to observe that, from time to time, the latter cast covert glances in his direction, glances that could hardly be described as friendly. Sophie turned to the Englishman, reverting to his language.

'I must introduce you, my friend,' she declared. 'This is Major Ernst Wilhelm, who has come all the way from Berlin to give me a letter. Is it not kind of him.' The underlying note of sarcasm was quite lost on Wilhelm. He returned the Englishman's bow stiffly when she presented Foster as, 'A friend who has helped to make my holiday in England and Hungary very pleasant. I have persuaded him,' she added, 'to come with me to Berlin, when I return. Englishmen who have not seen Berlin do not realise what they miss. Is that not so, Major Wilhelm?'

Her eyes shot a challenge at the German officer, who had frowned a little at the announcement that she had invited Foster to accompany her to Berlin.

'It is only natural,' returned Wilhelm in excellent English, 'that the Germans should be proud of the capital of their country.'

'I have often promised myself a visit,' proclaimed Foster. 'The baroness has helped me to make up my mind.'

He wondered why she had taken the trouble to declare that she had persuaded him to agree to make the journey. Could there be any harm in making a plain statement of fact that it was actually he who had insisted on going with her? Would such a declaration have caused trouble, and was she attempting to shield him from that possibility?

'I can assure you, Mr Foster,' observed Wilhelm, 'that you will like Berlin – if you go.'

The significance of the last phrase was not lost on either Sophie or Bernard. The latter, however, laughed lightly.

'Oh, I have quite made up my mind now,' he asserted.

Begging him to excuse her, and reminding him that they would meet at dinner, Sophie went up to her suite with Major Wilhelm.

Foster sought his own palatial apartment and, strolling out on to the narrow balcony, surveyed the scene below and in front of him. He felt that he had failed rather badly up to date in the task set him by the Chief of the Secret Service. All his endeavours to persuade the baroness to speak had proved abortive. He was unable to appear too insistent for fear that her suspicions against him should be raised. Yet she had more than once given him to understand that she was anxious to confide in him, but was prevented by a vow of secrecy. She had also declared cryptically that she would ask his assistance to connect a chain of some sort once she had found a link that was missing. It rather seemed that she was playing a double game. For the first time it really occurred to him that she was actually antagonistic to the German regime, though he had already guessed she was not in favour of the bellicose intensions which secret military plans, poison gas, and a wireless ray suggested. Could it be possible that she had obtained the confidence of von Strom for the very purpose of betraying him? Was that why she felt herself in danger? Expecting all the time that her motives would be fathomed she daily feared exposure. It seemed very much like it. If so, Foster was absolutely certain that she was not acting thus for any desire of gain. There was nothing ignoble about Sophie von Reudath; apart from which she was a wealthy woman. What was the oath of which she had spoken? Was it one she had given to the Marshal not to divulge whatever he told her? If so, how could she expect to be relieved of such a vow? He knew very well that she would never voluntarily break it.

He gave vent to an ejaculation of impatience. What was the

use of all this speculating? It did not help in the slightest. He had a duty to perform and, whatever it cost him personally, it had to be done. He would try once again to get Sophie to speak before she left for Berlin. If she would not, and he felt quite certain in his heart that nothing he could say or do would persuade her, he would be compelled to rely upon eavesdropping, searching her house in Berlin, and other unpleasant undertakings. The fact that such attempts would be fraught with considerable danger did not bother him. It bothered him very much, however, that he must be compelled to act in such a manner towards the girl he loved. His gaze wandered vaguely along the Corso; then suddenly he started, returning to the full realisation of mundane affairs with a little exclamation. At the end of the Hungaria terrace under the shade of a tree a man and a woman, of a different class to the majority of those sitting or strolling not very far from them, stood talking. It was not difficult to recognise even at that distance the stocky figure, hawklike face and flashing teeth of the man Carl. It was easier still to assure himself that the woman was Hanni Rowohlt, Sophie's maid. She was tall and angular, but was quite good-looking, if one overlooked the hardness of her eyes and mouth. Foster had seen as much of Carl as he had of her, for the man was indefatigable in his attentions. Sophie and the Englishman were allowed to make very few excursions without Carl shadowing them. Foster knew this quite well, but Sophie did not. The former was more amused than otherwise at their being trailed in a manner so assiduous. It was all wasted effort, for they had not gone anywhere which could have caused distrust or particular interest. Neither Foster nor Sophie had visited any of the legations; had had, in fact, very little to do with members of the diplomatic corps of their own countries or of any others.

Foster wished he could have been in a position to overhear the conversation going on. It must be of interest, he reflected, for he knew the man and woman seldom met. Once when disengaged he had observed Hanni going out upon what had proved to be an entirely innocent nature. He had once come upon Carl hurrying along the broad avenue called the Jósef Korút. The man had not seen him, and Foster had promptly taken on the role of shadower, only to find that Carl was bent on having a night out. It was then very late – Sophie had gone to bed – and Foster had had the doubtful pleasure of watching the German spy go from one drinking house to another until he eventually staggered home to his lodgings in a state of intoxication. He remained where he was interested in this meeting of Hanni and Carl, despite his inability to discover what it was about. Before long he had the satisfaction of observing the tall military figure of Major Ernst Wilhelm making its way along the terrace. The man had not been long with Sophie, he thought, until he glanced at his watch to discover, to his surprise, that he had been on the balcony for well over half an hour. A little heap of cigarette ends at his feet bore testimony to the profundity of his thoughts, since he had no recollection of smoking any of them. Major Wilhelm joined the other two, stood talking earnestly to Hanni for a few minutes, then walked away with Carl, the woman hurrying back to the hotel. Foster watched the two men until they were almost out of sight, after which he re-entered his room, and deeper in thought than ever, proceeded with his dressing.

He found Sophie down before him, sitting alone in a secluded corner of the lounge. She greeted his arrival with a little sigh of relief. He searched her face anxiously, but saw no sign there of any dismay or perturbation. She seemed, in fact, in a happy, contented frame of mind; took care in the selection of a cocktail, as though that was the only matter of importance that exercised her. When their wants had been supplied, however, and they were entirely alone, she bade him draw his chair closer to hers.

'It was as I thought, Bernard,' she told him. 'His Excellency is anxious that I return to Berlin at once. There are many things, he says, of which he must speak to me.'

Foster made a grimace.

'I am glad you can take it with such calmness, Sophie,' he declared. 'I hope that indicates that you have discovered your fears were groundless.'

She shrugged her shoulders.

'It is of no use to be upset,' she returned. 'I confess that I have dreaded very much the necessity of going back since I – since I—' she paused, and the colour suddenly flooded her cheeks. Gazing at her questioningly, a ray of light suddenly illuminated Foster's mind. A wondering happy smile suffused his face, and he was about to speak, when she went hastily on, 'I feel now that perhaps I was foolish to imagine that danger threatened me. The latter is very charming, though the messages sent by the mouth of Ernst Wilhelm are not so nice.'

Foster choked back the words which her hesitation and blush had brought tumbling to his lips instead.

'What were they?' he asked. 'May I know or is it forbidden?'

'There is no harm in your knowing, my dear friend,' she replied quietly, and he wondered to find that she was avoiding his eyes. 'One is that I am expected to be in Berlin without fail by the day after tomorrow; another is that Major Wilhelm is to travel with me and act as my escort; the third—' she hesitated and for some moments gazed silently down at her satin shoes. 'The third, Bernard,' she resumed with a deep sigh, 'is that His Excellency does not approve of my association with the young man who is my constant companion, and hopes I will leave him behind when I travel to Berlin.'

Foster was quite unable to speak for some time, but the look of indignation on his face was eloquent of his thoughts.

'Good Lord!' he burst out at last. 'What a confounded cheek! What right has he to dictate to you like this? Sophie, you're your own mistress, aren't you?'

'I am not his,' she replied vehemently, 'and he treats me as though I am.' She was looking up at him now, and he loved the angry way in which her eyes were sparkling. 'I assure you, Bernard, that after receiving that third message, I would not go back to Berlin were he a hundred times more powerful, if it could be avoided.'

'Are you so certain it cannot be avoided?' he asked earnestly.

'Absolutely, my friend. I must go.'

'Sophie, tell me: What hold has he on you? You don't love him or anything like that, do you?'

'Love him!' she repeated scornfully. 'I hate him as I hate the snakes and the vermin. He is loathsome to me, because—' She stopped suddenly, went on in a quieter voice. 'I am saying too much, but there is one thing you know now, Bernard. It is that I have a great hatred for Germany's Supreme Marshal of State.'

'Then why in the name of all that's amazing,' he demanded, 'does he behave as though you belong to him; as though he has a right to dictate to you, to order your life, choose your friends for you, and – oh! Every other damn thing.'

'Because he thinks that he has. I tell you, one day I will explain everything to you; then you will understand.'

'Why not now?' he pleaded. 'At least tell me before we leave Budapest.'

She shook her head.

'I cannot. It is impossible? Oh, my friend, you would not look as exasperated if you knew how great the longing is in me to tell you. You could perhaps be so much assistance. But I cannot tell you – yet. Please try and understand.'

He touched her hand gently.

'I'm trying very hard, Sophie,' he assured her. 'I will be patient and wait.'

'Thank you,' was her grateful response to that. 'It is very kind of you to bear with me like this, for I know how you wish to help me. But just now you said, "before *we* leave Budapest". Do you still intend to go to Berlin in spite of what the Supreme Marshal has said?'

He laughed.

'Of course, you can break off your association with me and, as far as you are concerned, leave me behind. Nevertheless, I shall go to Berlin and, if you are ever in need of me, I will be at hand, to help you. You will only have to send for me.'

'Even if it means defying von Strom?' she smiled.

'Even if it means defying him,' he repeated firmly.

It was not a particularly cheerful meal that evening. Rosemary Meredith and Dora Reinwald hardly spoke at all, Foster only occasionally, then on topics of little or no interest. Conversation was left in consequence mainly to the baroness and Major Wilhelm. Sophie did her part nobly, but even she could not prevent it from being extremely perfunctory. It must have been a great relief to all when dinner was finished and they repaired to the terrace for coffee. It was Foster who suggested that they should make up a party and go to the Dunapalata Roof to dance. Wilhelm declined, pleading fatigue after his journey, greatly to the relief of the others. Foster, with the consent of the baroness, promptly invited two Bavarians, August Keller and Franz Minck, who had been introduced to them a few days previously, and had become friendly with Rosemary and Dora. The invitation was enthusiastically accepted, and Wilhelm took his leave. Foster politely accompanied him to the taxicab that had been ordered for him.

'Beastly sorry, don't you know,' he remarked, as he shook hands, 'that you don't feel up to treading the light fantastic, and all that. We shall miss your cheery smile.'

Wilhelm eyed him doubtfully.

'I have little time for nonsense of that kind,' he observed stiffly.

'Oh, I say,' protested Foster, screwing his monocle back into the eye from which it had fallen, and succeeding in looking thoroughly fatuous. 'I wouldn't call dancing nonsense, you know. Why, dash it all, Wilhelm, old boy, give the – er – devil his due, and what not. The jolly old world wouldn't go round if people didn't dance. You try it, old son, and you'll get my meaning, what!'

The German ignored the trivialities.

'Am I to understand,' he asked, 'that you are determined to accompany the baroness to Berlin?'

'Yes, rather, wouldn't miss it for anything. Couldn't possibly let her go without me, though I must say she doesn't seem very keen on the idea now, I don't know why.'

'Has it not occurred to you that she may resent your attentions?'

'By Jove, no! Dash it all! Don't suggest such awful thoughts. Why, man, I'm potty about her, and one of these days, if I can get up enough courage, I'm going to ask her to marry me.'

Wilhelm laughed harshly.

'Don't be a fool!' he advised. 'Has she ever given you any cause to anticipate that she would be willing to become your wife?'

Foster rubbed his chin ruefully.

'Can't say that she has,' he admitted. 'She's been jolly decent to me, and all that, but she's not the amorous sort, is she?'

'She could be with the man she loved. But you are not, and never can be, Mr Foster. You have a saying, "Keep off the grass". I think you will be well advised to follow it. It will be much better if you do not go to Berlin with her.'

'I say, are you giving me orders?'

'By no means. I am merely giving you very good advice.'

'Thanks, old top. I've no doubt you mean well. But if it's all the same to you, I intend to follow my own inclinations in this matter. I'm coming to Berlin, if only to learn German. Cheer ho!'

Wilhelm turned abruptly away, entered his taxi, and was driven off. Foster walked back to the others chuckling softly to himself.

CHAPTER SEVEN

Foster Buys Perfume

They travelled together to Berlin, passing through miles upon miles of wheat fields in Czecho-Slovakia. On this occasion Foster did not have Sophie to himself, the courier insisting on carrying out his duties to the letter. He regarded the Englishman with an air of disapproval throughout the journey, but made no further reference to the inadvisability of his accompanying the baroness to the German capital. At the border Foster's belongings were subjected to such a keen examination by the Customs, and his passport scrutinised with such elaborate care, that he was forced to the conclusion that an excuse was being sought to detain him. That was significant. Everything was in perfect order, however – he had previously made certain of that – and the officials were left with no alternative but to permit him to proceed. Sophie made no comment concerning their officiousness, but inwardly she was intensely indignant.

It was very late when the train ran into the Anhalt Station. Having received her permission to call on the following morning, Foster watched her drive away to her house in the Grunewald quarters still escorted by the German officer. He then took a taxi to the Esplanade Hotel, where he had reserved a room by telegram at the suggestion of Sophie. She had declared that though by no means the most up-to-date, the Esplanade was the most charming in Berlin. His apartment had nothing of the magnificence of the one he had vacated at the Hungaria Hotel in Budapest, but it was well-furnished, large and comfortable. He found the bed admirable, and was quickly asleep. On waking the following morning to find the sun streaming into the room, he sprang out of bed, and walked on to the balcony. Then he knew why the baroness had described the hotel as charming. Enclosed by old grey walls, the Esplanade was apparently placed in the centre of a beautiful garden. Trim lawns, intersected by graceful shady paths, looked most enticing. There were ornamental pavilions nestling amid petunias, a circular fountain, from which the soothing music of the water reached his ears, backed by a riot of geraniums. Everything looked deliciously pleasant. The solicitude with which the spotless maids presently waited on him, the polite and quick-witted manservant, who prepared his bath and later brought his breakfast, helped to add to the effect of peaceful serenity which the place had produced on his mind. He discovered that the hotel had once been a palace. It was modern, yet in line with the old glory of Berlin. Situated in the Hohenzollern quarter it spoke of a spirit that had passed, but which still retained its influence. Descending to the reception hall, immaculately dressed as usual, his fair hair gleaming under the effect of the careful brushing it had undergone, his monocle stuck in his eye, his was a figure that attracted attention. Indolent in manner, guileless in expression, there was yet something about him that promptly claimed the notice of people, particularly of members of the opposite sex. A little stout man, magnificent in his morning attire, hurried up to him, and bowed low. Introducing himself as the assistant manager, he enquired solicitously after Foster's comfort, begged to be informed whether he had slept well and if the servants had attended to his requirements adequately. The Englishman was amused at this concern for his welfare; reflected that there were many hotels, with which he was acquainted, that would be the better for following the example set by the Esplanade. He assured the assistant manager that he had had an excellent night's rest, and was entirely satisfied with everything. The little man, who was gratified, expressed himself as delighted. Foster expected him to withdraw then, instead of which an expression of apologetic concern appeared on his face.

'I regret mooch to inconvenience you, sare,' he remarked regretfully in his laboured English, 'but I must ask you into mine office to step. A gentleman is there who mit you would speak. It is only the formality, you understand.'

'Who is he?' asked Foster curiously.

'That he himself will tell you. Will you mit me come, please.'

Foster followed him into a luxuriously furnished office. There he found awaiting him a young man of about his own height and colouring, attired in the uniform of a Nazi officer of high rank. The latter greeted him with a pleasant smile, and held out his hand, which Foster grasped readily enough, though he felt somewhat puzzled.

'My name is Schönewald,' announced the officer in perfect English. 'Yours, I believe, is Foster.' The Englishman nodded. 'Sit down, won't you?'

He turned to the assistant manager and dismissed him as Foster sank into a chair. When the door had closed behind the little man, Schönewald held out his cigarette case to his companion. 'I haven't any particular liking for my job,' he remarked apologetically, 'but

I have been told to do it, and there it is. I would have come up to your room, but didn't want to bother you until you were dressed. I have been here for nearly an hour as a matter of fact.'

'Sorry,' murmured Foster, 'but I had no idea—'

'Of course you hadn't. It was my own choice to wait rather than hurry you.'

There was an awkward pause, during which the two smoked, Foster placidly, the other puffing furiously, occasionally regarding each other with speculative eyes.

'You speak topping English,' observed Bernard at length, 'I would have thought you were English if I had met you elsewhere.'

'And not in this garb, I suppose,' laughed the German. 'I was at Haileybury and Oriel, so I'd be a queer bloke if I didn't speak the language as well as my own. It's because of my knowledge of English that I have been selected to interview you.'

'I see.' There was another pause. 'I don't want to hurry you, you know,' went on Foster presently, 'but don't you think it would be rather a good idea if you told me what the trouble is.'

'Yes, I suppose I'd better get on with it,' agreed Schönewald reluctantly. 'Don't run away with the idea that there is any trouble, though. I have been commissioned to extend to you a little friendly advice.'

He blew a perfect smoke ring towards the ceiling.

'How nice,' murmured Foster.

The other suddenly became businesslike.

'Look here,' he said, 'you met the Baroness von Reudath in England, became very friendly with her, and accompanied her to Budapest. You came to Berlin simply and solely because she was summoned there. That is correct, isn't it?'

'Quite,' nodded Foster. 'If it hadn't been for her, I don't suppose

I should have left England – not just yet, anyway. I did intend wandering round the continent a bit later on.'

'Why did you accompany her?'

'Oh, I say, that's rather an intimate question, isn't it?'

Schönewald smiled.

'I'll answer it myself, shall I? You followed her – I mean to say accompanied her, because you are infatuated with her. Is that correct?'

'Not infatuated,' objected Foster. 'I admit that I am very much in love with her. But dash it all, man! I don't see that that is anybody's business but my own.'

'Personally, I agree with you – officially I can't. Although I sympathise with you, it is my duty to inform you that any idea you may have in your mind of marrying the baroness must, at least for some time, be removed. I have been instructed to inform you that your association with her is not regarded with favour.'

'And who gave you those instructions?' asked Foster quietly.

'Does that matter?'

'It matters very much. I cannot see that anyone has the right to interfere with a friendship which is very precious to me and is perfectly innocent. The baroness, as far as I am aware, don't you know, is her own mistress. If she indicated to me that my companionship was distasteful to her, I would clear out at once, of course. As she has done nothing of the kind, I— well, dash it! I resent interference by anyone else.'

He screwed his monocle more firmly into his eye, and glared at the Nazi officer. The latter smiled grimly, and leant forward.

'My instructions,' he declared with deliberate emphasis, 'come from the Supreme Marshal himself.'

Foster looked amiably surprised.

'Is that so,' he commented. 'Well, I have a great admiration for His Excellency; he's a great man without a doubt. All the same, I don't see where he comes in in this affair.'

'Perhaps you don't; nevertheless, he has chosen to make it his affair, and it would be as well to remind you that he is all powerful in Germany. You may not know that the baroness is concerned with him in very important matters, and, until he decides to dispense with her services, she is pledged to him.'

'But I am not interfering in those matters.'

'We know that. Care has been taken to ascertain that you have not.'

'Oh! Indeed!' muttered Foster, looking interested. 'How?'

'That I am not at liberty to tell you. There was no objection to your becoming friendly with the baroness in London – she was on holiday. The same thing applied to Budapest. But here it is different. She will have no time for friendships – His Excellency will demand all her time. You will be wise, therefore, if you realise that you can only see her on rare occasions; you will be wiser still if you do not attempt to see her at all.'

'But hang it all!' cried Foster in real dismay. 'How can I agree to that when I – when I—'

'When you love her! Exactly! It is beastly hard for you, I know. As I have told you, I personally sympathise with you. I should hate to receive the – er – advice I am giving you, if I were in your position, but there it is.'

'I have an appointment with her this morning.'

'Well, keep it, but I earnestly urge you to make it the last. She will probably tell you herself what I have told you. Her life is bound up in affairs of great importance; there can be no room in it for the kind of thing your presence is possibly bringing into it. It is likely to unsettle her, and cause grave complications. You must forgive me for asking a question which concerns her. Has she ever given you to understand that she was the possessor of confidential information?'

Foster laughed.

'Never,' he declared, with such apparent frankness that Schönewald could hardly help but be convinced. 'There was a vague sort of rumour in London that she was on air with Germany's political intentions, but I was not interested. I know jolly well she would never speak of German affairs to anyone. She discussed His Excellency of course, with me and with others. She has such a warm admiration for him that it would be strange if she didn't, don't you know.'

Schönewald nodded.

'That goes without saying,' he agreed. 'Her husband was one of his staunchest supporters when he was climbing, and the baroness entered wholeheartedly into assisting. She did a lot for him. But she is a woman, and when a woman has an affection for a man she is liable to become injudicious.'

'Affection!' echoed Foster ruefully. 'I wish she did feel an affection for me. She's friendly enough, but I don't think there is anything else. She has always treated me as though I amuse her.'

'I do not wonder at that,' murmured the Nazi in German.

'What did you say?' asked Foster.

'Nothing,' was the hasty reply. 'I might tell you this, my friend: our information regarding you and her was that you were both in love.'

'Well, you can take it from me, old boy,' retorted Foster, 'that as far as she is concerned, that's all bosh. I only wish it were correct.'

'You forget that love is generally presumed to be blind,' smiled the German. 'Others may have noticed what you were blind to. But that is not exactly my business.' He rose. 'I am to assure you that there is no objection to you being in Berlin, and hopes are expressed that you enjoy your stay immensely. I earnestly advise you not to endeavour to continue on the same footing with the baroness, however, and urge that, after your visit to her this morning, you discontinue seeing her.'

'And what will happen if I insist on continuing my association with her?' asked Foster.

Schönewald shrugged his shoulders.

'No restraint will be imposed upon you,' he declared, 'but the consequences might be unpleasant to you – and to her.'

'To her!' echoed the startled Englishman.

'Exactly. If you do not consider yourself, at least I think you will consider her.'

'But why should anything unpleasant happen to her?'

'I am not at liberty to go further into the matter. I must apologise for detaining you so long, Mr Foster.'

He held out his hand, which the Englishman took readily enough. Whatever instructions Schönewald may have received, there was no doubt that he was a good fellow himself. Absurd to bear resentment against him.

'Aren't you going to question me about myself?' asked Foster sarcastically. 'I may be a villain in disguise with a dark and murky past, don't you know.'

The Nazi officer laughed.

'We all know about you,' he declared, 'including the fact that you became so bored with that English army that you resigned your Commission. We even know of your athletic records. I must admit that your history has been well read. There is nothing about you we don't know.'

He nodded and went out. Foster smiled at the closed door.

'Oh, yes there is, my well-informed Nazi,' he murmured. 'Quite a lot in fact.'

He resumed his chair, then mindful of the fact that he was in the assistant manager's office and not his own room he rose again and walked out. His mind was in a state of trouble. The warning conveyed to him by Schönewald was definitely disturbing. It was all very well to protest that his friendship with the baroness was nobody's business but his own. The Marshal of State had chosen to make it his business, to object to its continuation. He could not defy one of the most powerful men in a foreign country of which he was a guest. Yet, if he discontinued his friendship with Sophie, apart from all personal considerations, how could he possibly obtain the information he was expected to acquire? If he were unable to speak to her, he could not expect to learn anything from her, if he could not enter her house, gone was all the hope of being able to search any documents that might be hidden there. In addition there was the fact to be faced that insistence on his part might mean that the consequences, as the Nazi officer had put it, would be unpleasant to her. He did not bother about the fact that the implied threat referred equally to himself. It was part of his job to face risks and, if he alone were concerned, would not have hesitated a minute. It was a different matter, though, to endanger her. He was perfectly convinced that Sir Leonard Wallace would forbid him to take any steps that would react injuriously on the baroness. It began to look as though the brunt of the investigations would have to fall on the shoulders of Rosemary Meredith. Such a thought was extremely distasteful to him, not because of any dislike of the girl – on the contrary he liked her immensely – but because it would mean that he had failed in his part. He decided that the sooner he got in touch with Gottfried the better. The Berlin representative of *Lalére et Cie* perhaps already had orders for him.

In the reception hall he came upon the assistant manager, who smiled at him cheerfully.

'So!' he exclaimed. 'The so-liddle formality of which I speak is finished – it is all over.'

'Yes; it is all over,' nodded Foster. 'I found Mr Schönewald a very nice fellow.'

'Oh, the Herr Colonel indeed a very nice man is. I am glad you like him.'

'He's a colonel, is he?' commented the Englishman. 'Surely he is young for such a rank.'

'A most brilliant man he is. In Berlin many like him we have. Now, sare, at your disposal a guide I will place. He will you everything show.'

He beckoned to a stalwart man whose face reminded Foster of Carl the spy.

'I don't require a guide, thanks,' he intimated courteously. 'I prefer to wander about on my own.'

'Most tiring that would be,' protested the manager. 'Nothing you can know, but everything he knows.'

He persisted so eagerly that it was not long before Foster was convinced that the man was a member of the secret police who had instructions to keep him under observation. Momentarily he was filled with a sense of helplessness. What could he possibly accomplish when so many restrictions had been placed upon his movements?

'Always at your disposal, Herr Foster, he will be,' he heard the manager saying. 'If it is that sometimes him you do not want, then it does not matter. He will go mit you behind, then you will only have to call when it is that you his services require. So!'

Foster accepted the inevitable. He succeeded in forcing a smile.

'I did not know,' he observed. 'That German hotels were so thoughtful of the needs of their foreign guests.'

'At the Esplanade it our custom is,' the little man assured him.

'Liar!' thought Foster. Aloud he asked: 'Can he speak English?'

'Very goot English I spik,' announced the man himself in deep guttural tones.

'Excellent,' drawled Bernard. 'I'm sure you and I will get on very well together. What is your name?'

'Johann Schmidt it is.'

'Dear old John Smith – how I love it! Well, Johann, you can help me right away. I want to buy some scent for a lady. Where do you suggest I should go?'

'In the Friedrich-Strasse there many shops for scent are, also in Unter den Linden and the Leipziger-Strasse. Gome mit me, mit pleasure I will them show you.'

'But I want something special. In Paris there is Doty and Du Barry and Lalére and others. Have none of those branches here, where I can speak to the manager, and receive his personal attention?'

The man smiled happily, and said the very thing Foster hoped he would say.

'Lalére haf here mooch goot place. Gome! We to it will go.'

'Good. I'll get my hat.'

He was conducted along the Unter den Linden, and expressed great delight in the broad thoroughfare with its lime and chestnut trees although he already knew it very well. Johann Schmidt stopped at length outside the premises of the famous Parisian perfume firm *Messieurs Lalére et Cie*, and pointed at it with a stubby forefinger. The more Foster looked at him the more he appeared like Carl, though a taller and altogether bigger edition. He wondered if they were related by blood as well as by profession. Leaving the supposed guide outside, the Secret Service man went in. To the assistant who immediately attended to him he announced that he wanted something special in the way of scent, and would like to consult with the manager about it.

'He is engaged at present, sir,' was the reply. 'Will you wait or call again?'

'Perhaps you will ask him when it will be convenient to see him. My name is Foster.'

The assistant went away; returned a minute or two later to announce that Herr Gottfried would come and speak to him. The burly form of the man he knew well presently appeared. Gottfried with his round, closely-cropped head and bristling moustache, looked a typical Prussian. Yet he was as British as Foster, though he had spent most of his life in Berlin where no one had the slightest idea that he was anything but a pure German. One of the most reliable men in the Secret Service, his presence as an accepted German in the capital of the country had, for many years, been of the utmost value to Sir Leonard Wallace. He was on various municipal and other committees, mixed in the highest circles, and generally was recognised as a man of shrewd common sense whose love for the country amounted to a passion. It was little wonder, therefore, that he was on numerous occasions consulted upon highly confidential matters. No sign of recognition passed between the two as he and Foster faced each other.

'I understand,' commenced Gottfried in English which had the slightest trace of accent, 'that you are in search of a perfume of a special nature. If you will accompany me to my office, which is also something of a laboratory, I will be able, I think, to place before you that which will meet your requirements.'

'But I understand you are engaged,' objected Foster. 'I will call again.'

'By no means. The two gentlemen with me are very much

interested in scent. They will not mind.' Foster went with him, feeling rather puzzled that he had not been given an appointment for another time. They could certainly not discuss anything of importance before strangers. He was more perplexed and definitely perturbed when he was inside the office facing the two men – Germans of the most obvious type – Gottfried, having made certain that the door was fast closed, announced that he had expected him.

'Don't bother about whispering, when you speak,' he went on. 'This room is absolutely soundproof.'

Foster stared at him with incredulous eyes. Was the man crazy? His gaze encountered that of one of the Germans, a bronzed, hearty-looking man in the uniform of a naval officer. He had a round, jolly face and fair hair parted very much on one side. The other was small and extremely fat with hair standing up like bristles and a moustache of fierce proportions. Foster was not prepossessed in his favour. His face was wreathed in a smile that was apparently intended to be friendly, but rather failed in its object. The naval officer was smiling also; much more attractively, thought the young Secret Service man, though there was a suggestion of mockery in it. He turned back rather helplessly to Gottfried, who was regarding him with amused eyes.

'What about that perfume?' he asked. 'I want something special that—'

'Will be a worthy present for the most wonderful girl in the world,' the sailor went on for him, and he spoke in the voice of Sir Leonard Wallace. Foster swung round with a cry of sheer amazement and stared incredulously at him. 'Well, our disguises seem to be pretty good,' laughed Wallace, 'since they have taken in both you and Gottfried.'

'Good heavens!' ejaculated the astonished Foster. 'Is – is this one of us also, sir?' he asked, weakly indicating the small, fat man.

'It is most reprehensible,' came the voice of Cousins, 'for a junior to speak of a senior as this? To quote Mallory—'

'Cousins!' yelled Foster. 'Good old Jerry!'

'How dare you interrupt a quotation! You youngsters have no manners.'

'It's a lucky thing this room is soundproof,' commented Gottfried drily. 'Foster's yell might otherwise have reached to Potsdam.'

That young man did not heed his remark. He seemed unable to tear his eyes from the two men smiling at him. Although he knew Sir Leonard and Cousins were past masters of the art of disguise, he had never seen a more complete transformation than this. Foster sighed. He already knew there was a great gulf between himself and the 'experts' in many phases of Secret Service work. He felt he never could hope to aspire to such complete success in this very necessary branch.

'Well, if you have finished studying us,' laughed Sir Leonard, 'we will proceed with more important matters. I am extremely anxious to know if you have discovered anything of importance yet.'

Foster sank into the chair pushed up for him by Gottfried.

'I'm rather afraid I've failed pretty hopelessly, sir,' he confessed, 'and there doesn't seem much chance now that I will have any more opportunities of getting the information.'

'What do you mean?'

The young man told his story, carefully taking his listeners over every incident that had happened since he and the Baroness von Reudath had left London, except of course those of a nature intimate to himself and her. He repeated everything she had said to him that was in any way relevant to his object in being with her.

He then went on to describe the arrival of Major Ernst Wilhelm in Budapest with a summons to Sophie to return to Berlin, and the courier's attempt to dissuade him from accompanying her. Finally he told of Colonel Schönewald's visit to the Esplanade Hotel, repeated word for word what had been said, and informed his hearers that he had been saddled with a guide who, he was sure, was a member of the secret police who had orders to keep observation on him.

'He is outside now,' he concluded, adding with a grim smile: 'He guided me here, after I had asked him where I could purchase some extra special perfume.'

Sir Leonard appeared very thoughtful when Foster had ceased speaking. For some moments there was a profound silence in the room; then he smiled at the anxious-eyed young man.

'I do not consider that you have failed hopelessly at all,' he declared. 'It is true you have not yet obtained the information I want, but I did not expect you to do that at once. I think I told you your job would require patience, tact, and ingenuity. You have certainly succeeded in becoming *persona grata* with the baroness.' He smiled. 'Much more so than I anticipated, in fact. She has even told you that only a vow she has taken prevents her from confiding certain facts in you. What those facts are we can guess. Altogether, young man, you have done very well. I am certainly pleased with you.'

Foster flushed with deep pleasure. Praise of that nature was extremely gratifying. He had not expected it.

'I seem to be up against a blank wall now, sir,' he reminded his chief. 'If by continuing my association with the baroness, I am likely to bring harm upon her, it seems to me that I shall have to try some other way of obtaining the information.'

'It is obvious,' commented Sir Leonard, 'that von Strom is

very worried about something. Either he regrets now that he has confided in her to the extent he has – we actually have no proof that she is his confidante—'

'No positive proof, sir,' interposed Gottfried, 'but there is little doubt about it.'

'Well, as I was saying, he either regrets that he has given her his confidence or else he is jealous of you, Foster. Probably it is both. Cousins and I noted the arrival of Major Wilhelm in Budapest and drew our own conclusions from your sudden change of plans—'

'Were you in Budapest, sir?' asked the astonished Foster.

'We were. We have been with you all the time like a couple of guardian angels. Surprised?'

'Very much so, sir, I had no idea.'

'Naturally. Nevertheless, we travelled on the train with you to Budapest; we were on the same train to Berlin. We crossed the Channel on the boat on which you and the baroness crossed.'

Cousins chuckled.

'Do you remember seeing your friend Carl sitting on a seat at the stern, Foster?' he asked. 'I noticed you glanced that way.' The young man nodded. 'Did you happen to observe that he was sitting between two old ladies?'

'Yes, I did, now you remind me of it.'

Cousins chuckled again.

'We were the two ladies,' he declared.

CHAPTER EIGHT

A Surprise for the Baroness

Sir Leonard turned suddenly to Foster.

'You are calling on the baroness this morning, aren't you?'

'Yes sir,' was the reply. 'Apparently no objection is to be raised to that, but it is expected, I gather, to be my last visit to her.'

'H'm! We shall have to consider that point: we must consider ways and means. When you see her this morning warn her that she is being watched by her maid Hanni. I think it is time she knew. If she remains ignorant she is likely to bring trouble on herself. You can tell her of the conversation you overheard in the garden of Lord Ashington's house.'

'I am not supposed to know German, sir,' Foster reminded him. 'Am I to say the conversation was in English?'

'No,' was the unexpected reply; 'you can admit to her that you do understand and speak German. In fact, Foster, you have my permission to come right out into the open with her. Cousins and I have made a very complete study of her and, from the information with which you have supplied us, I am very certain she is utterly reliable. Furthermore I am convinced that she is working against, not for, von Strom. It has not been difficult to put two and two together. The key which has opened the door, and revealed a lot to me, is her love for Austria. She is an Austrian – she knows the Chancellor's ambition to rule Austria as well as Germany; thus her hatred of the man who is implementing his ambition. I had gathered that already, when you told me of the look of hatred that flashed across her face once when you spoke of von Strom being her friend. You could not understand it, and wondered if it had been directed against you. I reached the conclusion then that it was the thought of von Strom that had caused it. Events have proved that I was right. By some means she has been forced to take a vow of silence regarding certain things which she feels she cannot break unless she can discover a link in some chain of events. How that link can release her from her vow it is impossible to guess without knowing more. I have come to the conclusion, however, that for your own sake, and for the sake of the job you have on hand, the time has arrived to tell her who you are and assure her that the British Secret Service stands behind her. It is a rare thing for us to take a step of this nature, but it is not a gamble. For one thing I am perfectly convinced of her honesty, and another she is deeply in love with Foster. She would never think of betraying him, even if she were working at cross purposes with the British Intelligence.'

Foster's face was scarlet.

'You – you think that, sir? You really think she loves me?'

Sir Leonard smiled.

'I don't think,' he continued. 'I know. Any fool, with half an eye, could see it, as easily as he can see that you are in love with her. No doubt von Strom has been informed of the fact, and he is either seething with jealousy or he fears what love may cause to be revealed. Anyhow, you can tell her everything – you have my full permission. In return, beg her to confide in you. She knows very well that Great Britain is in sympathy with Austria, and that if Germany is plotting against her country she can be certain that support against any aggression can be looked for from ours. Probably she will be a little bit upset to learn that you were more or less sent to spy on her originally, but I've no doubt you will be able to smooth that out. I'm sure also that you will be glad to be able to be frank with her.'

'Glad, sir!' cried Foster. 'It will be marvellous.'

When Foster visited Sophie in her residence near the Grunewald Forest, he told her first of the visit he had received from Colonel Schönewald and of the warning given to him under the guise of advice. Sophie's eyes flashed angrily. With great indignation she commented upon the manner in which her freedom of action and his were being curtailed; informed him that she had received a visit from von Strom early in the morning. He had been very nice to her up to a point, but had insisted that her friendship with Foster must cease. She had vehemently demanded the right to have friends, and to choose them herself, but he had proved adamant.

'He fears, I think,' she added, 'that I may divulge to you certain secrets of his that I possess. I reminded him of the vow I had taken, but he was so much rude as to say that, under certain circumstances, a woman thinks nothing of breaking a vow. I was very angry, and did not part on amicable terms. I find now, my friend Bernard, that I am virtually a prisoner in my own house. You have seen the two storm troopers in the garden?'

He nodded.

'By what right does he treat you like this?' he demanded. 'It is shameful.'

'He is all-powerful,' she reminded him. 'He can do what he likes.'

'But why does he act in such a manner? Why cannot you and I be allowed to carry on a companionship that cannot hurt him?'

'He fears, as I have said, that I may tell you something of the schemes which are known to me. It is certain that he regrets now that they were ever confided to me. I know too much, Bernard, and, as he has lost a lot of confidence in me, I am in very great danger. I tell you this because I think soon I may perhaps die suddenly. In England you have a saying – "Dead men tell no tales". When I am dead I cannot speak. He will then not be worried.'

'Sophie!' cried Foster in agonised tones. 'Please don't speak like that. You make me feel – oh, I can't tell you! Surely he is not such a fiend – he would not harm you.'

She smiled wistfully. He was amazed at her calm.

'You do not know him,' she remarked. 'Always he was arrogant, I think. Now that he is bloated with power and success, he is many times worse. In everything he must have his own way. He is relentless, ruthless, domineering and implacable. My husband helped him to rise; he became fond of me, and it was then I was admitted to his confidence. He is of that type of man who likes to strut, and appear great and wonderful to a woman. Praise to him is the food of life – without it he would starve. And I also helped him in his efforts. But now his love for me is filled with fear. I know so much. Only the Chancellor and the Minister of Propaganda possess the knowledge that I possess. They also fear that someday I will let out the secret. That is why, my Bernard, I believe I may die suddenly, if I do not quickly convince them that there is, after all, nothing to fear.'

'This is awful, Sophie,' he groaned.

'Do not worry about me, Bernard. Our association has been very dear to me – it will remain always as a happy memory. But it must cease. After this morning you will please see me no more, and do not attempt to write to me. You will help me most by leaving Berlin. When you are gone, I think I can quickly chase away all doubts and fears from the mind of the Supreme Marshal.'

He turned a white, miserable face to her.

'But why must you?' he asked hoarsely. 'Sophie darling – leave Berlin with me. I want you so. Surely you must know that I love you. I—'

'Ah! No,' she cried pitifully; 'please do not say it, please do not. I have known for a long time, Bernard. I have seen it in your eyes; heard it in your voice. Of course I know, and my heart has yearned with a great ache for you, because I also love you with all my soul.'

'Sophie!' His voice, despite the torture he was suffering, was glad, triumphant. A wonderful, incredulous light broke through the expression of pain in his eyes. 'My Sophie!' he added reverently.

'I can never be that,' she sobbed, 'except in thought. Life is very cruel, Bernard, but, at last, now we must part, we can seek a little consolation from the knowledge that we have told each other that which is in our hearts.'

'Sophie,' he murmured again, this time very brokenly, 'must this cruel thing go on? Is there no hope that together we can seek happiness?'

She shook her head, the unheeded tears rolling down her white cheeks.

'Listen,' she whispered. 'I have told you of my love for Austria.

It is because of that that I cannot, I must not, run away. These things which I know, if they are used in an aggressive sense, will mean the destruction of my beloved country. I must remain here to find the link that will complete the chain of which I have spoken to you. I will find that link,' she added fiercely, 'even if I have to give myself to von Strom.'

He started back, a little horrified, a little awed.

'You would do that?' he asked.

'I would do that for Austria,' she told him simply.

The time had come for his revelation, but already they had been out in the garden too long. At any moment interruption might come. He must hurry.

'Let us walk,' he suggested.

She accompanied him readily, stopping every now and then with the pretence of admiring the flowers. He obtained a pledge of secrecy from her; then plunged into his story without preamble or any attempt at excusing himself. He told her of his connection with the British Secret Service, of the task that he had been set of obtaining from her, if possible, full information of the suspected German military plans, of the gas invented by a man names Hans Mohrenwitz, and Joachim Brau's wireless ray. She was obviously tremendously startled, but listened to him without interruption as though enthralled. The only time she spoke was when he informed her of the conversation he had overheard in Lord Ashington's garden between Carl and Hanni and described Carl's subsequent espionage. She admitted then that she had for some time suspected Hanni. He kept nothing back, even telling her that he had been instructed to appear infatuated with her, and was expected to do his utmost to cause her to fall in love with him in the hope that thus she would be inveigled into betraying State secrets.

'Told as I have told it,' he concluded, 'it all sounds horrible, loathsome, but we in the Secret Service have often to perform rotten jobs. All the time, Sophie, I have been aching to confide in you, to tell you the truth. I discovered at once that you were not at all the type of woman you were spoken of as being. I learnt to know you as the finest, noblest of God's creatures that is why there was no necessity to pretend to be infatuated with you. I fell deeply, helplessly in love with you at once, and to be compelled to live a lie in your companionship has been a hideous nightmare to me.'

She was silent for several minutes after he had ceased speaking. At length she looked up at him, and he sighed with profound relief to find there was no scorn in her eyes.

'This is all very much surprising, Bernard,' she admitted. 'It is difficult at once to adjust my mind. I have thought you were a man of leisure, of no profession, and I find you are engaged in the most dangerous work in the world. You are clever, my friend, to have deceived me so completely. I had thought I had learnt to know you so well, and I find I have known so little. So! You are of the famous British Secret Service. I think I am glad!'

'Glad!' he echoed. 'Then you are not angry with me? You feel no contempt for me?'

She shook her head.

'Of course I do not. I am not without understanding. You had your duty to do, and although, I know, it must have been very painful for you, you strove to do it. But I am sure,' she added, with a faint smile, 'if you had pretended only to be infatuated with me, I should have known. My own great love would have told me. I know so well that your heart was really mine. There was no doubt of that.'

Foster brushed his hand roughly across his eyes, forgetting the monocle, which he dislodged. He took some time readjusting it. It was in a very husky voice that he presently spoke.

'Sophie,' he muttered, 'you're more than wonderful. I think sometimes you are very nearly divine.'

'Hush! You must not say things like that. Tell me, Bernard: why is it that you have told me now all this?'

'I was told this morning that I could,' he informed her. 'The chief has gathered that your motives are all for the benefit of Austria. I am to let you know that the British Secret Service stands behind you. It is ready to come to your assistance whenever it may be needed.'

She clutched his arm involuntarily, her glorious blue eyes sought his almost feverishly.

'Is that true?' she cried. 'Really true?'

'Absolutely,' he assured her.

'Oh, it is wonderful, amazing! I feel already that perhaps now I may escape from the danger that threatens me.'

'You will,' he vowed. 'You can depend upon that.'

'I have heard so much of the work of the British Secret Service, and of the man you call the chief. It is Sir Leonard Wallace, I know. He was pointed out to me at the house of Lord Ashington. I think perhaps he is in Berlin?' She laughed softly as Foster remained silent. 'I see I must not ask questions like that. Oh, my Bernard, I feel that a new lease of life has come to me.' She was silent for a few seconds, and he wondered at the quick tumultuous rise and fall of her bosom; then: 'Perhaps,' she uttered in a voice so low that he had to bend down to hear, 'after all we shall go together to seek the happiness of which you spoke. No longer I feel alone.'

A wave of great emotion surged through him. It was all he could do to resist the impulse to take her into his arms.

'You were never alone, Sophie,' he reminded her gently. 'I was always ready to do anything you required of me.'

'I know that, my Bernard, but I was fearful of dragging you into danger with me. Now everything seems so different. I find that your life is passed in danger. You are working for your country, and the interests of your country are identical with mine. It is very comforting to know that you are of the English Secret Service and are at hand to help me.'

'Oh,' he sighed impulsively, 'how I wish I could kiss you.'

The colour immediately mantled her cheeks, but she looked up at him frankly, her eyes eloquent of her love.

'How I wish you could!' she murmured. 'You must go now, and remember you must not see me again. It is impossible. What you have told me cannot alter that. When I find that link of which I have spoken, I will find some way of communicating with you, if you do not leave Berlin.'

'Leave Berlin!' he repeated with a laugh. 'Not likely.'

'It would be better if you did. Listen! Tell your chief that it is true I am in full possession of the secret military scheme of the Chancellor. I know also all about the gas of Mohrenwitz and wireless ray of Joachim Brau, but the vow I have made prevents me from revealing them. I cannot break such an oath, if Germany's policy is pacific. It is possible that the military scheme, the gas, and the ray will only be used in the event of aggression by another power. They may be defensive measures. It is that which I am so anxious to discover – the link in the chain. If that link shows me that Germany's intentions are offensive, not defensive, then I will consider that I am at liberty to break my vow. An oath means nothing if by breaking it I am able to prevent Europe from being plunged into a terrible war. I could not break it, when I was certain

Germany had no belligerent aspirations. You do understand that, do you not?'

He smiled fondly down at her, though he felt a little disappointed at her decision.

'You are very scrupulous, Sophie,' he asserted, 'but I greatly admire you for it. You do not feel you can give me a little hint concerning just the military scheme?'

She shook her head.

'I cannot. I must be honourable to myself. I could never again feel peace if I betrayed what has been confided in me without the reason I have given.'

'I understand.'

'But,' she went on, 'there is one thing I will do. I will write everything down; then, if anything happens to me, you will have the knowledge I possess.'

'For God's sake!' he protested, 'don't talk like that.'

'It is possible, dear,' she persisted softly. 'The danger is present. Even now von Strom may have decided that it is better I should not live. You see the naiad on the fountain?' He nodded miserably. 'Well, she is sitting on a part that is hollow. There is a small hole a little way down, hidden by her left leg. Inside that hole I will put the document. But promise me that you will not search for it or allow others to come and search, unless – unless I am threatened.'

He promised, begged her to be careful, then swore that, if any harm came to her, he would not rest until he had avenged her. She smiled fondly at him.

'Of what use will that be to me?' she queried. 'You must remember that you are pledged to a great service. You must do nothing to bring harm upon yourself which may result in your country being robbed of you.'

They strolled back to the fountain, their conversation being now devoted to intimate personal topics. For a little while they remained listening to the soothing melody of the running water; then went on to the house. They had almost reached the terrace when two men strode from the library, stood gazing down at them. Sophie's face suddenly became drained of all colour.

'The Marshal!' she gasped. 'Why has he come back?'

CHAPTER NINE

His Excellency The Supreme Marshal of State

Foster regarded the man who had so large a part in deciding the destinies of Germany with a good deal of interest. He had never seen him in the flesh before, though he had studied numerous pictures of him. He was stockily built, a mass of unruly hair falling carelessly low over his forehead. A well-clipped moustache gave him a military appearance. His eyes were dark and held a penetrative quality. The face on the whole suggested obstinacy rather than strength, sullenness rather than force. On acquaintance, however, one became aware of the personality and magnetism of the man.

Sophie quickly recovered herself. She succeeded in greeting him with a smile as she and Foster ascended the steps to the terrace. The man in attendance, a tall, broad-shouldered individual in uniform with a row of medals across his breast, stepped back; stood by the French windows opening into the library. Beyond Foster caught a glimpse of the pale, anxious face of Dora Reinwald.

'This is an unexpected pleasure, Your Excellency,' cried Sophie gaily. 'Have you come to lunch?'

'No, I have come to talk to you,' replied von Strom in a harsh, unpleasant voice. 'Is this the young man who has pestered you with his attentions?'

Foster was careful to show no sign that he understood what was being said. The baroness now knew that he was familiar with the German language, but it was essential that no one else should be aware of the fact.

'Do not be unkind about him,' laughed Sophie. 'After all, he is in love with me, and that is no sin, is it?'

'It is a sin when it does not meet with the approval of the Supreme Marshal of State,' declared that gentleman. 'You are certain he has no knowledge of German?'

'He would not stand there looking with eyes of admiration at you, Excellency,' retorted the girl pointedly, 'if he understood the language.'

He turned and surveyed Foster. He saw before him a tall, fair-haired typical Englishman, good-looking, but with a naive not over-intelligent face. Apparently he decided that the man whose association with the Baroness von Reudath had caused so much commotion was, after all, of a harmless type. He actually smiled, and bade Sophie present Foster to him. The latter appeared overwhelmed with gratification at the honour. He stammered, dropped his eyeglass, screwed it back in his eye, and generally comported himself as though thoroughly confused. Von Strom watched him with a smile of half-veiled contempt. His English was not very good, and he refrained from airing it to any great extent. Presently he turned back to the girl.

'I am surprised,' he commented, 'that a woman of your great intelligence should find any pleasure in the company of such a man. He is good-looking, yes possesses a fine figure, no doubt, but he is only a fool. The rumours I have heard that you were in love with him are absurd. You, Sophie Von Reudath, could not love a man of his type. I must admit the sight of him has eased my mind.'

The baroness stole a look at the innocently bland countenance of her lover. She felt she would have given a lot to have been able to laugh at that moment. There was certainly a fool at the top of these steps, she reflected, but it was not Bernard Foster.

'You are cruel to him, Friedrich,' she protested. 'He is really very nice and he amuses me.'

'Have you made it clear to him that he must discontinue his friendship with you?'

She sighed.

'Yes; and he has submitted to your decree, but it has upset him very much. He told me Colonel Schönewald had already made that apparent. What harm can there possibly be in his association with me, Friedrich? I confess I do not understand. I like him, and he loves me. It is nice to be loved.'

'Have I not proved that I love you?' demanded the Marshal. 'Is not that sufficient for you? You should know that being a woman who has knowledge of great matters, it is unwise to possess too many so-called friends, more particularly when they are foreigners. I expect you to remember that your life is devoted to Germany and to me. I can make you great – what can a man of his type do?'

'You talk as though there was a question of my choosing

between you,' she protested in reply to his bombastic utterance. 'Why should you do that?'

'Choose between us!' he sneered. 'How absurd!'

'That is exactly what I thought. There is no question of a choice at all.'

'So! Let us have no more foolishness then. What were you and he talking about in the garden for so long? I am told that you have been there for an hour and twenty minutes.'

'Why is it that my movements are being spied upon?' she cried passionately. 'Why am I made to feel a prisoner in my own house?'

'I desire to protect you from fools,' was the reply. 'Tell me what you spoke about!'

'There were so many things that it is difficult to remember. We spoke of the flowers – he thought the garden lovely – about places we had visited in Budapest, people we had met. He asked me a lot of questions about the beauty spots of Berlin and its suburbs, about the restaurants, bathing places, and the best dancing resorts, and – oh! A lot of other trivial matters.'

'It took an hour and twenty minutes for rubbish like that,' commented von Strom. 'What a waste of time! Did he ask you any questions concerning the army, the navy, or the flying service?'

'Not a single one. Why do you ask?'

'Foreigners are apt to be inquisitive on those points. Very well, dismiss him. You and I will walk in the garden for a little while, then you shall entertain me to lunch.'

Sophie turned to Foster, and held out her hand.

'Goodbye,' she said. 'I have enjoyed your companionship on my holiday. It has been very nice. When you go back to England, give my love to Mrs Manvers-Buller and all my other friends.'

'Is this really goodbye?' asked Foster as he held her hand in his.

'Is it quite out of the question for me to come and see you again?'

'Quite, I am afraid. You will find many friends in Berlin, however, if you decide to stay here for a little while. I will ask people to call on you.'

'Come, Baroness!' called the marshal. 'I am waiting.'

She left him with a smile intended only for him – a smile which conveyed many things. He bowed to von Strom, received a curt nod by way of reply, and entered the library. The officer standing on the threshold of the French windows moved aside to let him pass, favouring him with a contemptuous glance as he did so.

After an exceedingly lonely dinner at his hotel, during which he was oppressed by memories of Sophie, his partner at so many meals during the previous fortnight, he went to the Gourmania roof, the indefatigable Schmidt accompanying him as before. By that time he had given up protesting against the fellow's presence. It was merely a waste of breath. Schmidt reiterated with monotonous regularity that his main duty was the protection of the visitor.

'You do not the Sherman spik,' he repeated. 'If you got lost what you do?'

Foster, therefore, resigned himself to the inevitable. The man did not obtrude at the Gourmania which was one blessing. The place was so crowded that the Englishman felt it would have been an easy matter to have given his follower the slip had he desired to do so. No doubt, though, Johann Schmidt was lurking in the vicinity somewhere. The Gourmania was very modern. There seemed to be music and dancing on every floor. The roof was narrow and long with a circular dance floor at each end. The ceiling, of opaque glass from which a bluish illumination was diffused, was supported by columns of burnished copper; the walls were panelled in blue glass. A large jazz band supplied the music. There did not seem to be a vacant table in the place, but a seat was found for him at one where a man and girl were sitting, apparently unconscious of anyone but themselves. Foster was rather embarrassed. He did not like intruding on what was so obviously a love affair. It seemed the custom at the Gourmania, however, for strangers to share tables. He ordered coffee, rejecting the waiter's suggestion that he should try the almost universally popular drink, a sickly-looking concoction in long narrow glasses. It surprised him to observe that little beer was being drunk. At one table not very far from his, however, a small, remarkably small, very stout man, with a fierce moustache and hair like the bristles of a brush, was very busily engaged in drinking beer. A succession of glasses of Pilsener seemed to reach his table, be emptied and replaced. The Englishman frowned thoughtfully. Where had he seen the fellow before? Suddenly it dawned on him. He was Jerry Cousins! It was stupid of him not to have remembered at once, but the disguise was so marvellous. Foster wondered, what he was doing there. As he took no notice of the other people sharing his table, it was to be presumed that he was alone.

At the table beyond Cousins' were two beautifully dressed young women and a fair-haired, good-looking man. Foster recognised the latter at once as Colonel Schönewald, and immediately became deeply thoughtful. Was it possible that his colleagues were keeping watch on the young Nazi officer? He grew so interested that it was some time before he noticed that the waiter was patiently standing by expecting him to pay for the coffee. He took out a handful of change and was looking for the coin he needed, when a voice asked if he was having trouble.

He looked up to find Schönewald smiling down at him.

'I thought you were in difficulties,' remarked the German. 'Money is always a beastly nuisance when one first tries to understand it in a foreign country. Allow me!'

He selected a mark from the heap in Foster's hand.

'That isn't enough for a tip as well, is it?' asked the Englishman.

'Heavens, yes! More than enough. Don't spoil the fellow.' The waiter departed, well satisfied. 'Would you like to join my party?' went on Schönewald. 'It must be beastly lonely for you. If you're keen on dancing, you'll find that the two ladies with me are A1.'

Foster rose with real gratitude.

'I say that's sporting of you,' he declared. 'Are you sure I won't be butting in?'

'Of course not. Bring your coffee along.'

Foster followed him to the other table where the two girls watched his approach with smiling friendly eyes. Though neither of them was particularly good-looking, they both had attractive faces. One was exceptionally dark, with a magnificent pair of eyes that more than made up for the shortcomings of her other features. The other had brown hair, blue eyes, and an excellent complexion. Schönewald introduced the first as Fraulein Marlene Heckler, the second as Fraulein Hilda Zeiss.

'They both speak English as well as I do,' he added with a laugh, 'so you need have no qualms. By the way, have you learnt any German yet?'

'Oh, I say, give a fellow a chance,' begged Foster. 'I only arrived last night. I find, though, that one can get along very nicely by saying "ja" and "so" every few minutes.'

The three laughed.

'It might come a trifle awkward on occasions,' commented

Schönewald. 'For instance,' he added. 'I wouldn't recommend you to say "ja", if asked whether you are in this country to learn the secrets possessed by the Baroness von Reudath.'

Foster inwardly felt a sense of perturbation. Had he been invited to that table, not altogether from motives of friendliness but more with the idea of subjecting him to an innocently sounding kind of third degree? The thought put him very much on his guard. He eyed Schönewald with an air of complete innocence.

'Does she possess any secrets of importance?' he asked. 'I can't help feeling mystified, don't you know. We're all friends here, and all that, so I suppose you won't mind my asking you a question.'

'Not at all,' murmured Schönewald. 'Go ahead!'

Foster noticed a swift look pass between him and the black-haired girl.

'What is it all about?' he asked. 'You came to me this morning and warned me to cease showing any interest in the baroness. You also asked me whether she had divulged any matters of importance to me, and hinted at state secrets and what not. I find it all jolly mysterious and can't make head nor tail of it. Can't you give me some sort of idea about what you're all driving at?'

Schönewald smiled.

'I'm sorry,' he replied regretfully, 'but I can't. If I could, I assure, I would.'

Foster sighed.

'I tried to get the baroness to tell me what the trouble is,' he observed, 'and why I was forbidden to see her, but she would only say that her holiday was over, and that, as she is a busy woman, she could not spare any more time to me. Of course she said she was sorry about it, and all that sort of thing, but it's beastly hard on a fellow, don't you know. At least I think someone might tell me why I'm regarded as a jolly old plague spot.'

'You take it too seriously, my dear chap,' laughed Schönewald. 'Forget all about the baroness, if you can. It will be better for both of you.'

'Forget her!' repeated Foster. 'Sounds easy enough, doesn't it? I'd like to see you try it, if you felt as I do about her.'

'You see,' observed the Nazi in rapid German to Marlene Heckler, 'he is just in love with her – nothing else. A young fool with more money than brains, but a nice fellow all the same. There is no guile in him.'

'I think you are right,' she answered, 'but I will see what I can do.' She turned to Foster with a smile. 'The Herr Colonel has told me that you are very much fond of dancing,' she remarked in English. 'I also like it. One can forget much when waltzing or foxtrotting. Would you like to dance with me, and afterwards with Hilda?'

'Rather,' he assented eagerly. 'I was about to ask you myself.'

They rose, Schönewald, at the same time, inviting Hilda Zeiss. It was at that moment that Cousins, in the person of the little fat German at the next table, rose and somehow or other tripped. He plunged headlong into Foster, sending him staggering back. If the latter had not grabbed him, he would have fallen to the floor. In the short time that it took to steady him, however, Cousins whispered urgently:

'Be careful of Marlene Heckler – one of Germany's most dangerous spies.'

Foster's face retained its ingenuous expression. The accident seemed only to have amused him. He patted the little man on the shoulders.

'You're not built for violent gymnastics, don't you know,' he remarked.

Schönewald laughed.

'Clumsy little beast,' he commented. 'More than half drunk I expect.' He added a reprimand in German to which the disguised German responded by apologising profoundly. 'Now,' continued the Nazi officer, 'let us on with the dance.'

Foster found that Marlene Heckler was an excellent exponent. She was as light as a feather and very adaptable, but her dancing only made his heart ache the more for Sophie. He almost felt that he was acting the traitor to her in dancing with another woman. But Fraulein Heckler gave him little leisure to allow his thoughts to dwell on Sophie. All the time they were dancing, she was questioning him with devilish, insidious cleverness. If he had not been on his guard, it is almost certain that he would have, more than once, fallen into the cunningly prepared traps set for him. It is a tribute to his astuteness that on returning to their table she told Schönewald that it was obvious that he was no more than he seemed; a perfectly harmless, wealthy Englishman whose brains were certainly not his strong point. Having made that statement, she turned to Foster, and thanked him for the dance.

'I was telling the Herr Colonel,' she added, 'that you are one of the best dancers I have ever been with.'

Foster bowed as though delighted at the compliment. He said nothing, but thought a great deal.

He stayed with them until very late, alternatively dancing with Marlene and Hilda. The latter made no attempt to cross-examine him or, in fact, to question him at all. She spoke mostly about the life of Berlin, anxious apparently to supply him with information which would enable him to enjoy himself during his stay in the capital. On the other hand Fraulein Heckler continued her task of delving deep into his history. She was amazingly skilful in her questioning, which had air of the utmost innocence. To all intents and purposes she was merely a woman interested in a man who rather attracted her. Being a foreigner she was curious about his mode of life. Yet every question had its point, most of them being concerned with the period subsequent to his leaving the army. Foster found the inquisition nerve-racking; he felt mentally tired when, at last, the party broke up.

CHAPTER TEN

Certified Insane

That night in the seclusion of his comfortable room he wrote out a detailed account in code of his interview with the baroness, taking special care to emphasise the pleasure she had shown at the knowledge, that she could rely upon the British Secret Service to support her if necessary. He repeated her undertaking that she would confide everything she knew to a document, which she would hide inside a pedestal containing the naiad on the fountain; described the exact position. He stressed the fact that he had given his word that search would not be made for the papers unless any calamity befell her. He wrote of his meeting with von Strom, repeating almost word for word that which had been said. He then went on to tell of the events of the evening. Cousins, he knew, would already have reported that he had been invited by Colonel Schönewald to join his party at the Gourmania. He confined himself, therefore, to describing the manner in which Marlene

Heckler, had cross-examined him and had attempted to trap him into a disclosure which might have ended in his real purpose in Berlin becoming known. The completed report was folded into as small a compass as possible, and sealed in an envelope. He placed it on the writing table, while he proceeded to collect and destroy the scraps of paper, he had used to enable him to transcribe his statement into code. He was meticulous in the care he took. Each was torn into minute fragments, after which he carried the heap to the fireplace, and set it alight.

While it was burning, he stood wondering where the best place would be to keep his report safe while he slept; came to the conclusion that the pocket of his pyjama jacket could hardly be bettered. His eyes strayed to the writing table and, at once, he stiffened apprehensively. As it was placed close to one of the windows, it was natural that the curtains should come within his range of vision. They were moving gently, to and fro as though swayed by a breeze. He had taken care to close both windows before commencing to write, this was therefore, to say the least of it, surprising and distinctly disturbing. It was impossible for the wind to flutter the curtains unless the window had opened. He remembered clearly fastening the catch. It could not have been blown open, therefore. But it would not be a very difficult matter for someone, provided with the necessary implements, to open it from the outside. There had been no sound, but an expert would be able to work quietly. Foster was convinced that a man had climbed up to the balcony, had possibly watched him while he wrote through a gap between the curtains, then, as soon as he had moved, had set to work on the window. But what was his object? The answer came to him immediately. The intruder was bent on stealing the letter. It still lay on the table, and quickly but noiselessly he walked across to pick it up.

As he was about to take possession of it, the curtains moved inwards and, from behind it, came a hand, broad and sinewy. The fingers were in the act of clutching the envelope, when Foster gripped the wrist with all his strength; at the same time he picked up the document with his other hand, pushing it into his pocket. A low but startled cry reached his ears. The intruder tried desperately to draw his hand away, but the Secret Service man held on. He endeavoured to sweep the curtain aside. The other, however, probably with the desire to escape recognition, kept it before his face. Foster immediately grappled with him, curtain and all, with the result that before long, it was torn from its fastenings. Then ensued a fierce struggle rendered more bizarre perhaps by the utter lack of sound from the Englishman's opponent. To and fro they swayed, but his very anxiety to avoid showing his face proved the downfall of the fellow. The curtain had fallen more on him than on Foster, and he was rapidly becoming enveloped in its folds. They collided with a large pedestal, sending the ornaments it contained crashing to the floor. A moment later they themselves went over, making noise enough to rouse the whole hotel. Slowly but surely now Foster began to get the upper hand, wrapping his antagonist more and more in the curtain until, at last, he was rendered helpless and, indeed, must have been half suffocated by the thick heavy material enfolding his head. He was a burly fellow. The Secret Service man reflected that, if he had not had the curtain to assist him, the chances are that he would have had the worst of the struggle. Now that the other was unable to make further resistance the Secret Service man enveloped him more tightly, and sat on him to await events. He took from his pocket a letter he had that evening written to his sister, and threw it on the writing table. It was not long before there came a loud knocking, accompanied by the sound of excited voices. Foster left his human seat, strolled across the room, and opened the door. Outside was a dozen or more people all but two who were porters clad in night attire, the majority of them looking thoroughly startled. Eyes stared at the Englishman with the crumpled shirtfront, disordered hair, and general appearance of dishevelment; a babel of excited questions burst on his ears. He smiled at them, shook his head to indicate that he did not understand and stuck the monocle in his eye. The night porters pushed their way to the foreground. One had a little English.

'Sare,' he demanded with painful care, 'vot is it dot are the – the pig noise make?'

For answer Foster pointed to the struggling bundle lying over by the window. Immediately there was a rush in the direction.

'Take care!' warned the Englishman. 'He is a burglar. He might be armed.'

Apparently some of the invaders of his privacy understood English. They stopped, and began to draw back, passing on the information to the others as they did so. The result was that the man in the curtain was left severely alone, while a debate took place concerning him. The position had its amusing side. Foster was beginning to enjoy himself. After all, no harm had been done. Of course the fellow was a spy not a burglar. He had been instructed, no doubt, to watch the room. Possibly he had become curious, when he noticed that the light had been kept burning – Foster had not bothered to draw the curtains very closely before the other window – and had climbed up to see what the Englishman was doing. The letter must have interested him vastly. It suggested so many possibilities. The man, therefore, had resolved to obtain possession of it. All this was conjecture, of course. There were flaws in it. For instance it was curious that the intruder had possessed the means at hand of opening a locked window. The thought occurred to the Secret Service man that it might have been his intention to burgle his way into the room while the occupant slept, and search his clothing. It seemed very likely. Foster sighed. These Germans took an awful lot of convincing of the bona fides of a man once they had become suspicious of him. The debate went on with increasing vehemence. One of the porters went off to rouse the manager. For a moment the Englishman was forgotten. It was then that he received a surprise.

'What was he after?' breathed a voice in his ear.

Foster had some difficulty in preventing himself from starting. He looked hastily at the man standing close by his side. It was Sir Leonard Wallace – or rather the bronzed, jolly-looking naval officer with the round face whose person cloaked that of the Chief of the British Secret Service. Sir Leonard was clad in pyjamas of a loud pattern. Like others he had not bothered to don a dressing gown. There were women among the throng – they also wore nightdresses or pyjamas without any other covering, but nobody bothers about trifles like that in Berlin.

'He climbed up,' whispered Foster, bending down in order that his lips could not be seen moving, 'opened the window, and was after the report I had written for you.'

'You'd better give it to me now – safer for you. My room's next door on the right, if you want me, knock three times on the wall.'

Foster withdrew the document from his pocket cautiously. It was transferred cleverly to Sir Leonard, who seemed to perform a conjuring trick. At all events it vanished right under Foster's eyes. The chief moved away and joined in the discussion with gesturing of his right hand. The left as usual, was hidden in the pocket of his jacket.

The manager, the assistant manager, the porter who had gone to rouse them, and other members of the hotel staff hurried into the room. The burglar had not, up to that time, succeeded in freeing himself from the folds of the curtain. He was lying perfectly still now. Foster became rather alarmed lest he had suffocated. The manager, who spoke very good English, asked courteously to be told what had occurred. The Secret Service man decided that it was safer to tell the truth or, at least, give the semblance of truth to his story.

'I had been writing a letter,' he declared, and nodded at the envelope lying on the writing table. 'I walked away, and was about to prepare myself for bed, when I noticed the curtain by that window blowing to and fro. As I had shut the window, that struck me as curious. I went to investigate and had almost reached the spot when a hand appeared. I caught hold of it. There was a bit of a fight, during which the curtain was pulled down, so I wrapped him in it. There he is.'

The story was translated to the others. Great indignation at the attempted burglary was expressed as well as admiration for the conduct of the Englishman. At the manager's orders the curtain was unwound and the burglar released. He was blue in the face and semiconscious, but Foster recognised him at once. He could not forbear a little chuckle.

'Well, well, well!' he exclaimed. 'If it isn't my guide, philosopher and friend, Johann Schmidt. Protector of the lonely stranger by day, burglar by night.' He picked up a carafe of water, and emptied the contents on the face of the half-suffocated man. 'That should bring him properly round,' he observed.

It did. Schmidt gasped and struggled to his feet, assisted by the porters, who kept a tight grip on his arms. Foster noticed, with a feeling of amusement, that the manager and assistant manager were regarding each with eyes, in which perplexity, embarrassment and annoyance struggled for mastery. Johann looked at the young man sheepishly, commenced to speak, but the manager immediately cut him short. He ordered him to be taken below, after which he turned to the Englishman, and apologised profusely for the burglary.

'It is most terrible that such a thing in my hotel should happen. It is more terrible because he is a man that we have much trusted. Measures will be taken to see that he is punished. I will the police send for.'

'Yes, do,' murmured Foster.

'In the morning you will a statement make to them – no?'

'Yes. I shall be very glad to make a statement.'

The manager bowed. He requested the guests to return to their rooms, begging them not to be alarmed. They had a good deal to say about burglars in general and precautions that hotels should take against outrages of that kind, but eventually they all dispersed. The manager and his assistants bade Foster good night and followed them.

'Don't let him escape!' the Englishman called out as they left the room.

He sat on the edge of the bed and chuckled softly to himself. He felt he would be greatly surprised if he saw or heard any more of Johann Schmidt. It had been a narrow escape, though. The thought of the consequences, if his report had fallen into the hands of the German secret police, caused him to grow serious. He smiled again, however, at recollection of the surprising appearance of Sir Leonard. It was comforting to know the chief was close by; it was more comforting to know that he had the document. Foster walked across to the fireplace and stamped the ashes of the papers he had burnt into dust. When that was done to his satisfaction, he undressed, and went to bed.

Anticipating that the early morning visitation of Johann Schmidt to his room would be conveniently forgotten by the hotel authorities who, he believed, were under the thumb of the police, he was surprised at breakfast to be told that certain officials were waiting outside his room to interview him. He at once gave orders for them to be shown in. When three solemn-looking gentlemen in frock coats entered, followed by two burly fellows, who were probably policemen in plain clothes, he became greatly interested. The frock-coated men looked more like doctors or lawyers than officials of the police. Apart from that, he was amazed that so many apparently important individuals should take the trouble to visit his room to interview him about a clumsy attempt at burglary.

'Will you be seated, gentlemen?' he invited. 'I have just finished breakfast, and am quite at your disposal. Oh! I forgot. I hope you understand me. I'm afraid I cannot speak German.'

'So!' nodded the man who appeared the senior, a short, stout individual with grey hair, a mouth like a rat trap, and a pince nez. 'It is well. We all the English speak.'

The three solemnly took chairs facing Foster, the other two men remaining by the door. The Secret Service agent grew puzzled. He was perplexed by the way in which they were staring at him. He looked from one to another wondering what was the reason for their intense scrutiny.

'Your name,' remarked the spokesman presently, 'is Bernard Foster. That is so?' Foster nodded. 'You are an Englishman, residing in London, who on a holiday to Berlin have come. Correct?'

'Quite correct, Mr Inspector or Superintendent, or whatever you are, but don't you think we can dispense with all that formality?

Everything possible must be known in Berlin about me by now. You have come for my statement, of course. Well, suppose you get out your notebook and pencil, and I'll tell you all I know.'

The three men looked significantly at each other. The leader cleared his throat importantly.

'I see that it is necessary to introduce mineself and these gentlemen to you, Herr Foster. I am not superintendant or inspector, as your poor mind leads you to think. I Doctor Keller am; these gentlemen Doctor Hagenow and Doctor Spraght are.'

Foster stared unbelievingly at them, then he sat back in his chair, and laughed heartily.

'This is the first time,' he chuckled, 'that I have heard of doctors being sent to investigate a criminal case.' Again came that significant look between the three men. Foster stopped laughing, and frowned. 'Perhaps,' he begged, 'you will be good enough to tell me what it all means.'

Dr Keller addressed his colleagues in English.

'You note, mine friends,' he remarked, 'the moods how quickly they change. There is first impatience, afterwards laughter, that is not controlled mit itself; then comes again the change. He frowns; a question he asks mit abruptness.'

Foster attempted to speak, but Dr Keller held up a pudgy hand.

'One minute,' he begged; 'afterwards, all you wish you can talk. There have not to us yet been signs of violence,' he resumed to the other two, 'but the evidence that before us has been given by the porters and the guests and the man Schmidt himself cannot be ignored. The possibility of violence at any time must be considered – no doubt in him a tendency there must be. If agreed mit that we are, under restraint he must be put. Mine colleagues and I will to a home for mental rest send you. Every care and attention you will have, and perhaps someday quite well again you will be.'

As full realisation of the vile plot being hatched against him dawned on Foster, he felt sick with horror. These men had come to certify him insane, and have him confined in a mental asylum, perhaps for ever. Of course, the Supreme Marshal was the instigator. Though proofs of Foster's harmlessness must have been put before him, he still insisted on regarding him with suspicion. Probably information had reached him of the happenings of the night. The fact that Foster had been writing at such a late hour had appeared to him significant, and he had decided to make certain that neither the Englishman nor the letter he had written would ever leave the country to spread any secret information they might possess. The Secret Service man threw a glance at the writing table. The letter for his sister still lay there. She would never receive it now. Thank God, the other, the vital document, was safe! Had Sir Leonard Wallace anticipated something like this happening when he had asked for it? Remembrance of the chief sent a sudden wave of hope through him; then again his spirits fell. What could even Sir Leonard do to save him from the living death of a mental home? If he had been an ordinary traveller the British embassy could have been informed. English doctors to examine him could have been insisted upon, his removal to England demanded. But he was a member of the British Secret Service, for whom no steps could be taken when in difficulties on foreign soil.

CHAPTER ELEVEN

The Baroness Speaks Her Mind

When the doctors had gone Foster sat in his chair for a long time, hardly moving, his mind working quickly, desperately. It was imperative that he must communicate somehow with one or other of his colleagues, but how? Once he was taken away, he would never have the chance, and the possibilities were all against their ever discovering where he had gone, or what had happened to him. His greatest anxiety was concerned with asking them to keep watch on Sophie. He had a horrible feeling that something unpleasant had happened, or was about to happen to her. A man who would not hesitate to have a foreigner certified insane, who to all intents and purposes was innocent of any word or act detrimental to the state, would certainly not scruple to safeguard himself by removing a woman who possessed his secrets, and was suspected of being in love with that foreigner. Once or twice he looked at the telephone, only to reflect that it was probably disconnected. At all events it was certain that any call he attempted to make would be ignored. Eventually he rose and, in order to test his supposition, took up the receiver. He had not been wrong; the line was blank. He then walked to the door, but the massive custodian barred his way, making it very evident that they had no intention of allowing him out. He argued with them vehemently. He would have obtained as much satisfaction in addressing the door or the wall. They merely regarded him with sheepish grins. Presently he wandered on to the balcony, and contemplated the garden below. It looked infinitely alluring; cool in shadow, bright in the brilliant sunshine. Some of the hotel guests sat there in the shade, lounging in long chairs with books or papers on their knees, or chatting idly to each other. Foster wondered what they would think or do, if they saw a man climbing to the ground from his room. Useless to try, of course. His guardians would tackle him before he could clamber over the balcony railing, besides – yes, there was a man on watch. He recognised Johann Schmidt with a grimace of disgust. Would he never see the last of the fellow! It was rather surprising that his services had not been dispensed with. His masters were of the kind that would not tolerate blunders. Schmidt had certainly blundered the previous night in allowing himself to be caught. Possibly he had been permitted to continue his duties in order that credence should be given to the tale that had been concocted. No doubt by that time the lie had been spread among the guests, at least among those who had heard the noise and had invaded Foster's room, that there had been no attempted burglary, but that the Englishman was insane, and had attacked the poor innocent fellow who was looking after him! Foster wondered whether Sir Leonard had heard the story. If so, he would have immediately put two and two together and comprehended the whole plot. Hope rose again in the young man's breast. He wished ardently that he could have given the signal that he was in difficulties. At least, he could have made certain then that Sir Leonard would investigate. Bernard's custodians would naturally enough become suspicious if he tapped on the wall, apart from which the chances were that Sir Leonard would not be in his room. Almost as that thought struck him, he observed the very man he most wished to see sprawling comfortably on a chair on the next balcony, only a few yards from him. Sight of the chief did him good, while the encouraging smile he received – even though it could hardly be described as Sir Leonard's own smile – raised his spirits immeasurably. He became aware that Wallace was tapping his pipe monotonously on the floor, and it was borne to his mind that his attention was being called in Morse. Quickly he ascertained that he was correct. He knocked his own pipe on the railing, denoting that he was listening, then rapidly the following message was rapped out to him:

Know what has happened. Do not worry. Go wherever they take you without resistance. We will not be far away.

Foster was naturally relieved, but his thoughts were still centred on Sophie. He signified that he understood, after which he conveyed to Sir Leonard his anxiety regarding the girl. Back came the reply:

Cousins on the job. Has been watching at her house since early morning.

That indeed was excellent news. A feeling of tremendous relief surged through the young Secret Service agent, as well as an immense sense of gratitude to Sir Leonard and Cousins. What a wonderful pair they were, he reflected. They were ubiquitous; always managed to be in the right place at the right moment.

After lunch he returned to his seat on the balcony, carrying a book with him. He noticed that his custodians took turns in going off for a meal. They had apparently decided that they need expect no trouble from him, or had become convinced that one alone would be quite able to overcome him if he suddenly became obstreperous. A clock somewhere was just striking three, when he heard a commotion going on outside his room. He started to his feet as the door was flung open, the attendant then on duty making an attempt to clutch it, but failing. Foster gave vent to a great cry. Standing on the threshold, her little fists clenched, her eyes flashing angrily, was Sophie. Behind her were the manager, his assistant, and two or three other members of the hotel staff, all looking thoroughly startled and ill at ease. She glared at the man on guard.

'Go out!' she ordered. He began to protest. 'Go out!' she repeated, stamping her foot. 'Stay outside, if you wish, but go out!'

He went without another word, and she slammed the door after him. Immediately she turned to face Foster, and now all the anger was gone, her eyes had become definitely soft and gentle.

'My Bernard,' she cried, 'what is this I hear? What are they trying to do to you?'

'Oh, Sophie, dearest,' he groaned, hurrying to her and taking her hands in his, 'you should not have come. God knows what may happen to you, when it is known. Why did you come?'

'Do you think I would allow them to do this terrible thing to my man without protest or expostulation?' she demanded. 'If you think that, you do not know me yet, Bernard.'

'Am I really your man, Sophie?' he asked very softly.

She smiled gloriously; then all in a moment was in his arms, their lips meeting, for the first time, in a kiss that was delicious rapture to both. He held her closely, almost convulsively, to him as though he feared they would come and attempt to drag her away. For several minutes they remained thus, neither uttering a word, their hearts being too full for speech. He fondled her lovely, glossy hair, buried his face in it, his own soul concentrated on the joy of that moment. Whatever happened afterwards, nothing, nobody, they each felt, could ever rob them of an infinitely precious memory. At length she stirred in his embrace.

'Oh, Bernard,' she whispered. 'I thought I was a woman so strong, who had dedicated herself to one object, and see what love has done to me! It has made me weak and a coward. I am so fearful for you; I am so frightened lest anything happen to me and I should thus be deprived of the happiness you have brought to me.'

He placed her gently in a chair; sat down opposite and very close to her.

'I am afraid that, by coming here,' he remarked, his voice expressing the anxiety he felt, 'you have placed yourself in a very dangerous position. How did you know about – about my predicament?'

'The Marshal of State himself, told me,' she replied. 'He came to me gloating – oh! It was terrible – just as I had finished luncheon. "You will no longer be troubled by that foolish Englishman," he said. "Last night he did something which made it necessary for doctors to examine him. Without doubt they were satisfied he is insane. He is to be moved to a private asylum, where great care will be taken of him." Can you imagine how I felt, when he told me that, Bernard? I knew of course, that it was a wicked plot, and the thought came to me that perhaps you would think I had betrayed the confidence you had reposed in me.'

'Good Lord, no! Such a thought never even occurred to me.'

'I am glad. It was very much difficult for me to control myself – the shock to me was so great. I asked him what it was you did last night but he only laughed. He would not say. What was it, Bernard?' He told her what had happened. 'So! I see,' she nodded. 'In spite of everything, they still have suspicions. That letter alarmed them. That you should take the trouble to write at an hour so late has caused them much concern. What has happened to it? The letter I mean?'

He nodded in the direction of the writing table.

'A letter to my sister is still lying there,' he observed. 'It was there last night, and it still remains unposted, as you see. I asked one of the fellows guarding me to take it to the post, but he refused. Nobody shows any concern in it.'

She smiled slightly.

'It is quite innocent?'

'Of course.'

'You may be quite sure that it will be examined. Everything you possess will be searched. It is inevitable.'

He told her of his meeting with Schönewald and the two women, and of the clever cross-examination to which he had been subjected by Marlene Heckler.

'An expert, that woman!' he declared. 'She made her questions sound so thoroughly innocent, yet setting traps for me. Luckily I was on my guard!'

Sophie gasped.

'Marlene Heckler is one of the cleverest members of the Espionage Service,' she confided in a low voice. 'One of her principal duties is to know members of the secret departments of other countries. How, she does it, I do not know, but somehow she becomes acquainted with them. I once visited her flat. In it there is an album full of photographs of men who do espionage work for their countries. Among them were portraits of Sir Leonard Wallace, Major Brien, and others of your famous Secret Service.'

'Mine could hardly have been there,' he whispered. 'My connections have been kept very quiet always. I am quite convinced, from what I heard her say to Schönewald in German, that neither she nor he suspected me of being anything but a brainless fool with more money than sense.'

'That may have been said for your benefit in case you did understand German. You cannot be sure what is in the brain of a woman like Marlene.'

Foster looked a trifle uncomfortable.

'You make her appear a very formidable person, Sophie,' he grunted.

'She is very much formidable.'

'Does von Strom know you are here?'

She shrugged her shoulders.

'If he does not, very soon he will. My house, I know, is full of spies. I came to you as soon as he had departed, and I did not make a secret of my intentions.'

'Oh, Sophie, Sophie!' he gasped. 'Why did you do it?'

'I could not help it,' she returned; 'I had to. You mean so much to me, Bernard,' she bent forward, and clasped his hands, 'so very much. I cannot let them treat you in a manner so wicked, besides I had to make sure that you did not suspect me of betraying you.'

'I would never have done that,' he assured her earnestly.

'From here,' she went on, 'I will go straight to the Marshal. I will tell him I have been to see you, and that it is absurd and wicked to say you are insane.'

'Please, dear,' he pleaded, 'don't do that. Keep out of this business, if you possibly can; though I fear that this visit will have very grave consequences. You need not fear me. They can shut me up in any asylum if they like, but, I assure you, it will not be for long.'

'How do you know?' she demanded. 'Once you are there, they will never permit you to go free again.'

He smiled.

'I repeat, I shall not be there long. Von Strom and all his satellites will fail to retain me, once a certain individual decides it is time I was free.'

'You seem very confident.'

'I am. There is another thing, which it may relieve your mind to know, you are being watched for fear any steps of an inimical nature should be taken against you. Once anything of that kind happens or, is thought, is about to happen the British Secret Service will not rest until you are safe.'

'Are you sure of that?' she asked, her eyes shining.

'Positive. Now go back to your home, Sophie, and do your best to remove the bad impression this visit will have created in the mind of von Strom. Tell him you have been to see me to assure yourself of my condition and, if you think it will help, agree that I certainly do not appear quite normal. Say anything to make him believe that any suspicion of you would be absurd. Please! I ask you to do this for your own sake. The thought of what that man might do, if he decides finally that you are dangerous to him, makes my blood feel like water.'

'Why should I fear him now I know that the wonderful English Secret Service is watching over me.'

'The Secret Service is not infallible, dear, and you must remember we are in Germany where the Supreme Marshal's word is law. He does not need warrants to help him do things. You could be whisked away to a prison or fortress without the slightest warning. Even then it is possible your escape might be arranged, but supposing that you could not be traced. I beg of you, Sophie, do as I say. Don't worry about me. I shall be perfectly all right.'

'You are quite certain of that?'

'Absolutely.'

'Then my mind is greatly relieved, my Bernard.' She rose. 'I will go now and, if it will be of any comfort to you, then I will promise to do my best to allay any suspicions my visit to you has perhaps caused.'

She held out her hands to him, and again he took her into his arms, kissing her hair, her eyes, lingering with a sense of wonderful ecstasy on the lips surrendered so frankly and eagerly to his. They were so entirely lost to thought of all but themselves and the rapture at that moment that they did not hear the door open. Von Strom himself, accompanied by the Minister of Propaganda and Colonel Schönewald stood on the threshold. At sight of the two wrapped in an embrace that was eloquent of their love, he frowned angrily, his teeth viciously biting his nether lip.

'So!' he snarled. 'The Baroness von Reudath is so lost to all sense of decency and honour that she rushes to a man who is known to be insane, and shuts herself up in his bedroom with him.'

Sophie and Bernard turned with startled faces to confront him, but she still clasped her lover's arm. The hot blood flushed her countenance a deep crimson at his remark; her eyes flashed with angry indignation. Foster never quite knew how he refrained from giving himself away at that moment. A heated reply rushed to his lips to be stifled barely in time. He came very close just then to betraying his knowledge of German. However, he succeeded in looking merely embarrassed.

'You lied to me,' von Strom snapped at Sophie, his harsh voice sounding more unpleasant than usual. 'You told me you did not love him; that he only amused you.'

'I did not lie to you,' she flashed back, her head raised defiantly. 'I did not tell you I did not love him. It is true that I also did not say that I do, for why should I? I am the mistress of my own heart. What right have you to say whom I shall or shall not love? I have been a good friend to you, sir, but I have never given you the right to order my life for me. Since you have intruded in this unwarrantable manner, you may as well know the truth. I do love Herr Foster with all the power of love I have in me and I am going to marry him.'

He contemplated her, for several seconds in silence, making no attempt to veil the sneer that curled his thick lips.

'So!' he commented at length. 'You are going to marry him! That is indeed news. Do you think by so doing you may restore his mind to health?'

'He is no more insane,' she cried scornfully, 'than you are. Far less in fact, for I am beginning to believe, on account of your behaviour and manner, that there is something wrong with your mind.'

Foster suppressed a groan. All hope of her escaping the vengeance of von Strom was rapidly evaporating. Instead of attempting to conciliate him she was deliberately defying him. It is true that the intimate scene he had interrupted had rendered extremely doubtful any possibility of Sophie being able to resume her old position of trusted friend and confidante. Nevertheless, Foster felt that something might have been done to save the situation. He pressed her arm in an effort to convey a warning to her, but she seemed determined now to champion the Englishman to the limit, and at the same time, convince the autocrat that his domination over her was at an end. She was a glorious picture of outraged dignity as she stood there her beautiful head raised proudly, her great blue eyes expressing her feelings without restraint.

'I was not even permitted to take a holiday away from Germany in peace,' she declared. 'Everywhere I went I was spied upon, my actions noted, my words reported. Because I formed a friendship with a charming Englishman which developed into love, you became alarmed. He and I also were regarded with suspicion. Since he has arrived in Berlin he has been harassed and watched by men instructed by you. Is that the way Germany should treat her guests? I have been subjected to espionage in my own home, made to feel myself almost a prisoner. Why has all this been done? Why have you committed the terrible crime of having Herr Foster certified as insane? Is it any wonder that I should begin to think that it is you who are mad?'

Von Strom had listened to her without interruption, but his brow had grown blacker and blacker as she spoke. She had barely finished, when the storm broke.

'How dare you speak in this manner to me, you wanton!' he raged. 'I wonder I do not strike you down at my feet. So this is the result of the friendship and privileges I have extended to you. You stand there and confess to a ridiculous love for a fool who may have money but has no position. You would scorn me, turn me aside – I, Supreme Marshal of Germany! – for a foreign nonentity. I was right. I suspected your duplicity. It was for that reason that I personally conveyed to you the news that he was to be confined in a home for mental cases. I wished to see how you would react. You were distressed. It was apparent, though you tried hard to hide the fact. After I had gone, you came here to your lover, to his room, where you threw yourself into his arms like any abandoned woman.'

'Stop!' she cried. 'You have no right to say things like that. You may be—'

'I have the right to say whatever I will. And I will add this. I am convinced that he is nothing but a spy, who has inveigled you into loving him in order to learn from you that which is not yours to impart.'

At that she laughed scornfully.

'So!' she cried. 'It is that which is behind it all. The great Marshal of State is in fear, he trembles lest his guilty secrets should be made public. What would the great German people think if they knew you were afraid? What would the Chancellor himself think? You have never had cause to distrust me, Excellency. I have not once, in the slightest particular, betrayed anything you have confided in me. As I say, it is only a guilty conscience that makes you fear. You have admitted me to your counsels with the Chancellor and the Minister of Propaganda. Why? Because you had a respect for what you called my woman's instinct, and sense, also because you were infatuated with me. You hoped one day I would submit to the proposals you were continually making to me.'

'Enough! Enough!' roared von Strom. 'You go too far, Baroness. If you—'

'Ah! You are again afraid. Afraid this time that I may tell

these gentlemen of the manner in which you entreated me to—'

'Wait outside!' ordered von Strom sharply turning to his companions.

They went at once. Sophie gave a contemptuous little laugh, and sank into a chair.

'You sent them away too late,' she observed quietly. 'They know now why it is the Baroness von Reudath was admitted to the confidence of his Excellency the Supreme Marshal of Germany. No doubt they suspected the reason, but now they are certain. They also know that your object failed.'

He stood glowering down at her, his whole attitude making it plain that she had gone beyond any hope of pardon or mercy from him. It was not difficult to guess at the thoughts that were passing through his mind. Foster's heart had sunk until a feeling of the most utter despair filled him. Why had she done it? She must have known that she was only rendering her position desperate. Von Strom completely ignored the Englishman; he seemed to have forgotten his presence.

'What did you mean,' he demanded, endeavouring to keep the passion from his voice, 'when you spoke of guilty conscience and guilty secrets. How can my conscience and my secrets be guilty?'

'You know very well,' she returned at once. 'Is it not your ambition, as soon as your preparations are complete, to plunge Europe into a war? You have—'

'Who told you that?' he shouted, all his rage rising to the surface again.

At that moment he looked a thoroughly startled man. There was a gleam in Sophie's eyes, and Foster thought he was beginning to understand her apparently reckless defiance. She had roused him to his present state of anger purposely. She was endeavouring to bluff him into disclosing the information which would either mean her divulging what she knew to the world or retaining, for ever, her silence. She was engaged in a gamble, quite unconcerned that whichever way it went her life would be forfeit. Foster listened fascinated.

'I do not betray matters confided to me,' she replied to his question. 'You ought to know that.'

'Answer me! Who spoke of war to you?'

She shook her head, looking up at him with insolent unconcern.

'Let it suffice that I do know. Are you so sure that you did not tell me yourself, Friedrich?'

'I certainly did not,' he stormed.

'But, my dear man,' she protested, her drawl being a model of calculated impudence, 'what of the confidential military plans? The secret concentration of troops on the Polish, French and Austrian frontiers, particularly on the Austrian frontier! That was not arranged for amusement.'

'It was a measure of defence. You know it. Have I not many times told you so?'

'You have and although I wondered why the most powerful army was to be sent to the Austrian frontier, I accepted your word. But since I have learnt differently. They are to be concentrated for offensive not defensive reasons, and it would be absurd of you to deny it.'

For a moment he was silent, staring malevolently down at her; then he bent and catching her roughly by the arms dragged her to her feet. Foster made a movement to go to her help, but paused. She would never forgive him if he interfered at that moment. He stood by therefore, biting his lip to restrain himself as von Strom cruelly shook the girl.

'Who has told you this?' shouted the man almost beside himself with passion. 'I will know. You shall tell me.' Then came the admission she had striven to obtain. 'Other than the Chancellor only two people beside myself know of my plans – one of them must be the traitor. Who is he?'

'What does it matter? You have told me yourself now.'

CHAPTER TWELVE

Charged with Treason

He released her and stood trembling with his anger. His eyes, boring into hers, certainly looked just then, as though they were those of a madman. Suddenly he let out a cry that must have been heard some distance away.

'God in Heaven!' he shouted. 'You were not told, you trapped me into an admission. What was your reason? Answer!'

She looked at him calmly, steadfastly in the face.

'Because I am an Austrian and love Austria,' she said quietly.

'And you would betray my plans, eh? What of your oath, you devil; what of it, I say?'

'When I believed Germany's intentions were merely defensive your secrets were safe with me. But I would be a wicked, degraded creature were I to keep silent, and allow her to throw the world into another war, permit you to devastate and ruin my own country. I withdraw my vow. At least I owe it to tell you that.'

'You traitress!' he hissed. 'You scheming, plotting creature of the devil! You will never have the opportunity of betraying me. You have signed your own death warrant. And,' he added with a laugh that sent a shiver through Foster, 'you can die with the knowledge that it is our intention to make your precious country a province of Germany. All my efforts are directed to the attainment of that object.' He gripped her again cruelly, shook her with savage force. 'Think of that and carry the thought to the grave with you, you infernal traitress.'

She shook her head.

'I am not a traitress,' she replied quietly. 'It is you, Supreme Marshal of Germany, who are the traitor, the renegade. You may kill me, if you will, but I shall die with the knowledge that I have done my part to save Austria and preserve Europe from wanton bloodshed.'

'Oh, you will,' he jeered, continuing to shake her brutally. 'We shall see.'

Foster had endured as much as flesh and blood could stand. He strode forward now and, gripping von Strom by the shoulders, swung him away from Sophie with such force that he went staggering across the room.

'I don't like your ways,' he drawled, 'and you'll keep your hands off the lady who is going to be my wife.' He caught sight of a bruise on Sophie's neck. 'God!' he exclaimed, 'I'm tempted to knock you down, Supreme Marshal or not.'

Von Strom stood glaring at him, in far too great a fury to reply in anything like passable English. However, he did his best.

'You – you – I haf forgot. On me the handts dare you to place! I – I—'

He almost frothed at the mouth.

Then abruptly he turned and left the room. They heard the sound of the door being locked. Sophie was very white, but she smiled up at her lover.

'I have obtained that link to my chain, Bernard,' she murmured.

He nodded miserably.

'But at what a cost,' he groaned. 'I didn't understand at first why you were going out of your way to defy him. I gathered what you were up to afterwards, of course. Sophie darling, was it worth it?'

She nodded her head emphatically.

'Certainly,' she declared, 'there is now nothing to hold back your friends from obtaining my statement from— where I have placed it. You told them?'

'Yes. So you have already put it there! You are sure nobody saw you?'

'I took very great care. It was at midnight, and there is no moon.'

Their conversation had been carried on in an almost inaudible whisper both feeling certain that ears were listening at the door eager to catch whatever was said. There suddenly came a knock, a slight pause; then Colonel Schönewald entered. His good-looking face wore a look of distress, his manner was a trifle embarrassed. He closed the door behind him, and bowed to the baroness.

'Nice of you to knock, Schönewald,' remarked Foster. 'At least you are a gentleman. There seems to be a remarkable shortage of them in Berlin.'

Schönewald ignored him. He addressed Sophie in a low apologetic tone.

'I very much regret, Baroness, that I have been ordered to arrest you on a charge of treason and to escort you to the Wannsee prison.'

He spoke in German, and Foster once again had great difficulty in refraining from betraying his knowledge of that language. He bit his lip to suppress the cry of anguish that was on the point of breaking from him. Sophie's face went perfectly bloodless, but even in that moment she could remember her lover's necessary pose of ignorance.

'Will you kindly speak in English, Herr Schönewald,' she requested. 'I would like Herr Foster to understand.'

The Nazi bowed.

'Very well, Baroness,' he said in that language, and turning to Foster added: 'I have been ordered to arrest the Baroness von Reudath on a charge of treason.'

'What an awful lot of rot!' exclaimed the Englishman angrily. 'Is it treason for her to visit a man who has been falsely certified insane by the orders of your precious Marshal of State? Is it treason for her to—?'

'I cannot enter a discussion about the matter,' interrupted the other sharply. 'I have my orders, and they must be obeyed.'

'You, a gentleman,' commented Foster scornfully, 'obeying the orders of an upstart bully!'

'Sir,' protested Schanewald angrily, 'you are speaking of His Excellency, the Supreme Marshal of Germany. A remark of that nature is quite enough to get you a severe term of imprisonment.'

'Have you forgotten,' drawled the Englishman, 'that three men who represent themselves as Berlin's most famous doctors have declared that I am a lunatic? I can, therefore, say anything I like with impunity. If what I say is taken seriously, and I am punished for it; then those doctors will have to reverse their decree.'

Schönewald turned from him impatiently.

'There are some men here awaiting my commands, Baroness,' he informed her, 'but it is my intention to save you from humiliation and as much pain as possible by sending them away. Then you and I can enter your car without anyone guessing that you are under arrest.'

She drew herself up proudly, but her little hands were tightly clenched.

'You are very good, Colonel Schönewald,' she acknowledged. 'I am ready.'

'I will go and dismiss them. In ten minutes I will return, if that is suitable to you.'

'Thank you,' she murmured gratefully.

He went out locking the door after him. Immediately she had thrown herself sobbing into Foster's arms. He held her close to his heart, doing his best to comfort her, while he himself was in an agony of grief.

'Oh, Bernard, Bernard,' she moaned, 'how can I leave you. It is not what they may do me that is breaking my heart – I am not afraid. But I cannot bear to lose you, dear, and this, I know, must be the end of all my hopes, all my happiness. Nobody can do anything for me now. Your wonderful Secret Service men cannot help me once I am in the Wannsee prison. Those gates I know will close on me for ever. How can I leave you, Bernard, my beloved, how can I? Oh! How can God be so cruel?'

'Keep up a stout heart, Sophie,' he implored. 'Somehow you will be rescued – I know it. Sir Leonard will find out what has happened, and he will leave no stone unturned to save you from that fiend.'

At last came the knock they were both dreading. They rose to their feet, stood facing the door. It opened slowly. Schönewald entered. His eyes fell quickly when he noticed the ravages that sorrow had made on the face of a beautiful woman, and a usually cheerful happy man.

'I am sorry, Baroness,' he remarked, with a note of infinite regret in his voice, 'but I fear we must go now.'

'I am ready,' she declared bravely.

'Look here, Schönewald,' commenced Foster, but she placed her fingers gently on his lips.

'Do not make his task harder, Bernard,' she begged. 'You can see he loathes it. He can do nothing. Goodbye, my beloved, my man.'

One long last kiss, and she was gone swiftly from the room, leaving Foster staring after her, a figure of abject tragedy. Schönewald told him that he had ordered his custodians to remain outside and not intrude, but the Englishman made no sign of having heard. He remained where he was standing like an image carved in stone.

The hours passed and dinner was brought to him, but he could not touch a morsel. He had partaken of a very meagre luncheon, knew that it was necessary to eat to retain his strength, but he felt that he would choke if he attempted it. For all he knew, Sophie was even then lying dead in the cold, horrible surroundings of a prison cell, a victim of the hatred of a man who had once pretended to love her. Desperately he tried to shake off such thoughts, feeling that he would indeed go mad if they persisted. Backwards and forwards in his room he paced, a prey to the most terrible anguish a man could possibly be called upon to endure. The shades of evening began to fall, the heat of a brilliant June day was now tempered by the fresh breeze which blew in the open window. The room became darker, but he did not switch on the light, continuing his restless walk to and fro until he was unable any longer to discern clearly the objects in the room. He found a certain measure of relief in the coming of night. Soon now, he reflected, they would be taking him away; strove to fix his mind on his own position, wonder what sort of a place it would be in which he was to be confined. It was all no use, however, his mind was unable to dwell on anything but the agony of the one all-absorbing thought.

Suddenly he thought he heard a sound on the balcony, as though someone had dropped lightly on to it. At once he hurried out, wondering if another attempt was being made to break into the room, and, if so, what sense there could possibly be in such a venture, when he was so utterly at the mercy of the people who insisted on spying on him. He could do nothing to prevent their searching either his person or his belongings if they so desired. A dim form confronted him, a hand grasped his arm.

'S'sh!' came in a low warning. 'Not a sound. There are two men below now as well as those in the corridor. You will be taken away at ten. Into the room! It is safer there.'

The overwhelming sensation of relief that surged through Foster at the sound of Sir Leonard's voice almost caused him to cry out. He entered the room walking rather like a man in a dream, closely followed by the chief.

'Shall I switch on the light, sir?' he asked in a voice that trembled.

'No. You can hear me, and that's all that matters. I shall not stay long. As a matter of fact I came to do my best to cheer you up.'

'I can hardly feel cheerful unless – unless—'

'Yes; I know. It's a devilish position for you. I can pretty well guess how you feel.'

'You know what has happened, sir?'

'Of course. The baroness is in the Wannsee prison. She is to be tried in camera there tomorrow. It will probably be something of a relief to you to know that. No doubt you feared that she would have been murdered off-hand.'

'I did, sir,' muttered Foster. 'The thought has almost driven me mad.'

'Well,' murmured Sir Leonard sympathetically, 'you can relieve your mind a little anyhow. Of course, there's no doubt but that she will be condemned to death. Von Strom will see to that.'

An involuntary groan broke from the young man.

'Can – can nothing be done?' he asked.

'You'll have to pull yourself together, Foster,' was the reply. 'If it is at all possible to save the baroness, it will be done. You can neither help her nor yourself by giving away to despair. Cousins and I will do all that is humanly possible.'

'I know that, sir; thank you. I feel much more confident and happier now that I have seen you.'

'You can hardly be said to have seen me,' retorted Sir Leonard drily. 'There is one thing I should like to say, Foster. The Baroness von Reudath is one of the bravest women I know. The way she defied von Strom was magnificent, and the courage when she left you to go to her death, as she must have thought was sublime. In winning her love you have obtained something beyond price.'

'I know that, sir,' murmured Foster. 'I can't think what she sees in me to love. But – but how did you know all this, sir?'

Sir Leonard laughed softly.

'I took rather a risk,' he admitted. 'I happened to be in the lounge when the baroness arrived. I anticipated that she would be informed that you had been declared insane and her impulse would be to come here at once. That was why I was in the lounge. I was waiting for her. She was a bit later than I expected. However, I followed her up, witnessed her clear that fellow out of the room, and thoroughly confound the manager and his crowd. Her coming, I guessed, would be at once reported, and somebody sent to arrest her or at least take her to his Excellency to give an account of herself. I must confess I did not think our friend Friedrich would have come himself. That was all to the good. I had decided that I would like to hear what the emissary had to say. I went to my room and put on a suit of overalls to make it appear that I was a workman. I then went to the balcony and climbed to the railing, pretending to be engaged in doing something to the wall to deceive anyone who happened to look up from the garden. I was not worried about the guests. My only fear was that a member of the staff might see me and want to know who I was and what I was doing. However, that was a risk that had to be taken. I had a microphone with me, and, from my vantage point I succeeded, after a good deal of effort, and several bad shots in landing it just inside your window behind the curtain. The baroness really had made my plan possible by turning out your guard. While he was in the room, no doubt, sitting by the door and facing the windows, it was not possible. He would have seen the microphone swinging to and fro before landing. It was padded with felt. It made little noise when it dropped therefore. Obviously neither you nor the baroness heard it. I climbed back to the balcony again, taking care that the leads I was carrying did not grow taut and drag the microphone from its position. I then re-entered my room and, clamping on the headphones, sat down to listen-in. I must admit that most of the time von Strom was there I felt a trifle jumpy for fear he would walk on to the balcony and discover my little scheme. As luck had it, he did not, and I heard everything that took place.'

'By jove!' exclaimed Foster. The enterprise and daring of Sir Leonard rather took his breath away. Once again a warm glow of hope filled him. It seemed that nothing was impossible to this man. If there was a possibility of Sophie being saved, he would do it. 'How did you get across to my balcony now, sir?' asked the young man.

'Jumped,' replied Wallace laconically.

'But it is quite eight feet from your railing to mine,' murmured the impressed Foster, 'and it is pretty dark too.'

'Eight feet is not much of a distance. It would be nothing to you. Well, keep up your pecker, my boy. I'm afraid you'll have to put up with a few days in the asylum. Cousins and I, and Gottfried too, will be very much engaged looking after the baroness for the present. I am not going to make any rash promises, but we'll spare no efforts to get her away. I must go. They are coming for you at ten – I overheard those scoundrelly doctors decide upon that this morning – and it is nearly that now.'

'I can't tell you how deeply grateful—' began Foster.

'Wait until there is something to be grateful for,' interrupted Wallace. He took his assistant's hand in his; shook it warmly. 'No more despair mind. I would have come to you before, but I dare not take too many risks. Cheer-ho!'

'What about that microphone, sir?'

'My dear chap, I pulled it back hours ago. I'm off now to find the document hidden in the Baroness von Reudath's garden. Goodbye!'

He was gone, leaving Foster happier and more composed than he had been since Sophie's dramatic arrival. His mind was wonderfully relieved. So much so that, for a while, his reflections were chiefly centred on the amazing athletic feats of his one-armed chief. He was smuggled out of the hotel and taken away in a closed car promptly at ten. His guards were greatly relieved that he made no attempt at resistance, though there were enough of them to render anything of that nature futile. His baggage was taken possession of by the police and removed to headquarters. With it went the letter addressed to his sister.

CHAPTER THIRTEEN

Remorse

Still disguised as a round-faced, jolly-looking naval officer, Sir Leonard Wallace left the Esplanade Hotel at half past ten and, hiring a taxicab, directed the chauffeur to drive him to the Grunewald quarter. During the journey he sat for the most part with his chin sunk on his breast, a deeply thoughtful figure. Nobody realised better than he the stupendous task he and Cousins would have, if they were to rescue the Baroness von Reudath. Gottfried would be required to help, of course, but his part would have, of necessity, to be performed from the background. Sir Leonard made it a rule that men who represented the firm of *Lalére et Cie* must on no account expose themselves to risk of recognition when acting for the British Secret Service. No suspicion must be allowed to fall on the great Parisian scent corporation. Still, with his influence, Gottfried would prove almost indispensable. He it was who had discovered for Sir Leonard the orders of von Strom concerning the

Baroness von Reudath. She was to be tried for treason in a room of the prison in which she was confined. The trial was to be in camera, and would start at ten o'clock on the following morning. Wallace had hoped to have been able to plan to rescue her when being conveyed to or from the courts of justice. It would have been a desperate venture, of course, but nothing like as desperate as it would now prove to get her away from a strongly guarded fortress. Even his great heart fell a little at thought of the stupendous task before him and Cousins. He wished now that he had made the attempt when she was being taken by Colonel Schönewald to the prison. But there had been no time to plan anything, and he well knew that to attempt an enterprise of a nature so desperate it is imperative to have the whole scheme cut and dried beforehand. Every contingency must be provided for, the whole thing planned down to the smallest detail, alternatives arranged in case of an unexpected alteration in some particular, possibilities of failure through some unseen cause guarded against. Entire secrecy was absolutely essential. Once the slightest suspicion was sown in the minds of the authorities that an attempt might be made to rescue the baroness all hope of success would automatically be destroyed. At present it was unlikely that thoughts of such a nature had occurred to them. The only person who, to their knowledge, would have been likely to have tried anything so hare-brained was Foster, and he had been certified and, by that time, was in a place as safe as a prison. They would, therefore, be in a state of unsuspicious equanimity. Sir Leonard intended that they should remain in that frame of mind. He was resolved that he would move heaven and earth, if necessary, to free the girl. In a sense he felt responsible for her terrible predicament. If he had not directed Foster to become acquainted with her with a view to learning from her the information she possessed, the chances were that she would have returned to Berlin without rousing von Strom's anger or suspicion. She would not have defied him as she had done in Foster's room in the hotel and shown him her hand so openly. Perhaps sooner or later she would have discovered that which she had been anxious to learn and, in consequence, have notified him that she no longer intended keeping silent. She was so essentially honest and scrupulous that she would, as indeed she had done, tell him she withdrew her vow. But the chances are that, before doing so, she would have, at least, arranged for her escape from his clutches. Apart from all this, she and Foster were deeply in love with each other, and Sir Leonard was determined, somehow or other, to save her for the sake of his young assistant. He felt also that he owed it to the country of her birth, for which she possessed a devotion of such deep nobility, to rescue her. The problem, however, was extremely intricate, difficult in the extreme. All the way to the Grunewald he was turning it over in his mind, only to reach the conclusion that the first essential was to obtain a complete knowledge of the routine in the prison and a thorough acquaintance with the prison itself. Gottfried would be required to pull more strings. Either Sir Leonard or Cousins or both of them must pay a visit to the place and, while being shown round, make notes of everything in preparation for the rescue they would plan.

The taxi driver, obeying instructions, stopped his cab in one of the streets of the villa colony some distance from the Baroness von Reudath's magnificent residence. He was directed to await his passenger's return. Sir Leonard became very cautious as he drew near the house. He anticipated that it would be guarded, and had no intention of being found wandering about the premises. He proved correct. A sentry stood inside the gates. He heard the man humming softly to himself as he crept silently up. Stepping softly, in order to avoid making the slightest sound, he went on by the side of the high wall until he came to a fine old chestnut tree. By the dim light of a lamp burning some distance away he was able to assure himself that a branch was overhanging the top of the wall. There were no pedestrians about and only an occasional car passed. It was a fortunate circumstance that the house was in such a secluded district. Watching his opportunity he presently commenced on one of those feats which were the admiration of his colleagues. Although badly handicapped owing to the fact that he only possessed one arm, he climbed the tree, a trifle awkwardly perhaps but with something of the agility of a monkey. Reaching the branch which was his objective, he lay at full length along it, and wriggled his way towards the wall. Once there he remained still for some time, his eyes endeavouring to pierce the gloom. At length, satisfied that there was nobody in his vicinity, he let himself down on to the top of the wall. He sat there for a little while wondering if he would be able to get back as easily as he had reached there. Deciding that he would find a way, and that his most pressing task at the moment was to secure the document for which he had come, he let himself down at arm's length, dropping softly on a flower bed below.

Moving like a shadow he encircled the house, avoiding the terrace, at length reaching the lawns at the back. He was quite familiar with the place. Cousins and he had reconnoitred it, thinking it might be useful to become acquainted with it, on the night of their arrival in Berlin. There were several lights showing from the house but, apart from the man at the gates, there seemed no one about. He paused for some minutes listening intently, but the only sound to reach his ears was the musical flow of the water in the fountain. Gradually he approached, and was only a few yards away when he stopped dead. His keen eyes had caught, even in the gloom of that moonless night, the outlines of a figure. It seemed to be sitting on the verge of the pool and, as far as he was able to ascertain, was quite alone. It was clothed in a garment of some light material, and Sir Leonard quickly decided that it was a woman. One of the servants perhaps. He quietly lowered himself to the ground, afraid that she might catch sight of the silhouette of his figure against the lighter background of the house. There he waited, the minutes passing slowly, and no sign of movement coming from the woman. Studying her, it seemed to him that she was leaning forward as though her head was sunk upon her breast. She certainly looked a very dejected person. Presently above the sound of the water, he distinctly heard a sob, and everything became plain to him. She was sorrowing for her mistress, and no wonder. Wallace had heard that the servants of the baroness were utterly devoted to her. This poor girl had apparently gone out there to be alone with her grief. He sat listening, wishing he could go to her and offer her words of comfort.

Suddenly she rose to her feet and he was able to observe her much more distinctly. She stood, as far as he could gather, looking down into the pool. The next moment he was up and running towards the fountain. The woman had either fallen or thrown herself in. It was not deep enough to drown anyone unless the person herself deliberately meant to drown or perhaps had fallen in in a faint. Arrived at the side, Sir Leonard looked in. She was lying face downwards, her hair floating on the water above her. Throwing himself at full length he bent down and clutched at her. Directly she felt his hand she struggled violently to free herself; there was no doubt about it now, she was bent on committing suicide. Grimly he ignored her frantic efforts to evade his grasp, pulling her slowly but surely from the water and wishing then, perhaps as much as he had ever wished it, that he possessed his left arm as well as his right. He was very thankful that she did not scream or cry out. He had feared that, as soon as her face was free from the water, she would have made a clamour. She did nothing of the sort, fighting desperately in a kind of dogged silence to seek the death she had planned for herself. Twice she succeeded in squirming away from him, but he obtained a grip on a leg and at length dragged her up the bank on to the grass. She gave up the struggle then and, lying quiescent, burst into a storm of weeping, the sound of which caused his heart to ache. He reflected that if all those tears and her determined attempt to drown herself were caused by her sorrow at the fate that had overtaken the baroness, she must possess an amazing devotion for that gallant lady. He sat by her side, making no attempt to interrupt her grief until she showed signs of regaining control of herself. Then he spoke to her with infinite gentleness, his attractive voice imparting to the German language a quality which it seldom seems to contain.

'What is the trouble, fraulein?' he asked. 'Tell me, and perhaps I will be able to help you. There are no troubles so great in this world, you know, that no remedy can be found.'

'Why did you not leave me alone?' she sobbed passionately. 'I wished to die. Who are you? What business is it of yours to interfere. If you think that you have saved my life, and deserve thanks, you will not get it. I hate you for doing it – do you hear? I hate you.'

'Calm yourself, fraulein,' he begged in the same soothing voice. 'By taking your own life you do not end grief. Think of those who love you – there must be many, I am sure. Is it fair to stifle the grief in your own heart by killing yourself and thus bring sorrow into the hearts of those who love you?'

'Oh! Go away! Leave me alone! Leave me alone!' She sat up and covered her face with her hands.

'I will go if you promise me not to act foolishly again.'

'I will not promise! I will not! I have determined to end my life, and nothing will prevent me. For the time you have succeeded, but you will not always be there. I must die. It is the only way I can get away from the hell that is tormenting me.'

'What hell?' he asked curiously.

She was silent for a while; then once again broke into a paroxysm of wild weeping. It subsided, at last, and she regained sufficient control of herself to speak almost normally.

'I was the maid of the Baroness von Reudath. When she went away the police made me one of their secret agents and promised to pay me well, if I spied on her and reported all her actions and words to them. They sent a man also to watch, and to whom I was to pass on my information. She has now been arrested – tomorrow she will be tried for treason, and they will execute her. And I have done it – I have done it. I who love her.'

She sat rocking backwards and forwards, her sobs tearing at the heartstrings of the grim-faced man watching her. Sir Leonard felt that he had seldom witnessed grief like this.

'So you are Hanni!' he commended quietly.

'Yes, I am Hanni,' she moaned, 'the woman Judas who has betrayed her mistress for money.' Then he sensed rather than saw that she had taken her hands from her face and was staring at him. 'How do you know about me?' she demanded. 'Are you of the police? If so, I curse you and all your breed because you have made me what I have become.'

'No, I am not of the police,' he assured her.

'Who are you then? What are you doing here?'

'I think,' he returned calmly, 'that perhaps I was sent to save you from doing a very stupid thing, and to give you the chance of redeeming yourself.'

'I do not understand.' She had of a sudden become very quiet in her manner. He knew she was turning her head to pierce the darkness in an effort to obtain a glimpse of his face. 'You have not told me who you are.'

'That does not matter. I am as distressed about the trouble which has befallen the baroness as you are, though I have done nothing to bring it upon her. I cannot fail to see that you are sincerely sorry for the harm you have done. What would you do to try and repair it?'

'Anything,' she whispered at once. 'Oh, anything!'

'Do you mean that? Would you dare the anger of the Marshal himself?'

'Yes. He could kill me if he wished. Rather that than harm should overtake Sophie.'

'You call her Sophie, do you? Were you so familiar with her?'

'No, no. I should not call her that. I was only a servant. But I have become used to thinking of her as Sophie, and I spoke without thinking.'

'I see.' He was a little abstracted in his manner. An idea had occurred to him, and he was busily engaged in considering it from every angle. It all depended upon whether he could trust Hanni. Was she so sincerely repentant and desirous of making amends that she really would do *anything* to save the baroness? He reached a decision. 'You, of course, are quite unsuspected?' he asked.

'Unsuspected,' she repeated bitterly. 'I have been thanked and rewarded for what I have done. The money I have thrown into that pool. I would now be lying there as useless, if you had not dragged me out. Oh! Why did you do it? Why did you?'

She showed signs of becoming hysterical again.

'Calm yourself, Hanni!' he commanded sternly. 'I am going to give you a chance of saving her.'

There was a long pause; then:

'How?' she demanded in a tense whisper.

'You are still the maid of the baroness, are you not? You are allowed to see her?'

'I took some clothes to her this evening. Why do you ask?'

'Do you think you can go and see her tomorrow night after dark? You can take a dress or something she may be expected to require for the following day.'

'Yes,' she replied eagerly. 'I think I can do that.'

'Perhaps they will insist on taking it from you and giving it to her. What then? It is necessary for my plan that you actually go to her and see her alone.'

'They will let me go. Of that I am certain. They have no reason to suspect me.'

'Then listen! Wrap your face up well as though you have the toothache. When you are alone with the baroness change clothing with her, and send her out in your place, making sure that she wraps up her face well. I will be waiting outside the prison with a car for her. Will you do this? Think well I am asking you to run a great risk. It is possible you may be severely punished.'

'They may quite likely sentence me to death. But I will not mind dying to undo the harm I have done. Yes, I will do it.'

'Excellent,' he approved, 'but do not worry about being killed. I will see that you are rescued before they can do that – if they go so far. The main thing is to get the baroness out of their clutches as soon as possible.'

'You talk with great confidence,' she commented. 'Who are you?'

'A friend of the Baroness von Reudath,' he replied, adding: 'And of yours now, I hope.'

'How do you know that I will not betray you, as I have betrayed her?'

'I always know when I can trust men or women,' he told her quietly. 'I am ready to put absolute trust in you.'

A sob reached his ears out of the darkness. He smiled quietly to himself. He was confident he could rely upon this strangely complex being. The sob, he felt, gave him his final assurance. They discussed the details of the project, and she marvelled at the manner in which this stranger thought of all the eventualities and instructed her how to meet them. More than ever she wondered who he was, but he did not satisfy her curiosity. It was arranged that she should visit the prison in the morning before the trial began, and announce, when she was coming out, to the governor, or whoever she saw in authority, that the baroness had asked her to bring some things at ten o'clock that night ready for the following day and to take away certain articles she would have discarded. That was reasonable enough. Sophie was permitted to wear her own clothing and would probably not be disrobing before that hour. Hanni was to tell her in the morning the scheme that had been planned in order that she would be prepared. At ten o'clock Hanni would return, her face wrapped up, and complaining bitterly of toothache. She would insist upon being alone with her mistress, given some intimate reason as an excuse if any objection were raised. That she did not anticipate, however. She had been left alone with her that evening. Directly she was locked in she and the baroness would change clothes, and she was to make certain that the latter wrapped up her face well, and tell her to walk with her hand to her cheek as though in great pain. The baroness would be met as soon as she left the prison, and escorted to the car waiting for her.

'After that,' remarked Sir Leonard, smiling in the darkness, 'I shall have to concoct plans for rescuing you.'

'Make sure that the baroness is safely away first,' urged the woman. She then proceeded to give Sir Leonard a great shock. 'What about Fraulein Reinwald?' she asked. 'Can you do nothing for her?'

'Why? Where is she?' he asked in quick alarm.

'In the same prison as the baroness. She is to be tried with her for treason tomorrow.'

'Good God!' exclaimed Sir Leonard. 'Poor girl! What has she done?'

'Nothing. Of that I am certain. But she was a companion of the baroness and in her confidence. Also she is a Hebrew.'

'And what of the other girl?' asked the shocked and startled man. 'I mean Fraulein Meredith. Is she also in prison?'

'No; she is English. The Supreme Marshal dare not go too far with English people. She has been certified insane like the other young man friend of the baroness and is under guard in the house. Tomorrow she is to be sent to the mental home where he is at.'

'My God!' muttered Sir Leonard to himself. 'What a fiend the fellow is. It seems to me I shall be very busy during the next two or three days,' he added aloud. 'However, we must concentrate on saving the baroness first. Now go in and take those wet things off. It is a warm night, but you might get a chill.'

'I shall hate entering that house,' she declared vehemently. 'It is full of police, whom now I detest from my heart. They are searching everywhere for evidence to produce against my poor mistress.'

'Never mind them. Remember that you are about to wash out everything you have done of a nature treacherous to the baroness. You are going to prove that your betrayal was a mistake, and that your love and loyalty soars above all.'

He helped her to her feet. Impulsively she bent down and kissed his hand, then was gone. He waited for a little while, after which he took off his shoes and socks, turned up his trousers, and waded into the pool. He reached the naiad and, after some fumbling, felt the hole in the plinth. At once he inserted his hand, feeling eagerly within. A moment later he withdrew a long envelope folded in two. Placing it in a pocket, he waded back to the bank. There he quickly dried his feet with his handkerchief and replaced his shoes and socks. A few seconds later he had left the fountain and was creeping silently round the side of the house towards the wall. He heard voices a little way in front of him, and saw the glow of cigarette ends. Two men were there taking the air. There might be others about. He redoubled his precautions, moving away from the smokers, yet on the alert lest they were approaching other prowlers. He reached the wall safely, however, walked slowly along searching the darkness for a tree which would enable him to scale the obstruction. There appeared no trees inside that part of the wall at all, and, finding himself perilously near a gate, he turned and retraced his steps. Suddenly he caught his foot painfully against something lying on the ground. He bent down to find, to his surprise, a ladder there half-concealed in the grass. A strange place to leave such an article, he reflected, but the very thing he required. Peering cautiously round, he raised it, and placed it against the wall with great care. Then, for some moments, he stood looking back meditatively at the house. He was half-inclined to attempt to rescue Rosemary Meredith while he was there, but on consideration decided that it would be the height of folly. He did not know the geography of the house; had not the slightest idea where she was incarcerated. As the place was full of police, according to Hanni, the chances of his finding her and getting her away without capture were exceedingly remote. He dare not take the risk of losing his own liberty when so much was at stake, and Rosemary was in no actual danger. With a sigh he turned away. The whole affair was becoming distinctly complicated. Apart from the central figure, whom it was vital to rescue as soon as possible, there were now three others, and Hanni would make a fourth. He climbed the ladder and, sitting on the top of the wall, pushed it over. It fell with a thud to the ground, but he was certain did not make enough noise to be heard, unless there was somebody in the vicinity. Waiting a few minutes to make certain, he let himself down the other side, and went in search of his taxi.

The driver grumbled at being kept waiting so long, but grew mollified at the promise of a large gratuity. Sir Leonard directed him to drive to the Unter den Linden. There he dismissed the man, keeping his promise so generously that he was overwhelmed with thanks. He entered a telephone booth, and rang up Gottfried.

'My friend,' he remarked on hearing the latter's voice, 'I am bored with life. Is it too late for me to come up and spend an hour with you?'

'Come by all means,' was the hearty and indeed eager reply. 'I have a little party on here. We shall be glad to have you with us.'

Sir Leonard frowned a little.

'Ah! Then I shall not intrude. I will see you tomorrow.'

'No, no, no!' cried Gottfried urgently. 'Come now! They are friends of yours.'

Wallace went without further hesitation. Gottfried possessed a luxurious flat above his shop. He himself opened the door to Sir Leonard, and led him into an elegant sitting room. Two people rose on their entry. One was Cousins, still disguised as an acquisitive-looking Teuton. The other was Rosemary Meredith. Wallace eyed her without any apparent surprise.

'How did you get here?' he asked.

'I have been a prisoner,' she replied. 'I managed to escape.'

'That explains the ladder,' he commented.

CHAPTER FOURTEEN

The Revelations of the Baroness

He threw himself into the easy chair Gottfried pushed forward and contemplated the girl with a smile. 'Your escape,' he remarked, 'means that there is one less to rescue. How did you manage it? You were certified insane, I know, and were to have been sent to the same asylum as Foster.'

'That is true,' the girl replied. 'After the doctors had been – they gave me a terrible time subjecting me to a kind of third degree enquiry that drove me to the verge of hysterics – I was locked in my room, which is on the top floor of the house. I suppose it did not occur to them that I would or could escape from there. But as soon as it was dark I got out of one of the windows, climbed on to the sun blind and, from there, on to the roof which, as perhaps you know, is flat. It was an easy matter then to descend to the ground by way of the fire escape. Some distance from the house is a group of sheds used by the gardeners. I took a ladder from one, and used it to climb to the top of the wall. I had to let myself down at arm's length the other side and drop, but I managed it.'

'Good for you,' approved Sir Leonard. 'I found that ladder or rather it found me. I was wondering how I was going to scale the wall, when I walked into it.'

'So you were in the house, sir?' put in Gottfried.

'Not in the house – in the grounds. I went there for the document hidden by the baroness.'

'Did you get it, sir?' asked Cousins eagerly.

'I did,' nodded Sir Leonard, patting his pocket. 'Incidentally I prevented the woman Hanni from committing suicide and have enlisted her in our service.'

There was a surprised silence for a few moments.

'But she is a police spy,' objected Rosemary.

'She was. Apparently, however, she all along had a deep love for the baroness. At all events she had thrown the money paid her for her work into the pool and followed it in herself, when I happened along and dragged her out. She certainly made a very determined attempt to kill herself. Under ordinary circumstances the water is not deep enough to drown anybody, but she lay in it with her head under. I had rather a job with her at first, but when she realised that I was a friend of the baroness and was offering her a chance to redeem herself she listened to me eagerly enough.' He explained at length the scheme he had arranged with Hanni in the hope of rescuing Sophie. The others followed attentively. 'Of course,' he concluded, 'the chances are that it may fail. We must have an alternative.'

'Are you quite certain, sir,' asked Gottfried, 'that this woman will go through with it? The risks to her are enormous.'

'Quite so, but I am sure she'll do it. She is only too eager to make amends for her treachery, and she won't bother to count the cost. A girl who will make such a determined attempt to end her own life through remorse, will not hesitate, whatever the risk, at attempting something which will save her mistress from the fate overhanging her, especially when she considers herself responsible. But it is not altogether a plan with which I am satisfied. There are too many ifs about it. As I say, we must have an alternative. For that purpose, Gottfried, you will have to pull a few more influential strings. I want to see the inside of that prison. I want to make a thorough study of it from top to bottom in order that I can plan something a little more cast-iron in case Hanni's job goes awry. And I'd like Cousins to see the place as well. Do you think you can possibly arrange for us to visit it tomorrow morning?'

Gottfried rubbed his chin, looking very dubious the while.

'I know the governor pretty intimately,' he admitted, 'and at any other time, it would have been fairly easy. Tomorrow, though, with the trial taking place there, it is certain that the strictest precautions will be observed. I know the guard is to be doubled and only the judges, attorneys and witnesses connected with the case are to be admitted. Instructions have even been given that the ordinary tradesmen who call daily are to deliver their goods and receive their orders outside the main gates.'

'H'm!' grunted Wallace. 'I seem to have set you a pretty problem. Still, see what you can do. I must get inside that prison, even,' he added with a smile, 'if I have to go as a lawyer's clerk.' He looked quickly up at Gottfried. 'What witness can they have?' he asked.

The manager of *Lalére et Cie* shrugged his shoulders, while an expression of contempt spread over his rugged countenance.

'They have many,' he returned, 'all sworn to give false evidence of course. Von Strom intends granting the baroness what will appear a fair trial in order that he can point to his righteousness and justice afterwards if necessary, but he is taking care to provide witnesses who will swear the poor girl to her death.'

'Do you really think she will be sentenced to death?' asked Rosemary, regarding him with horrified eyes.

'Without the slightest doubt, and so will Dora Reinwald.'

'But what has she done? I have watched, as you know, and I am sure she is innocent of anything at all. She knows nothing of the secrets the baroness possesses.'

'Neither do you as far as the German authorities are aware,' Sir Leonard reminded her. 'Yet, you, like Foster, have been certified insane, and were to have been confined in a mental home where you probably were to be kept until you died or the Supreme Marshal was ready to strike in accordance with the scheme Germany has concocted. It is obvious that von Strom has resolved to wipe out all who may have any knowledge of their schemes. The baroness, of course, because she is acquainted with everything, and has made no secret of her intention to denounce him. You and Dora Reinwald because you were her companions and friends and may have been told, Foster for the reason that he is her lover. The trial, you say, Gottfried, is expected to last three days?'

'Yes, sir.'

'How soon after the verdict's given, do you think the execution or executions will be ordered to take place?'

'Almost immediately I should imagine, sir. The press has been muzzled, and an official notification of the trial will be handed to the editors of all the big papers for publication *after the baroness is dead*. That is His Excellency's little way. It prevents a great deal of trouble as well as criticism. It is not much use criticising or protesting when the victims are dead. But even in Germany it is impossible to keep matters of such importance secret for long. I should be prepared to bet, therefore, that the executions will take place on the morning after the sentence has been pronounced.'

Rosemary shuddered; her face was suddenly deadly pale. Cousins leant across and patted her hand.

'Don't you worry!' he urged. 'Sir Leonard won't let those girls be executed, and I shall do my little bit to help. "They rais'd them from that hellish pit, Despite the monster's dev'lish plan!"'

'So long as the baroness gets away in place of Hanni tomorrow night,' mused Wallace, 'all should be well. In the confusion that will afterwards take place, I think we ought to be able to rescue Dora and Hanni as well, another reason why we must know the prison. It seems to me,' he went on quietly, 'that even if the authorities have framed so many witnesses to bear testimony against the baroness, they would very much appreciate an additional two whose evidence bore the hallmark of truth.'

The three stared at him, unable to comprehend the drift of his remarks.

'I suppose they would, sir,' observed Gottfried in puzzled tones, 'but—'

'Listen!' enjoined his chief. 'Tonight Cousins and I shed our Prussian personalities. We become Bavarians who recently spent an enjoyable holiday in Vienna and Budapest, and have now come to Berlin to finish it off by – er – making whoopee in the capital of your own country before returning home. In Budapest we met the baroness and became very friendly with her and Foster and the things we could tell – well, we'll whisper them into your ear, my good Gottfried, directly your shop opens and we enter to buy perfume to be sent to the baroness – that sounds like a horrible play upon words but is not intended to be. You, being the good German citizen report at once our remarks to the Minister of Propaganda, who is quite a good friend of yours. If I am not mistaken he will immediately compel us to give evidence for the prosecution. Our tales, you see, will not be to the baroness's advantage. Thus we enter the prison.'

'Will you really give evidence against her, sir?' asked Rosemary.

'Why not? Nothing we will say can make things any worse for her, and it is essential we become acquainted with her surroundings. We will change our disguises here, Gottfried – you have all that is necessary. Then, when dawn breaks, we will make our way to Anhalt Station and, as soon as the early train from Prague arrives drive to the Adlon Hotel – more because it happens to be near than for any other reason.'

'You must go along to the British embassy, Rosemary,' continued Sir Leonard, 'and the sooner the better. You should have gone there direct instead of coming here. It was not very judicious of you to enter a place like this, which on no account must be allowed to fall under suspicion.'

'She did not come straight here, Sir Leonard,' Gottfried hastened to explain. 'he rang me up. I told her to walk up and down on the other side of the road for ten minutes or so and not to enter until she saw an amber light in my window. While she was doing that Cousins and I went out and made absolutely certain that she was not being watched. Then I re-entered and showed the amber light. Even then Cousins kept watch outside for a while.'

Sir Leonard nodded.

'I am glad you were so careful,' he observed. 'All the same it would have been better had Rosemary gone straight to the embassy. Cousins, you had better escort her there now.'

'Can I do nothing to help,' she pleaded. 'It seems to me I have been no use at all up to now.'

'My dear child, what nonsense! Why, we are indebted to you for supplying the information that first enabled us to act. Since then you have given us several valuable items of intelligence. You have done your job splendidly. Now the embassy is the place for you. You will be quite safe there. It is my intention to give the Chancellor an unpleasant problem to face. He will receive a note from the Ambassador informing him that you have sought the sanctuary of the embassy after escaping from the house of the Baroness von Reudath where you had been confined to your room, having, upon the instructions of the Supreme Marshal, been certified as insane by three German doctors. As you are a British subject, he will demand to know why the embassy was not informed, why you were to be removed secretly to an asylum, and whether it is a fact that another British subject, Bernard Foster by name, is now confined in an asylum. Furthermore, he will state that you have been examined by the embassy doctor – as you will be – and that you have not shown in the smallest particular any signs of insanity. I don't think von Strom will dare deny the statement concerning Foster. He will be compelled at least to allow English doctors to examine him. Neither you nor Foster are suspected of being members of the British Intelligence Service – we have quite ascertained that – action can be taken, therefore, without any possibilities of embarrassment to Great Britain.'

'Just a moment, sir,' ventured Cousins. 'There are drugs which render a man insane. Don't you think that, on receipt of the Ambassador's note, orders will be given to dose Foster so that, when the English doctors arrive to see him, they will actually find him, to all intents and purposes, a lunatic.'

Sir Leonard eyed his brilliant assistant in silence for a few moments; then he slowly nodded his head.

'You are right, Cousins,' he agreed. 'I would not consider even a diabolical act like that beyond von Strom. Before the Ambassador's note goes, we must get Foster away. He has been taken to Dr Hagenow's own private mental home at Neu – Babelsberg I gather. Do you know it, Gottfried?'

'Yes, sir. I was once taken there on a visit by a friend who had a relative inside. It is a beautiful place in grounds enclosed by very high walls, and as difficult to escape as a prison I should think.'

Sir Leonard sighed.

'We do come up against some snares in our life,' he murmured. 'I wish I had a few more men to assist us. However, we must do the best we can. It would be too risky to send for Carter or Shannon who, at the moment, are the only two available at headquarters. Besides, there is no time. I'll have to think it out. Now then, Rosemary, off you go. Give me some paper, Gottfried. I'll write a note for her to hand to the Ambassador explaining matters.' The paper was quickly forthcoming and, for ten minutes, Sir Leonard wrote rapidly. As soon as he had finished he sealed the letter in an envelope, and handed it to the girl. 'Give that to Sir Charles,' he directed. 'And now listen! You go first, Cousins, and keep watch. As soon as Miss Meredith emerges, follow her at a safe distance, but do not speak to her or, in any way, show that you know her. When she is safely inside the embassy, return here. If she is accosted and any attempt made to capture her don't go to her aid, but approach close as though curious. I don't suppose anything like that will happen, Rosemary, but if it does, take care that the letter you have does not fall into the hands of your captors. Drop it so that Cousins can pick it up and get away with it. You both understand?'

They intimated that they did, whereupon he bade the girl good night. Cousins quietly left the flat. A few minutes later Rosemary followed him. When she had departed, Sir Leonard looked up at Gottfried, who had remained standing ever since the arrival of the chief.

'What I should like more than anything else at the moment, Gottfried,' he murmured, his grey eyes twinkling, 'is a large whisky and soda.' With many apologies the burly Secret Service agent hastened to supply his guest's requirements.

'I am afraid, sir,' he admitted, 'I have been too interested to think of refreshments. I'm terribly sorry.'

'There's nothing to be sorry about. I've suddenly developed a thirst, otherwise I shouldn't have thought of bothering you.' He took a deep drink. 'You know, Gottfried,' he observed, 'I am not sure that I am altogether glad that Rosemary Meredith escaped. It was the natural thing to do, of course, but it is likely to cause complications, and heaven knows matters are quite complicated enough as it is. I certainly don't want our job of rescuing the baroness and Dora Reinwald not to mention Foster to be made more difficult than it is. I must confess that I am not too sanguine about the success of the woman Hanni's visit to the prison tomorrow night.'

'Do you think,' asked Gottfried anxiously, 'that, if you are ordered to appear as witnesses at the trial you and Cousins can go through with it without engendering mistrust? I shudder to think what would happen, if that took place and it was discovered who you are.'

Sir Leonard smiled.

'It would cause a bit of a sensation, wouldn't it?' he chuckled calmly. 'I have no intention of presenting von Strom with such a triumph, however, and, I'll see that Cousins does not. We shall be word perfect in our parts by the time we are called upon to give evidence.'

'How about the fellow Carl who was always spying on the baroness? Won't he declare that he has never seen you?'

'On the contrary, he will declare that he has. He is going to supply us with our bona fides.' Gottfried looked astonished but made no further comment. Sir Leonard drew the envelope containing the Baroness von Reudath's statement from his pocket. 'Now,' he declared, 'we shall find out all we want to know.'

He opened it, drawing out the several sheets of paper it contained and a smaller sealed envelope which he laid aside for the time being. Sophie had written in German in neat legible handwriting which presented no difficulties whatsoever to the reader. She commenced without superscription or, in fact, without address or date, plunging directly into the narrative she had to tell. Translated, it read:

I, the Baroness, Sophie Wera von Reudath, declare that the following is entirely true in every detail. It is drawn from my own personal knowledge and observation, and is not, in any one particular, obtained from hearsay. My husband, the late Baron von Reudath, was a great personal friend of the present leaders of Germany. He became acquainted with them when they were fighting to obtain recognition and, growing very impressed with the doctrines for the welfare of Germany that they preached, threw in his lot with them, thereby becoming perhaps their firmest and most steadfast helper. The Baron von Reudath, as is well-known, did a considerable amount of propaganda work for the

Chancellor, never sparing himself, and travelling all over Germany to raise support for the cause that, to him, had become almost a religion. But he was not a very strong man, and his hard work told on his health, as a consequence of which he eventually became ill and died. Before that event, however, I had been imbued with some of his enthusiasm and had also helped. I was sometimes admitted to their councils with the other leaders of their party.

After my husband's death, I automatically took his place. It became a habit of the Supreme Marshal of State to hold the most confidential discussions in my house. I took part in some of these. There were times, however, when he, the Chancellor, and the Minister of Propaganda, excluded me from their deliberations and conferred together behind locked doors. The subject of their discussions on these occasions was, I believe, the complete subjugation of all opposition parties in the Reichstag. Directly the Chancellor obtained full power, he set about planning secretly to place Germany once again in the position among the nations she had once occupied. He was resolved that the terms of the Treaty of Versailles should be revoked, but, before he was in a position to act at all defiantly, it was necessary for him to recruit a strong army, navy and air force. These, I was assured, were for defensive purposes only. I was told that when Germany declared her intention of ignoring the treaty it was very likely that France, Italy, perhaps Poland and Russia as well, would take aggressive measures. To guard against anything of that nature it was essential to equip and train a powerful force secretly. I had several long arguments with the Supreme Marshal concerning the

matter. I pointed out to him that it was Germany's duty
to respect her obligations, no matter how hard they were.
He would reply to that, sometimes by falling into a rage;
sometimes by pointing out to me that I myself had often
spoken of the harsh manner in which Austria had been
treated, and had said that she could not be blamed, if she
endeavoured to throw off the shackles in which she was
bound. That is true I had said it. I still feel very keenly
that Austria was made the scapegoat and, of all countries,
suffered the most.

About the time that these new plans were being formed
the Supreme Marshal began to show in no uncertain
manner that his interest and confidence in me was not
altogether due to my brains and judgment. His attentions
became more and more intimate as time went on, and,
he often attempted to make love to me. I was forced, on
several occasions, to remind him of his wife. She, I might as
well state, had enquired, I believe, why it was necessary for
him to continue to hold private conferences in my home
after the Baron von Reudath had died. I understand that
she pointed out to him that times and his circumstances
had changed. Whereas he had commenced using the house
of the Baron von Reudath when he had no convenient
place of his own, matters had vastly altered. Apart from
his private rooms at the Reichstag, there was his own
palatial residence. Why could he not use that for his secret
conferences? It will be seen that my position was becoming
embarrassing. What reply he made to his wife, I am not
in a position to state, but he continued to use my house
almost as though it was indeed his own. In addition, his

visits became more frequent and were not always due to conferences. Eventually I decided that I should have to leave the country. I had no regrets. In spite of the fact that I had married a German, I had never been able to feel myself a German subject. My heart is, and always has been devoted to my country, Austria.

I told him of my intention, and he was very much upset. He begged me to remain in Germany, and promised that, if I did, he would not pay me any attentions distasteful to me. In addition, he declared that he had need of what he called my cool, calculating brain. I allowed myself to be persuaded to stop. I feel now that his purpose in reporting his entire confidence in me from that time on was to keep me in the country under his power. As I had been entrusted with secrets of such importance, he felt he could insist on my remaining in Germany; if despite his injunctions I went, he could revenge himself on me by accusing me of treachery. I did not realise that then, of course. I have felt it ever since he showed such violent opposition to my leaving Germany even on a holiday. I know I am in great danger; that at any moment, I may be arrested, and tried for treason. It is because of this that I have decided to write these lines with the enclosed information and place the document where it can be found if anything happens to me, for it may be necessary for the sake of Europe and the world at large that all be made public before very long.

When confiding in me the matters of which I am writing, he made me take a vow that I would never divulge them. Before doing so I asked him if they were of a nature aggressive to Austria or other countries. He assured me they were not. I accepted his word and readily took the oath he imposed. As time went by, however, I began to feel he had lied to me; feared that a scheme conceived on a scale so gigantic must mean that, despite his declaration, his intentions were of an offensive character. But I had given my oath and until I was certain that he had misled me, could not break it. Since my suspicions were first roused I have searched diligently for what I have described as the link in the chain of knowledge, the link, in other words, that will prove to me beyond a shadow of doubt that directly Germany is fully prepared she will declare war. In my heart I know that I have been fooled; yet I feel I cannot break my vow without the proof I need. In writing these lines I am trusting to the honour of the great service I have suddenly discovered to my delight and gratitude, is ready to help me. I am confident that no attempt will be made to obtain this document unless I am arrested or killed. In conclusion I declare that I am not in the espionage service of Austria, am not in any way connected with the Austrian government. All desires to help my country and fears on her behalf are actuated entirely by my love for her. I ask the recipient of this to communicate at once with Vienna, giving all details as set down in the enclosed papers, if I am murdered, or arrested and executed. Sophie Wera von Reudath.

Sir Leonard looked up at Gottfried as he finished reading, and his grey eyes, for once in way, were eloquent of his thoughts.

'A woman worth saving,' he observed; 'a woman I am proud to serve.'

Gottfried, who, at his invitation, had read over his shoulder, nodded.

'I hope I have the pleasure of meeting her someday,' he murmured, 'Young Foster is amazingly lucky to have won the love of a woman like that.'

'He certainly is,' agreed Wallace.

CHAPTER FIFTEEN

Witnesses for the Prosecution

Sir Leonard tore open the second envelope, and withdrew the contents. Immediately he and the Berlin manager of *Lalére et Cie* became absorbed in that which was so clearly set out before their eyes. It was evident to them at once that here was no description of a scheme conceived for defensive purposes. From first to last the plan spoke of aggression. Throughout Germany, in workshops, factories, business houses men had for well over a year been secretly drilled and trained to carry arms. In schools and colleges the same exercises obtained until it was evident that Germany had become, on a greater scale than ever before, a vast military organisation. And not only men and boys, but women and girls as well underwent the training. At the same time, in several remote districts, hosts of aeroplanes and airships were being constructed and, while apparently little attention was being paid to the building of major warships, every new liner was being framed of armoured steel and made powerful enough to carry guns of a heavy calibre, thus assuring Germany of a fleet of speedy, dangerous cruisers. Above all a large number of submarines of great range and strength had already been constructed and more were being built. It was the intention of the Chancellor and his advisers to bring in conscription as soon as they were in a position to show their hand, then a force of five hundred thousand men, equipped with heavy and field guns, tanks, machine guns, and supported by a great air fleet, would move quietly to within easy distance of the Austrian frontier. An equal army similarly equipped would secretly take up its position near the French frontier while smaller ones would arrive in the neighbourhood of Czecho-Slovakia and the Polish Corridor. The baroness had even been made acquainted with the manner in which such vast bodies of men were to be moved without causing comment. The manoeuvres were necessarily to be carried out by degrees; they would take months to be completed, but Sir Leonard was unable to forbear expressing his admiration for the brain that had conceived an undertaking of a nature so gigantic. The people of Austria, France and Czecho-Slovakia would have awakened one fine day to find themselves invaded by vast, well-equipped armies against which they would be ill-prepared to defend themselves and their countries.

It was a mighty scheme, wonderfully conceived, but its greatest warrant of success was not the numbers of men, guns, aeroplanes, tanks and the submarines that would roam the seas, as much as the deadly gas invented by Hans Mohrenwitz and the wireless ray of Joachim Brau. The Baroness von Reudath included the formula of the gas and full details of the ray. No wonder, reflected Sir Leonard, that she was in such deadly peril. Gottfried drily commented that it was amazing what fools even the greatest and most ambitious of men will make of themselves because of infatuation for women. It was almost unbelievable that the Supreme Marshal of Germany could have confided to the girl who had taken possession of his senses matters of such vital and world-shattering importance. The gas was guaranteed to penetrate all but specially constructed masks and suits. It was stated to be able to enter the body through the pores of the skin and roots of the hair, and was swift in its deadliness. Sophie wrote of both the gas and wireless ray from the point of view of their being weapons of defence, but neither Wallace nor Gottfried took any account of that. They regarded the whole scheme, and they could hardly do otherwise, as a vast plan of attack. Joachim Brau had successfully demonstrated that his ray effectively disabled the ignition system of a petrol engine. It caused the entire magnets to melt within the space of less than two minutes, while it had an effective range of three miles and could be transmitted directionally in the manner of the beam wireless system. It did not take a great deal of imagination to conceive the use of such an invention in time of war. Not only would it put armoured cars and tanks out of action, but an invisible barrier of these wireless rays would stop the engines of enemy aircraft, and cause them to be hurled to destruction. Moreover the baroness stated that Brau's invention would penetrate any normal type of screening system. The only possible way to avoid its disabling effect would be to fit aeroplanes with engines of a compression ignition type which are without magnets or coil. The ray had been conceived on the basis that interference between wireless and an electrical ignition system is mutual.

Sir Leonard folded up the papers which contained information of such tremendous significance to the whole of Europe; handed them to his companion.

'You must go to Paris on important business concerning the firm tomorrow,' he directed. 'There must be no delay. Cousins and I will affect the rescues as best we can alone. It is essential that those must reach the Foreign Secretary as soon as possible. As soon as you reach Paris get Lalére to telephone to Carter to cross from London immediately. You will seal the papers, and hand them to him with instructions to take them at once to the Foreign Office. Understand?'

'Very well, sir,' Gottfried put them carefully away in an inner pocket of his coat.

'When you report what you have been told by your two Bavarian clients to the Minister of Propaganda, you can mention incidentally that you have been called to Paris for a conference. We don't want him to rope you in also as a witness against the baroness. Of course, if he does it, it can't be helped. You must make no objection, and postpone your departure for a day or two. In that event the delay cannot be helped.' Gottfried had refilled his glass as he was speaking. He raised it now, looked reflectively at its amber contents for a moment or two; then added softly: 'I drink to the safety of a very gallant lady.'

Gottfried hastened to raise his own glass. It was amazing the expression almost of reverent gentleness that crossed his stern, rugged face as he murmured, 'That Baroness von Reudath.'

A few minutes later came a ring at the door bell, and Cousins was admitted. In reply to Sir Leonard's questioning look the little man smiled, and nodded.

'Everything OK, sir,' he announced. 'Miss Meredith reached the embassy without incident of any kind, and is now safely inside.'

'Excellent,' remarked the chief. 'Now have a drink, and we'll start on our preparations.'

A few minutes after Wallace and Cousins commenced changing their disguises. First of all they removed all traces of their previous characterisations, and revelled in warm baths – a distinct and pleasing relief to both of them. It was only then that Sir Leonard gave his companions details of the fresh roles he had decided Cousins and he would play.

'Do you remember the two Bavarians living in the Hungaria at Budapest who became so friendly with Dora Reinwald and Rosemary Meredith?' he asked the little man.

'You mean August Keller and Franz Minck, sir?'

'Exactly. You and I will borrow their personalities. They had several conversations with the baroness and Foster, and dined with them and the two girls once. Keller was about my height and Minck was not much taller than you, though a good deal stouter, so there are no insurmountable difficulties.'

'Can you remember them sufficiently to deceive the spy?' asked the dubious Gottfried.

Sir Leonard nodded.

'I studied them on purpose,' he told the other. 'It occurred to me then that it might be useful to fix a mental picture of them in my mind with a view to impersonating them if fresh characters were needed. It will be more difficult to convince the baroness and Fraulein Reinwald who were in personal contact with Keller and Minck. It might be awkward if they declared we were imposters.'

He and Cousins set to work, Gottfried helping the chief from time to time in the adjustments of garments he could not manage with his one hand. While his fingers were expertly altering his face, Sir Leonard instructed Cousins in the story they would repeat to Gottfried when they entered the shop in the morning, and advised and directed him regarding his conduct if and when questioned by the Minister of Propaganda and afterwards when acting as witnesses. Cousins nodded and smiled from time to time. Neither he nor Wallace seemed to consider that there was any particular danger attached to the undertaking to which they were about to commit themselves. Gottfried felt differently, however, the worried frown on his brow testifying to the anxiety of his thoughts. He mentioned his doubts once, but Wallace smiled cheerfully at him.

'The very fact,' he declared, 'that we will be giving evidence against the baroness will be our greatest safeguard. Who would suspect people desiring to help her who were engaged in condemning her?'

Always thorough and extremely careful to leave nothing to chance, Sir Leonard and Cousins took a considerable time over their preparations. At length they were completed, and once again their individualities had changed entirely. Cousins, thanks to specially constructed shoes, was three or four inches taller than his normal. He had become stout, red-faced, and jolly-looking with sparse fair hair, and wore a pair of large glasses through which he looked benevolently out at the world. Sir Leonard was his own slim self, but had a long, narrow, rather sallow face and slightly protruding upper teeth. His hair was also fair, but thick and untidy; his nose was inclined to be pointed, while a straggly moustache surmounted his upper lip. A long scar suggestive of a student's duel ran the course of his left eye to his chin. Gold rimmed pince-nez over a pair of half-closed sleepy eyes completed his disguise. Gottfried inspected them both, expressing his admiration. He still felt very doubtful, however, of the welcome of the daring enterprise on which they were hoping to embark, but said no more. He knew it would not only savour of impertinence, but be utterly useless to attempt to persuade Sir Leonard to decide on a less risky method of finding out all he wanted to know about the prison. The chief regarded his artificial arm rather ruefully.

'I notice,' he remarked, 'that Keller had a habit of using his left arm rather a lot. That is something I cannot do. I dare not show my left hand at all. Yet it will perhaps appear strange to that fellow Carl if he is at all of an observant nature.' He stood in thought for a few moments, after which he smiled a little. 'I had an accident just before leaving Budapest – fell down and broke a small bone in my wrist. I shall want bandages and a sling, Gottfried, please.'

A couple of hours later, he and Cousins quietly left the flat, Gottfried having first ascertained that the way was perfectly clear. They went to the Anhalt Station by a circuitous route, and hid themselves in the vicinity, waiting for the coming of the early morning train from Prague. On its arrival they mingled with the passengers, and engaged a taxicab to drive them to the Adlon Hotel. Both carried bags well-labelled and indicating that they had come from Vienna and Budapest. They registered as August Keller and Franz Minck, and appeared a couple of men imbued with the determination to enjoy themselves, though perhaps Minck gave the impression of possessing a heartier sense of enjoyment than his companion. They were well-dressed, and seemed to be amply supplied with money. They ate excellent breakfasts; after which they strolled out of the hotel to see the sights both apparently looking forward eagerly to an enjoyable stay in Berlin. It would be difficult to imagine how either Sir Leonard or Cousins were able to appear so thoroughly bright and energetic. Neither had

had much sleep since arriving in Berlin by the same train that had brought the Baroness von Reudath and her companions to that city – on the previous night they had merely dozed for an hour or so, in Gottfried's easy chairs. Neither, however, showed signs of the slightest fatigue.

Shortly after nine they entered the imposing shop of *Lalére et Cie*, and informed the assistant, who hastened to attend to their requirements, that they wished to purchase perfume for three ladies. Gottfried had known the exact time they would arrive, and had taken care to be in the shop. He entered into conversation with them, joining in the important discussion on scent. When they confessed that they had no idea of the preference of the three ladies, he shook his head solemnly.

'That is a great pity,' he declared. 'I do not know how to advise you. You see, gentlemen, without knowing, you may present them with something they do not like. All Lalére's perfumes are beautiful, we do not deal in anything of an inferior or pungent quality; nevertheless, you must remember there are individual tastes.'

'We did not think of that,' admitted the sham Herr Keller. He looked at his companion. 'Do you know what the baroness or Dora or Rosemary like, Franz?' he asked.

The stout Herr Minck beamed cheerfully.

'No, I do not know. Perhaps, if we buy *Eau de Cologne* we will be safe.'

Herr Keller clicked his teeth impatiently.

'How can we present *Eau de Cologne* to the Baroness von Reudath!' he protested.

Gottfried and his assistant favoured them with looks of interest.

'Do you know the Baroness von Reudath?' asked the former.

'Of course,' returned Franz Minck. 'My friend and I had the privilege of much charming conversation with her. We were more friendly with her companions you will understand, but she was very kind.'

'And so delightfully frank,' added Herr Keller. 'She told us much of the confidence His Excellency reposes in her. His plans are very wonderful, do you not think so? He is indeed a great man.'

Gottfried suggested a perfume which he thought would appeal to the ladies, and, on the two visitors announcing their intention to take his advice, sent his assistant away to procure the selected bottles, and wrap them up. The manager then leant confidentially over the counter.

'I agree with you that His Excellency is a great man,' he declared. 'The baroness, of course is known to be in his confidence. Did she tell you much of his plans?'

'She could not tell us a great deal,' replied Keller. 'She would not reveal such secrets, but we could read between the lines. The scheme for equipping a great army, air corps, and navy, and the methods of obtaining them she did not divulge but we know there are plans on foot for the raising of men, building of ships and aeroplanes, and that the government possesses a great secret which, in time of war, would confound the enemy.'

'I see,' murmured Gottfried. 'She must have been very friendly with you to tell you all that?'

They raised their shoulders deprecatingly.

'We were more friendly with the two companions,' repeated Franz Minck. 'What lovely girls!' He raised his eyes ecstatically. 'Dora Reinwald captured my heart. Yet she is a Jewess, and hates His Excellency.'

'Did she tell you that?' demanded Gottfried eagerly.

'Words to that effect,' nodded the other. 'But we must not blame her too severely. She does not understand.'

The assistant returned with the package. Herr Minck took it, while his companion paid, and the two left the shop. Directly they had departed, Gottfried entered his office, and telephoned to the Minister of Propaganda. To that important individual he imparted what the two apparently gullible Bavarians had told him. Sir Leonard's scheme worked like a charm. The Minister was vastly interested, almost excited. He explained to Gottfried in confidence that the Baroness von Reudath was about to be tried for treason, and that it was possible the Bavarians would be required to give evidence.

'It would be useful perhaps,' he added, 'if you were also present.'

'I am sorry, Herr Minister,' replied the manager of *Lalére et Cie* regretfully, 'but I must leave for Paris today, for a conference with my directors. Of course, if you insist, I will telegraph to postpone my visit.'

'No, no,' came the voice over the telephone. 'It is not necessary, it does not matter. I will have a talk myself with these men. What did you say their names are?' Gottfried told him, adding the address. 'I thank you very much,' went on the Minister of Propaganda. 'Once again you have proved yourself a great patriot. Neither His Excellency nor I will forget.'

Sir Leonard and Cousins were sitting in the lounge of the Adlon Hotel when the manager approached them, accompanied by an officer. They both recognised the latter as the Major Wilhelm whom they had seen in Budapest, and who, they knew, had conveyed a summons then to the Baroness von Reudath to return to Berlin.

'These gentlemen are Herr Keller and Herr Minck,'

announced the manager, regarding the two a trifle doubtfully.

Major Wilhelm clicked his heels and bowed. He waited until his escort had left, then:

'I am to request you, gentlemen,' he informed them, 'to accompany me to the Reichstag. His Excellency, the Supreme Marshal himself, wishes to speak with you.'

Wallace and Cousins rose to their feet, giving a very good impression of men struck with amazement not unmixed with perturbation.

'His Excellency wishes to speak with – with us,' stammered the sham Franz Minck. 'Why?'

'That he himself will tell you. Come, gentlemen. His Excellency does not like to be kept waiting.'

They accompanied him, still looking astonished and dismayed. In the car he took no notice of them whatsoever, not even deigning to reply when the pseudo Herr Keller attempted to get into conversation with him. Apparently he regarded them as beneath his notice. They were shown into a small room in the Reichstag, with a sentry at the door. They were not detained there long, however. Major Wilhelm quickly returned and instructed them to follow him. He took them to a lofty, well-furnished chamber that had more the appearance of a drawing room than an office. When they had entered, he went out, closing the door behind him, and they found themselves confronting the Supreme Marshal and the Minister of Propaganda. They bowed awkwardly, and stood looking with alarmed and sheepish eyes at the men who held in their hands the destinies of Germany. The Marshal, standing with his hands behind his back, regarded them silently for a while, his dark eyes searching piercingly into theirs as though he were endeavouring to read their inmost thoughts.

'You are Herr Keller and Minck of Bavaria, I understand,' he commenced at last.

'Yes, Your Excellency,' murmured Wallace. 'I am Keller; my friend is Franz Minck.'

There followed several questions regarding their supposed homes in Bavaria, their holiday in Budapest, and the reason for their presence in Berlin, to all of which they answered promptly and confidently, being well-prepared. There was again silence, which von Strom followed by an entirely irrelevant query.

'What is wrong with your arm?' he asked, nodding at the bandages and sling enfolding Sir Leonard's artificial limb.

'I fell in Budapest and broke a small bone, Excellency,' explained Herr Keller.

'Oh! I am sorry!' Another pause, then: 'I understand you know the Baroness von Reudath?'

Herr Keller's apparently involuntary start was no less forcible that the exclamation that broke from the lips of Herr Minck. Their eyes met as though each was dumbly begging the other to do any explaining that might become necessary. It was Keller who replied however.

'We have met the baroness, Your Excellency,' he murmured in faltering tones. 'We cannot claim to have the privilege of being her friends.'

'Did I ask you if you were?' snapped von Strom. 'I have been informed that you became acquainted with the Baroness von Reudath in Budapest, and that she spoke to you of certain military schemes under private consideration by the government. Is that true?'

'Sh! Those unguarded tongues of ours,' sighed Herr Franz Minck, his jolly face screwing up into a comical expression of consternation. 'We intended no harm, Excellency, and if—'

'Is it true?' thundered von Strom.

'She spoke of you with great admiration for your brilliance,' Herr August Keller told him hastily. 'She let us know that she was in your confidence, and that you had wonderful schemes to build up the army, navy and air force into an organisation that would make Germany great again.'

'How is it to be done?'

'She did not tell us that, Your Excellency. She would not divulge matters of a nature so secret.'

'What else did she say?'

'Apart from the plans that are on foot for the building of many aeroplanes and ships, and the enlistment of great armies, she merely stated that you have in your possession a secret that, in time of war, will confound and rout the enemies of Germany.'

The Marshal's brows met together in an angry frown, while his companion looked significantly at him. Sir Leonard did not fail to note that a triumphant gleam showed in their eyes.

'Did she give you any idea of what the secret you speak about consists?'

'Oh, no, Excellency,' smiled Herr Keller. 'She would not do that. She only said what she did to prove to us the great things Germany could expect you to accomplish. She was full of enthusiasm for you and your work,'

'Ah! Bah!' sneered the other. 'You are great fools, August Keller, you and you friend, Franz Minck.' He turned away and began to pace to and fro, his hands clasping and unclasping behind his back, while the other three men in the room watched him, two with pretended fear showing in their expressions, the other with half-veiled looks of delight. Abruptly he turned back and confronted the disguised Englishman. 'You are sure there was nothing else of importance concerning me and my work?' he demanded.

'The baroness spoke always most highly of your great patriotism, and the brilliance of your mind, Excellency,' commenced Herr Keller.

His Excellency gave vent to an impatient exclamation.

'I do not wish to hear that stupid kind of talk,' he snapped.

He then proceeded to question them very closely and shrewdly with the intention of discovering if they were aware of any details concerning their disclosures, but they succeeded in convincing him that they were not.

'It is enough,' he declared at length, turned and spoke in whispers to his two right-hand men for some minutes. Presently he faced the pseudo-Bavarians again. He actually smiled at them. 'It is good that you repeated to a very loyal German the things you were told,' he proclaimed. 'Perhaps you did not realise the significance of such information being imparted to you. Fortunately, however, he did. The very fact that the Baroness von Reudath dared to open her mouth concerning such matters was treason. Do you follow me? Treason.' He held up a hand peremptorily as Keller and Minck were about to speak. 'You do not understand. This I will tell you in confidence. Sophie von Reudath has already done much to rouse our suspicion and distrust. We have discovered beyond doubt that she is a traitress and a menace to the safety of the Fatherland. She has been arrested, and today her trial is taking place. You will be required to testify against her.'

Looks of utter dismay appeared on the faces of the two.

'But, Excellency,' protested Minck, 'she always seemed so loyal, so devoted to you. She—'

'All pretence,' grunted von Strom. 'I was a fool myself. I trusted her. But I do not intend to allow my previous feelings of friendship for her to influence me now. She will be punished severely and the girl Dora Reinwald with her.'

'Not Dora, surely!' cried Herr Minck in agitated tones. 'She has done nothing, has she?'

'Did she not tell you she hates me?' demanded von Strom sternly. The little man groaned. 'Not that is of any account. Many hate me, many, that is, who have not the good of Germany at heart. I am convinced, and there is proof, that she has been concerned in treachery with the Baroness von Reudath. Besides, she is a Hebrew, and no good German,' he added significantly, 'has any affection for the Jews.'

'Must – must we really testify against – against them?' faltered Herr Minck.

'Have you any objection?' asked the Chancellor.

Sir Leonard almost smiled at the question. As though it would matter one way or the other if they had! He hastened to assure the man of destiny that they had not.

'It is naturally a great shock to us, Excellency,' he went on. 'We had no idea that the baroness was anything but a loyal and enthusiastic lady, but we are prepared to do our duty.'

'It is well. You will be conveyed to the prison where the trial is already taking place, and will tell the judges exactly what you have told us when you are called upon to do so. It is my wish that the baroness and her companion shall have an absolutely fair trial, but for obvious reasons it must take place in secret. You will leave at once.' He turned to the Minister of Propaganda. 'I am worried at the escape of the English girl.' Wallace heard him say in a low voice, and add viciously: 'The fools, to let her go! Do you think she has made for the British embassy?'

The Minister shook his head confidently.

'It has been under observation ever since her escape was discovered,' he replied. 'I do not think she has gone there.'

'She may have arrived there before it was known that she had got away. If so – it will be difficult to explain. See that these men are sent to the prison under escort at once.'

CHAPTER SIXTEEN

A Travesty of a Trial

They were handed over to Major Wilhelm, who was awaiting them outside. He received his instructions standing stiffly at attention, then, bidding the sham Bavarians accompany him, led them to a large car which was awaiting him below. The driver was in the uniform of a storm trooper, as was the man who sat by his side. Major Wilhelm with a sergeant took seats in the tonneau opposite the new witnesses. The speedy run to Potsdam was not marked by any more eagerness on the part of Major Wilhelm to enter into conversation with the men under his charge than before. For the most part he sat moodily silent, only occasionally addressing a curt word to the sergeant by his side. Sir Leonard and Cousins maintained an attitude of anxious discomposure as though feeling a guilty dislike for the task to which they were committed. Once or twice they essayed to speak to each other about the country through which they were passing, only to lapse almost immediately into silence again apparently having no heart for such a topic.

The Wannsee Prison had been itself a castellated palace before the Great War, but it had nothing of the stillness and lifelessness of its fellows. The high walls half hiding it looked grim and forbidding, the powerful iron gates menacing, the towers, rearing their grey bulk to the sky, suggestive of stern, unrelenting restraint. As a palace it must have been an unpleasant kind of place in which to reside; as a prison it certainly appeared to be fulfilling its real object. It was; in fact, the very building in which political prisoners would be expected to be confined. As he viewed it, Sir Leonard's lips pursed a little. If Hanni's attempt failed, the chances of getting the baroness away seemed very slender.

Major Wilhelm was subjected to a good deal of questioning and his orders carefully scrutinised before the gates were opened, and the car allowed to proceed. A powerful guard, with sentries posted every few yards it seemed, was on duty; in fact, the whole place simply bristled with armed men. Wallace had not expected anything quite like that. He wondered if von Strom possessed any suspicions that an attempt might possibly be made to rescue the Baroness von Reudath. To hold a secret trial, and then send a large body of Nazis to keep guard seemed a contradictory state of affairs. The very presence of the armed force was enough to rouse interest and excitement, thereby promoting rumours which would naturally spread like wild-fire, and rumour is ever apt to be dangerous. The German press was muzzled, of course, but matters which cause exceptional curiosity have a habit of percolating out of even the most guarded country. The Supreme Marshal certainly would not wish foreign newspapers to get hold of half a truth and from that deduct and publish an exaggerated report which would attract the suspicious eyes of Europe to his country.

Within the walls there remained more indication of the old glories of the palace that had become a prison. The courtyard still contained marble fountains, while the exterior cornices of the buildings, enclosing it on three sides, were supported on geometrically positioned pilasters. Through an open doorway beyond, Wallace and Cousins caught sight of flowers and hedges in stiff patterns, lilac and laburnum trees, festoons of bourgainvillea and lavender and white acacia. Further on terraces, still trim and neat, could be seen descending to the bank of the Wannsee. But neither the Chief of the British Secret Service nor his companion were particularly interested in searching for signs of ancient dignity and beauty just then. Their eyes were occupied, though not appearing to be thus engaged, in absorbing a picture of their surroundings and imprinting it on their minds for future reference. Not an item escaped them. The positions of the sentries, the guardhouse, everything likely to be of possible use, was noted, and all in the space of a few minutes during which the car traversed the broad courtyard and drew up on the farther side by the door of a great grim tower that seemed entirely out of keeping with the fountains and pavilions surrounding it and the masses of blooms beyond. Here, without doubt, the baroness and Dora Reinwald had been confined, here also, it appeared, they were being tried.

Wilhelm stepped out of the car, and curtly bade the supposed Bavarians follow him. They passed through the frowning portal between more guards into a great stone hall. There they were left in the charge of the sergeant and storm trooper, while the major disappeared through a doorway to the right of the hall. The formality of searching them was gone through despite their indignantly voiced protests. Fortunately, anticipating such a procedure, neither of them carried weapons. Sir Leonard and

Cousins listened intently to every scrap of conversation they could catch, but none of it was of any interest to them until two men descended the broad curving staircase to their left and, passing close by them, entered the room whither Major Wilhelm had gone. They were clothed in the sombre garments of lawyers.

'It will be all over tonight, without a doubt,' one was saying.

'And the verdict?' questioned the other.

'You will get it, of course, my friend. Guilty! It is a pity – they are very lovely women.'

Major Wilhelm reappeared, beckoned peremptorily to them. They promptly joined him, and entered the room with him. They found themselves in a long bare dining room, in which half a dozen men, all garbed in legal gowns, were eating at a table in the centre. Apparently the midday recess was on, though to Cousins and Wallace it seemed a trifle early for the meal. They were taken to a man who sat close to the head of the table, making unpleasant noises of enjoyment as he swallowed prodigious quantities of sauerkraut. He was a coarse-looking fellow with small, shrewd eyes, and thick, sensual lips. He looked up at the newcomers and nodded curtly.

'So! You are the two Bavarians of whom we have been told,' he commented with his mouth disgustingly full. 'Your evidence will be taken after the recess, though it is not needed,' he added with a leer. 'I could have closed my case with perfect satisfaction this morning, if I had not known you were coming.'

'We do not wish to testify if it is not necessary,' Herr Minck declared eagerly.

The other laughed roughly.

'It has nothing to do with you,' he returned. 'You are here to obey orders, not to say what you do or do not wish to do, Guertner!' he called.

A man a few places away looked up.

'Yes, Herr Doctor?' he asked.

'Take these two men up to see the prisoners, before the court sits. They are further witnesses for the prosecution, and I want them to be sure that they have not made a mistake.' He turned his eyes back to Wallace and Cousins. 'It would not do for you to enter the court, and then discover that the people you thought were Sophie von Reudath and Dora Reinwald in Budapest were not they at all. It may seem a little irregular to you to be taken to the prison cell to view the defendants, but it is best to make sure first that you will be giving evidence against the right people.'

It was irregular, most irregular, thought the two, but they were glad. They were being given an unexpected opportunity of finding out where the cell of the baroness was situated and how it could be reached.

'There can be no doubt concerning them,' remarked Herr Franz Minck, 'unless you have the wrong people here. We are quite sure we met the Baroness von Reudath in Budapest.'

'So am I, but the law requires proper identification.'

'Surely that would take place in court,' put in Wallace.

'Enough, I have my reasons for wishing you to see them before the trial is resumed. You had better go into the witnesses' room and obtain food. Herr Guertner will call for you there.'

They were conducted to a room on the floor above where a dozen men and women sat eating. They gave the impression of being out on a holiday, and the two Englishmen felt disgusted with the lack of any concern in their faces. Engaged in swearing away the lives of two innocent young women, through a mass of perjured evidence, they yet had no guilty thought, no regret for the crime they were committing. They were eating and drinking away as though their only concern was food. It has to be reported that Herren Keller and Minck quite failed to compare with their companions either as trenchermen or imbibers of beer, neither did they present the same self-satisfied, unconcerned front. It was a relief to them to get away from the noisy eating, the ribald remarks about the prisoners, above all from the neighbourhood of creatures so utterly vile who, for the sake of gain, were prepared to swear innocent victims into cruel oblivion.

Herr Guertner came for them long before they would have had time to have partaken of a meal if they had desired it. He was one of the men they had overheard speaking in the hall below, and appeared to be assistant prosecutor. He was quite a presentable young man who showed a disposition to be friendly. Leading them along a corridor and up a further flight of stone steps he spoke engagingly of Bavaria of which he seemed to have an excellent knowledge. Neither of his companions listened or replied with a great deal of interest, however. They were too much engaged in taking into those receptive minds of theirs every detail of their progress to the upper storeys. They ascended three further flights of stairs which brought them to the fifth floor. On the way they had hardly encountered a soul, but now they again found themselves in the presence of half a dozen well-armed Nazis, standing at intervals along a narrow stone passage in which every few yards appeared iron-studded doors. Although at such a height from the ground, the place was dark and gloomy as well as badly ventilated and stiflingly hot. A contemptuous smile appeared fleetingly at the corner of Herr August Keller's lips. The precautions taken to guard two delicate, inoffensive women struck him as ludicrous. It would have been amusing had it not been so tragic for them. How it would ever be possible to rescue them from the fate that threatened them was a greater mystery than ever now, and it appeared that there was only one night to do it in. If the two girls were found guilty and sentenced that day the chances were that they would be executed next morning. Sir Leonard had almost given up hope that the scheme he had arranged with Hanni would succeed. The more he had seen of Wannsee Prison, the more impossible it appeared that Sophie von Reudath would be able to walk out unsuspected as her own maid. He marvelled now that the girl had agreed to undertake such a foolhardy enterprise as to endeavour to change places with her mistress. He could only think that she was so desperate at thought of what she considered she had done that she was willing to risk anything and face whatever consequences might befall.

Guertner explained the reason for his coming with the Bavarians to the man in charge of the guard, and after a considerable amount of discussion, a door about halfway along the passage was unlocked and thrown open. Guertner beckoned to Wallace and Cousins to approach. They obeyed. Inside a tiny room, with small barred windows, bare except for a table, chair and little iron bedstead, was Sophie von Reudath, dressed neatly and elegantly as ever. She had been standing looking out of the aperture when the door had been opened. Now she turned and confronted them, her head raised almost with queenly dignity. They noticed, however, that her hands at her side were tightly clenched. Guertner asked her courteously to step out into the corridor in order that the men with him could have a good view of her face. She obeyed apathetically as though the hopelessness of her position had taken her in its grip. When she left her cell, however, she seemed to become aware of the two sham Bavarians for the first time, and started violently.

'Ah!' exclaimed Guertner. 'I see you recognise them.' He turned to the pair. 'This, I presume, is the lady you met in Budapest.'

'Without a doubt,' responded the bogus Keller, as he bowed to the baroness.

His heart went out to her. He would have given anything at that moment to have been able to whisper a few words of comfort and encouragement in her ear. Her ordeal had done nothing to impair her beauty, but the dark rings under her lovely eyes told their own tale.

'It is strange to meet you here, Herr Keller,' she murmured, 'and you also, Herr Minck, but I do not understand. Why are you here? Why have they brought you to see me?'

'Alas, Baroness!' interposed Guertner, before either could reply. 'They are here to give evidence against you.'

Cousins felt he could have shaken him by the hand for the note of contempt he detected in his voice.

'Give evidence against me!' she cried. 'How can that be possible?' She swung round on the two, her voice raised in outraged indignation. 'Surely, you two, who seemed men of honour, are not also going to add to the lies that have been told about me and poor Dora Reinwald. All the morning it has been lies, lies, lies. Mother of God! Surely it is not to continue. Is there nobody I can trust in this world? Nobody but one?' she added, as though correcting herself, and the watchers noticed the soft light that came into her eyes.

She was gently requested to return to her cell by Guertner, and a guard locked the door. Another was then opened, and sitting in an almost identical room, was Dora Reinwald. She rose slowly at their entrance, her burning gaze fixed on Cousins and Wallace. She showed no surprise at their appearance, and it became evident that she had overheard what had transpired. Her large eyes were smouldering with an unaccustomed fire in their depths, her face was as serene as ever. Her gracefulness as she walked slowly from her room to face them, drew a sigh of admiration from the lawyer.

'So!' Her words came quietly, but with an intensity of bitter contempt. 'You come all the way from Budapest to identify Sophie and me, and bear false witness against us. You are devils, not men, like all the rest of them from that hypocritical, bullying, lying Marshal of State down—'

'S'sh!' warned Guertner. 'Compose yourself, fraulein!'

'Compose myself!' echoed Dora, and laughed harshly. 'What does it matter what I say or whether I compose myself or not? The result will be the same. When is this farce of a trial to end? You are an advocate – one of them – you know the result was decided upon before it began. Tell me why such a travesty of justice is permitted to take place? Where is the old German blood – the blood that was red and of men – real men? Where is it now? Has it become water under the squeezing of that monster who has forced himself to power on misery? Why are these two here? In Budapest I thought they were friends. Has not the farce gone on long enough?'

Her accusing eyes sought those of Cousins in a long, challenging look; then suddenly she started. He knew at once she had recognised that he was not the real Franz Minck, he had not spoken for fear of giving himself away for he had never heard Minck's voice. As quick as thought he pushed her back into her cell.

'You speak too much,' he cried; 'you harm yourself.' For a precious moment they were apart from the others. 'We're disguised – trying to help you,' he breathed in her ear in English. 'Take no notice of what we say.'

It had all happened so quickly that he was out of the cell and with the others again before any of them, except Sir Leonard, who had been watching the girl intently, realised quite what he was doing.

'You seem in a hurry to get away from her or rather to push her away from you,' observed Guertner mockingly. 'Is your conscience pricking you, Herr Minck?'

'Why should my conscience trouble me?' the stout little man demanded. 'I did not ask to be brought here to give evidence. By talking in that hysterical manner she but damaged her own chances of acquittal.'

Guertner sighed. Almost he seemed to be sorry for her.

'She has already done that beyond repair, I am afraid,' he murmured, and signed to the men to close the door.

The last sight they had of Dora in her cell was a figure stiff and upright, immovable as a statue, but Sir Leonard thought to see a faint light of hope shining now from the depths of her great eyes. He had no means of knowing then, of course, but he wondered if, during the recent little episode, Cousins had managed to whisper a message of encouragement to her. Guertner conducted them down to the next floor, but not back to the room in which the witnesses had been given a meal. Instead he took them along a corridor and into a long unoccupied apartment. On a dais at one end were three large chairs placed behind a desk, below was a table covered by masses of documents and surrounded by chairs. Directly beyond this, and facing the dais, was a railed platform, and behind it were rows of forms reaching as far as the door at which the three men stood.

'This is the room which is being used as the court,' announced Guertner unnecessarily. 'Sit over there,' he pointed to a form near the improvised dock, 'and wait. In a quarter of an hour proceedings will reopen.'

There was a stir as the Nazi Guards came to attention and other people rose to their feet. Into the court, led by an usher, solemnly passed the three judges. The Englishmen eyed them curiously, and were not attracted. Not one of them looked as though he possessed a vestige of humanity in him. Their faces were hard, even cruel. They might have been brothers by blood as well as by profession, if a similarity in facial expression were proof of relationship. They took their seats; then came the prisoners, closely guarded, entering the dock. The baroness was very pale, but she held her head high and, in her eyes, was an unmistakable look of contempt. Dora made no attempt to hide her feelings in the slightest. She stood as straight as a ramrod, her lips curled scornfully, her whole air undeniably that of one who felt nothing but the most bitter disdain for her judges and in fact the whole farcical business.

The prosecutor was quickly on his feet. His coarse face glowed with delight in his own importance as he informed the judges that he still had two witnesses to produce.

'In the light of the overwhelming evidence that has already been offered against the prisoners,' he added, 'additional testimony may hardly seem necessary. I have proved, I think, beyond a shadow of doubt, that the women now being tried for treason are guilty. My learned friend who has the extremely difficult task of finding a defence where there is no defence, has in vain attempted to shake the evidence of the numerous witnesses you have had before you. He tried very hard –' this was said with a sneer which drew laughter from one or two '– but his task was a hopeless one. The two fresh witnesses, however, have an importance that we cannot overlook. They spent some time in the company of the prisoners in Budapest; they came to Berlin to visit them, as is evidenced by the fact that their first thought was to purchase scent for them.

From that it will be gathered that they have a friendly interest in them. They have no desire to testify against them, but the law can take no denial and their evidence will serve to convince you finally that Sophie Wera von Reudath has viciously betrayed a great, a precious confidence, has acted with the utmost treachery against the country of which she is a subject, and that her willing tool, her aider and abettor has been Dora Reinwald.'

He called the name of August Keller, and Sir Leonard stepped to the witness stand. He gave the impression of a man who was performing something utterly distasteful to him as he repeated, on demand from the prosecutor, what he had already told von Strom and Gottfried. Although his evidence sounded innocent enough in itself, was in fact calculated to show that the baroness had spoken only out of admiration for the Chancellor, the shrewd prosecutor succeeded in putting a suggestion of traitorous cunning into every word Sophie was reputed to have said. The baroness watched with an expression of utter indignation and horror on her face. Once or twice she seemed on the point of interrupting. Not so Dora. The latter seemed, if anything, a trifle amused. Her eyes never left Sir Leonard's face. The advocate for the defence made a sorry show of his cross-examination. It was perfectly obvious that he was making no real effort on behalf of his clients.

Cousins followed, and apologetically told the same story. Under examination he appeared to grow confused, sometimes contradicted himself. He deliberately got himself into difficulties, and in any honest court of law his evidence would have been regarded as utterly useless. Once or twice the prosecutor's gross face became suffused with rage, but he glossed over every mistake, insisted on his own interpretation of certain remarks being recorded. The defending counsel abjectly allowed him to go unchallenged, his cross-examination of the distressed Franz Minck was as inept as that of August Keller had been. Guertner gave evidence that they were actually the two who had been with the baroness and Fraulein Reinwald in Budapest, describing the manner in which steps had been taken to prove identity. Sir Leonard and Cousins appreciated the fact that he made no mention of Dora's remarks. Carl Schwartz was called to substantiate identity; told how he had seen the men often in the company of the companions of the baroness and, on occasion, with her and her English friend. After that the prosecution rested, and the attorney who had conducted it sat down with a self-satisfied smirk on his ugly face.

The only witnesses for the defence were the prisoners themselves. They, poor ladies, were badly handled by the man who was supposed to be there to prove their innocence. The prosecutor cross-examined them with ruthless cruelty. With diabolical cunning he strove to make it appear that their gentleness, their womanliness, even their beauty, were cloaks for the hearts of female Iscariots. Sophie von Reudath protested in vain against his innuendoes, Dora angered him by refusing to answer his questions, regarding his shouts and threats and the passionate antics into which her indifference threw him with an insolent mocking smile. The final speech by the defending counsel was as listless as all his other efforts on behalf of his clients had been; that of the prosecutor a thunderous, violent denunciation, a diatribe that was intended to make the two women appear the lowest of the low. Through it all ran his insistent demand for the death penalty. The judges conferred together for a brief period; they did not leave the court. Then they gave their verdict of guilty. The accused were asked if they had anything to say, whereupon Sophie made an impassioned appeal for her companion. With tears in her eyes she declared to the judges that whatever guilt might rest at her door, Dora Reinwald was utterly, entirely innocent. She declared she was willing to suffer whatever penalty they cared to impose on her, but begged them to exonerate the girl. Her plea was calculated to touch the hardest heart. It failed, however, to have any effect on the inhuman monsters who had presided over that pathetic farce of a trial. Only too well did they carry out the orders of the man who had succeeded in getting such a pitiless stronghold on Germany.

Sophie Wera von Reudath and Dora Reinwald were condemned to death. They were to be beheaded in the courtyard of the prison, at sunrise on the following morning.

CHAPTER SEVENTEEN

Two in a Lorry

Both Sophie and Dora received the sentence with wonderful calmness. Except that their faces went entirely bloodless, their eyes showed horror, and their hands gripped convulsively, they gave little sign of distress. They walked steadily away between their guards, passing close to the men who had vowed to rescue them. The baroness held her head high with a noble, touching dignity; she looked neither to the right nor to the left. Dora Reinwald, however, cast a long searching look at Cousins in which he read a tragic appeal. He and Sir Leonard watched until they had disappeared. They stood unheeding as the judges passed out and the room rapidly emptied. It was almost with a sense of surprise that they presently found themselves alone, except for a clerk who was busily writing in a large book at the table.

'Come!' muttered Sir Leonard. 'Let us get out of this.'

They descended to the hall below. At the entrance door their progress was stayed by a burly Nazi guard.

'Quarters for the witnesses have been provided in the pavilion over there,' he announced, pointing across the courtyard.

'Quarters for the witnesses!' repeated Cousins, almost making a muddle of his German in his surprise.

'That is what I said,' declared the man gruffly.

'But we do not require quarters,' Sir Leonard told him with a smile, though a dreadful suspicion had entered his heart. 'We have rooms at the Adlon Hotel in Berlin. It is our purpose to go there at once.'

'It may be your purpose,' grunted the fellow, 'but it is not ours. The orders are that no witnesses are to leave the castle until tomorrow afternoon.'

The suspicion had become fact. Realisation of what it would mean passed through Sir Leonard's brain in a flash, but he allowed no sign of his feelings to show.

'That is rather inconvenient,' he observed calmly. 'Surely such an order cannot apply to us. We are visitors to Berlin, and—'

'The order applies to all witnesses without exception. Paul,' he called to another man a short distance away, 'escort these two to their quarters.'

They went without further demur, but their thoughts were indescribable. They were shown into an ornately decorated building, the long corridor within, with its beautiful carved work, the trophies of the chase hanging from the panelled walls, speaking eloquently of a glory that had departed. At the door of a large room their guide left them, after informing them that they were at liberty to walk in the courtyard, but would be turned back if they approached the gates, or attempted to wander into the gardens or any other part of the prison. They entered the apartment to find the other male witnesses sitting on chairs or reclining on the camp bedsteads that had been provided. It was a large room with a wonderful ceiling, oak-panelled walls, and a great open fireplace. A long table ran down the centre, and was covered with papers and magazines, which had been provided for the entertainment of the reluctant guests. It was not possible for the two British Secret Service men to talk unheard or unnoticed there. Selecting their beds, therefore, they sauntered out into the courtyard. They chose a quiet spot, where they could reasonably expect to be free from interruption and were far enough from any sentries or other officials to be able to converse unheard. There they paced to and fro discussing the situation in low voices. The one essential they decided at once was that they must escape by some means or other, but try as they would that means refused to present itself to them. After dark there might be more hope, but the chances were that then they and the other witnesses would be locked in for the night. It was a terrible problem that confronted them. Already faced with the seemingly impossible task of rescuing the two condemned girls, they were now themselves prisoners, utterly unable to make arrangements for carrying out any scheme that might suggest itself to them in the event of Hanni failing in her purpose. Even if she succeeded, and they still remained in the castle, there would be no car to meet the baroness and whirl her away to safety, nobody to get Dora Reinwald away. Time was slipping by – it was already long past six o'clock. They stood watching a lorry coming through the gates. It was driven by a soldier, another sitting by his side, and seemed to be loaded with a variety of objects from sacks of vegetables and crates of groceries to articles of military equipment. After it had undergone the usual scrutiny at the entrance it was driven to a building that had the appearance of a storehouse quite close to where they were standing. There it was unloaded. A gleam showed fleetingly in Sir Leonard's eyes as he watched men throwing in bundles of empty sacks and crates from which the contents had been removed.

'If we could only get inside and cover ourselves with the sacking,' he muttered, 'our problem would be solved. Let us go and show how interested we are, Cousins.'

A little smile appeared in his companion's face. Sir Leonard's casual manner suggested to the little man that action was imminent. The chief never appeared more unconcerned than when he had resolved on taking a desperate chance. They strolled as though aimlessly across to the lorry, and stood within a yard or two of the back watching the men at work. There were four of them apart from the driver, who still remained at the wheel. After a few enquiring glances no notice was taken of them. They merely appeared a pair of individuals who, having nothing better to do, were taking a cursory interest in the proceedings. From where they stood they could only be seen from one part of the courtyard, and that was deserted; had been deserted for some time, a fact which had first decided Sir Leonard on taking the chance on which he was now bent. If the four men would only enter the building at the same time instead of in relays as they were doing, it would mean that there would be nobody within sight of the rear of the vehicle for any appreciable period, perhaps half a minute. Unfortunately as one or two went inside others came out, and thus it went on. Wallace managed to draw a couple into conversation, as they were departing for a fresh load of empty sacks, asking them casually what the sacks had contained, and why they were taking them away. They responded to his overtures genially enough.

'Why,' laughed one, 'you would be surprised how all the sacks are numbered and docketed. If we of the supply lose one there is a great fuss. They come here loaded with potatoes and other vegetables and when emptied, are carefully folded and stacked up. Empties – boxes, sacks and all – are collected once a fortnight like this, and taken back to the depot in Berlin.'

'You people up here are very particular,' remarked Herr August Keller. 'In Bavaria we do not bother much about trifles.'

'The quartermaster would have a fit,' commented the second man, 'if he heard you talk of his beloved sacks as trifles. So you are from Bavaria? I was once at Munich. It is a fine city. Are you witnesses for the trial?'

'Yes,' chuckled Cousins, 'and we are being given free board and lodging for one night. What a tale I shall have to tell when I get home. I shall horrify my friends by saying I was kept in a prison in Potsdam. That will shock them. They are all so good, and will think I am stamped with a blot that will not come off.'

There was a general laugh at that. The other two men came up, one carrying a couple of empty cases, the other a bundle of sacks. Sir Leonard adroitly drew them into the conversation. He now had the four together, which meant that they would depart together. For some minutes they stood talking; then one said:

'Come on, you fellows! There is still quite a lot of stuff to be loaded.'

'And we were told a meal would be given us soon,' observed Cousins, 'so we had better be going back to our little bit of the palace or we may miss it.'

'You look as though that would be a great grief to you,' observed the man, who seemed to be the senior.

'It would be – a great grief,' returned Cousins.

The four went off laughing. Sir Leonard cast a last look round. They still seemed to be unobserved, the part of the courtyard from which they could have been seen remaining unoccupied.

'In you get,' he whispered, 'and don't make a noise, or the driver may hear.'

Cousins promptly drew himself up and wriggled along to the far end. Wallace was up and in as rapidly; despite his handicap. They squirmed their way under piles of sacks, taking care that they were completely covered, and lay close behind the driver's cab. It was perhaps a fortunate circumstance that the latter did not possess a little window like so many. The man might have looked through, and thus put a complete end to their chances of escape. They could hear him singing softly to himself, as they lay hot and half stifled but now definitely hopeful. For some time they were filled with anxiety, fearful lest they had been noticed, but no hubbub rose, no sound of excited voices there came no sudden removal of their coverings and a curt demand for them to get out. From time to time they heard other crates and bundles being dumped in the lorry, occasionally caught scraps of conversation. It seemed a very long time before the lorry moved, and all the time they were troubled by the thought that they might be missed, and a search made for them. At last the engine was started.

They lay for a long time under the sacks without venturing to raise their heads. There was a possibility that a man was riding in the back with them in which case he would be bound to discover them if they moved their coverings. But Sir Leonard had no intention of riding to the depot and thus perform the time-honoured action, of falling from the frying pan into the fire. It was his design to descend at some quiet spot in the suburbs of Berlin. If there appeared to be a man riding in their part of the lorry, it would be a pity – for the man. Cautiously he moved the stifling, evil-smelling sacks away from his head, and looked out. They were alone. He nudged Cousins who sat up promptly, and drank in a great draught of fresh air.

'O – oh!' gasped the latter. 'What a relief! "Air so precious, air so divine, air that is—"'

'All right, Cousins,' grunted Sir Leonard in his ear. 'We'll think of other things than quotations just now. The first thing is to keep a sharp lookout, and slip off when we are close to Berlin. That is, if we can do it without being noticed. After that we shall have to rid ourselves of these disguises. They'll soon be on the lookout for Messrs. Keller and Minck.'

Cousins laughed softly to himself.

'I hope,' he observed, 'that the real couple will not suffer on account of our little impersonation.'

Sir Leonard shrugged his shoulders.

'If they are arrested, they ought to be able to prove an alibi. As far as we know they are still in Budapest. If by some unfortunate chance, they have come to Berlin, it may prove awkward for them. We cannot risk returning to the Adlon. I think the best thing we can do is to get a taxi and drive straight to the Esplanade. We'll book rooms there in fresh names, then when all is clear, get into the room I still retain in my – er – naval capacity – I left word that I might be away for a day or so. We can then shed these disguises and walk out as our previous selves or as an entirely new couple. Incidentally we can obtain possession of my own make-up gear which is locked away there. Now that Gottfried has gone to Paris we can't use his flat, and we shall possibly want several fresh personalities before we are done with this business. It is certainly proving rather a strain on our powers of disguise. Are you tired?' he asked, as Cousins yawned.

'A bit, sir,' admitted the little man, '"I lay me down in dead fatigue, As the arms of Morpheus to me are stretched. I call on thee—" Oh, sorry, sir.'

Sir Leonard laughed.

'You can't help yourself, can you? It has occurred to me that we haven't had much sleep lately, and we are not going to have any tonight. Before morning we must rescue the baroness, Fraulein Reinwald, and Foster. Possibly the woman Hanni as well. We've quite a busy time before us, Jerry.'

'Quite a busy time,' agreed the little man drily.

Whenever the lorry passed a populous district, they covered themselves again. At length they reached Berlin and the two of them, choosing the moment well, dropped off the back of the vehicle while it was passing along a temporarily deserted avenue. The pace was not sufficiently great to cause the undertaking to be dangerous. Cousins let himself down easily enough, but Sir Leonard, owing to his handicap, went down rather awkwardly lost his footing, and was thrown somewhat violently to the ground. His companion helped him to his feet.

'Are you hurt, sir?' he asked anxiously.

Wallace shook his head.

'A bit shaken, that's all,' he replied, cheerfully, as he proceeded to brush some of the dust from his clothing. He watched the lorry disappearing in the distance, and smiled. 'We've been lucky,' he declared. 'I was afraid that we should never strike an entirely deserted spot.'

They walked on for some minutes before they reached a shopping district. There they engaged a taxicab and were driven to the Esplanade Hotel. They booked rooms, explaining that their baggage was at the Atadtbahn. The reception clerk offered to send for it, but they declined with many expressions of thanks. There were certain dues and gratuities to be paid, they told him. When they had seen their rooms, and had washed, they would go themselves. They were accommodated on the floor above that on which was Sir Leonard's previous flat. Waiting until there was nobody about the chief descended and entered the other room – he had retained his key. A few minutes later, Cousins joined him. At once behind locked doors they proceeded to remove their disguises. After a little discussion they decided to revert to their previous characterisations. The clothes they had worn had, of course, been left in Gottfried's flat, but Sir Leonard had other garments at hand, and Cousins could continue to wear those he had on with certain alterations which would render them unrecognisable as the clothing of the fat little Bavarian who had that evening taken a room. Make-up, wigs, and all other necessary appliances were packed in a cunningly constructed secret compartment of Sir Leonard's large suitcase.

Working rapidly but carefully, the faces and figures of the two Englishmen were metamorphosed into the bronzed, hearty-looking naval officer with the round face and fair hair and the small fat man with the bristly hair, a fierce moustache and sagging, unhealthy-looking flesh. When they had done, they inspected each other critically, putting a finishing touch here and there. Discarded articles were packed away in the secret compartment, which had escaped the vigilance of numerous customs as well as other officials.

'The mystery of the disappearance of two Bavarian guests,' commented Cousins, 'will probably cause a good deal of conjecture.'

'Not if the authorities trace us to this hotel,' retorted Wallace.

'It will look rather obvious why we have come and gone so quickly. They will merely think that we had got wind of the fact that they were after us. I'd rather like to know how they will regard the escape from Potsdam. I only hope it won't cause them to suspect an attempt at rescue, and thus be more acutely on the *qui vine* than ever. Now we'll dine, then get the car and go to Potsdam.'

Casting a final look round to make sure that nothing of an incriminating nature had been left lying about, Sir Leonard unlocked the door, and looked out. The corridor was deserted, and they descended to the lounge, where the chief ordered cocktails. The assistant manager caught sight of them as they sat waiting for the drinks to arrive.

'Good evening, Herr Commander,' he bowed. 'You are back I see.'

'It is evident,' replied Wallace drily. 'My friend and I are not dressed for dinner, as you observe. Kindly give orders to the head waiter for a table to be kept for us in a secluded part of the dining room where our attire will not be noticeable.'

'It shall be done, but there are others who have not dressed. The Herr officer and his friend have no reason to feel embarrassed.'

'We shall not feel embarrassed,' murmured Sir Leonard in English to his companion when the manager had departed, 'but I am not anxious for us to be particularly noticed.'

In his character of the gross-looking man with the fierce moustache, Cousins had taken a room in the Fürstenhof. As he had not been back there the previous night, and had left no message to explain his absence, it was thought advisable for him to show himself for fear comment might be caused by his disappearance. Thither, therefore, the two repaired after dinner and, meeting the manager, Cousins confided to him that he had had a rather hectic night, as a result of which he had spent the day sleeping off the effects at a friend's house. The man laughed.

'You visitors to Berlin,' he commented, 'certainly do enjoy yourselves when you come here. By the way,' he added, 'a lady has several times telephoned for you today. She would not leave her name or a message. I was informed because you could not be found and your room had not been slept in last night.'

Cousins was barely able to repress a start of surprise. He stole a glance at Sir Leonard to find the latter smiling genially. The information must have equally disturbed the chief, but, if so, he showed nothing of it.

'Ah, ha!' he laughed. 'One of your peccadilloes seems to have found you out, Otto.'

'It seems like it,' agreed Cousins ruefully. 'Did she say nothing,' he asked the manager, 'to give a clue to her identity?'

'Nothing at all. The last time she telephoned was at about four.'

'I see. Thank you.'

Left alone, he and his chief repaired to a quiet corner of the smoking room.

'This is intriguing and highly disconcerting,' murmured Sir Leonard, appearing to be the least concerned of men.

'Who on earth can she be?' whispered Cousins.

'I am afraid conjecture is rather hopeless. It seems to me that someone has somehow got on your track, Jerry, unless it was Miss Meredith ringing up from the embassy. She knew you were staying here and the name under which you are going. But surely she would not be so foolish as to do a thing like that.'

'If she had something urgent to communicate, sir, surely she would be more inclined to get in touch with you. She is—' He stopped abruptly as a page boy poked his head into the almost empty room, and called a number. 'Mine!' he ejaculated, and beckoned the boy to him.

He was informed that he was wanted on the telephone.

'You'd better find out who it is,' muttered Wallace *sotto voce*. 'Be careful!'

As Cousins hurried away in the wake of the boy, Sir Leonard's hand involuntarily sought the pocket in which he had placed an automatic pistol when in his room at the Esplanade Hotel. A few minutes later Cousins was back. He slid into his chair quietly.

'It was the same woman apparently,' he whispered; 'she would not give her name – says that she had something of the utmost importance to tell me, and insisted upon coming round here at once.'

'H'm!' grunted Wallace. 'I can't say I like the sound of it. Still it is necessary to find out what it is about. I had better make myself scarce. If someone has tumbled to you, there may be still a possibility that I am unsuspected. Have you any idea how long she will take to get here?'

'She said she'd be here in five minutes, sir.'

'Then you'd better place yourself in a prominent position in the lounge, where she can't miss you. I'll go and get the car and wait for you a little way along the Potsdam-Platz on this side. If you don't join me by nine I'll go on. Good luck, Jerry.'

The two men quietly and unobtrusively gripped hands. Both knew that that might be the last they would ever see of each other. If Cousins's real identity had been discovered, his first duty as a Secret Service man would be to endeavour to cover all traces of his unsuspected colleague, even at the cost of throwing away his liberty and disappearing from the ken of his country and his companions without seeking or expecting the slightest assistance. It was a poignant moment for both, but they smiled cheerfully at each other. A few seconds later Sir Leonard left the smoking room. He walked out of the hotel in a casual manner, but was actually very much on the alert to note whether he was being observed. Taking the most elaborate precautions to avoid being followed, he eventually arrived at a garage in a turning off the Unter-den-Linden, quite certain that no attempt had been made to trail him. There he found a closed car awaiting him that had been arranged for by Gottfried. The driver was a man who looked as much a German as Gottfried himself, but was just as British, and belonged to the rank and file of the Secret Service. He was a member of the Guides Association, and very well known in the districts of Berlin, where tourists gather. Sir Leonard nodded to him, entered the car, and directed him to drive to the Potsdam-Platz, and draw up a little way from the Fürstenof.

After the chief had left him, Cousins sauntered into the lounge, and took up his position in a place where he could see and be seen by all who entered the hotel.

Only two or three minutes had gone by, when a young woman, perfectly dressed in an evening gown of emerald tinted tissue and carrying a black Spanish shawl on her arm, appeared. She stood for a moment gazing round her; then, catching sight of the disguised Englishman, hurried towards him. He recognised the beautifully waved brown hair, lovely complexion and blue eyes of the girl who had been the companion of Marlene Heckler and Colonel Schönewald on the night the latter had invited Foster to join the party at the Gourmania. She was Fraulein Hilda Zeiss. Involuntarily he stiffened. This appeared rather worse than he had anticipated. Marlene Heckler was one of Germany's greatest secret agents, a woman who was reputed to have an amazing knowledge of members of the espionage corps of other nations. It was not too much to imagine that Hilda Zeiss, who was so often her companion, was also employed in Germany's Secret Service. She reached him, and, glancing round her in a manner that suggested anxiety, spoke in a low voice.

'You are registered here as Otto Bräun, am I not right?' she asked.

'That is my name, fraulein,' he replied easily. 'I must confess that I am intrigued by this visit.'

'Take me somewhere where we can speak without being seen or heard,' she directed.

'My room would be the best place for that,' he remarked dubiously, 'but—'

'We shall go to your room then,' she decided.

Hesitating for a moment, he shrugged his shoulders and escorted her to the lift. A little later they were in the privacy of his own apartment with the door closed on them. She sank into a chair, while he stood two or three yards from her, regarding her curiously.

'I have been trying to find you,' she commenced, 'since noon today. It would have been better for you had you not returned to this hotel. As it is, I am here to warn you to leave at once and, if you can, get away from Germany.'

'Why, fraulein?' he asked, becoming more deeply interested than ever.

'This is no time for pretence,' she told him, her eyes holding his eagerly. 'I know your proper name is not Otto Bräun. I also know you are not a German.' She leant forward, and suddenly spoke in English. 'You are an Englishman who is suspected of being a prominent member of the British Secret Service, and your name is thought to be Cousins.'

The little man felt as though his whole world was tumbling about his ears. For a moment the room seemed to be whirling dizzily round him, but not by the flicker of an eyelid did he betray himself. Instead he smiled and twirled his fierce moustache.

'This is very amusing,' he commented, persisting in speaking German. 'I am afraid you have made a very grave mistake, fraulein.'

She clicked her tongue impatiently.

'Very well,' she decided, reverting to German herself. 'Since you intend being obstinate, I must convince you. Two nights ago you were at the Gourmania. You sat at a table next to one occupied by Colonel Schönewald, Fraulein Marlene Heckler and myself. Lest you do not know it, I must tell you that Marlene is in the espionage service of Germany. She has made it her speciality to know as many of the agents of espionage of other countries as possible. She knows Herr Cousins well by sight. When Herr Foster, who was suspected of being friendly with the Baroness von Reudath for the purpose of obtaining information from her, joined our party you stumbled against him on your way out. Whether it was an accident or intentional I do not know, but Marlene, who is always suspicious, sent a man to shadow you, find out who you were and all about you. She has many ways of communicating directions like that to others. A man or woman, or perhaps both, of her service are nearly always close by wherever she goes, and a finger raised, a nod of the head, or some other indication which nobody but they observe, gives them their instructions. You were followed, therefore, to this hotel, and information regarding you obtained. It was discovered that you had come from Budapest, which in itself was enough to rouse in Marlene greater interest than before, for Herr Foster and the Baroness von Reudath had also come from that city. Yesterday morning you were followed to the residence of the baroness, where you were seen to be keeping watch. When she went to the Esplanade Hotel you followed. Afterwards, when Colonel Schönewald took her to Potsdam to the Wannsee Prison, you followed again. But on that journey you were also trailed by Marlene herself, who had been informed of your activities by that time. You had lunch in the Polast Café at Potsdam and, while you were eating, you were under observation by her from behind a curtain in an adjoining compartment. What it was that made her guess who you were I do not know, but she is certain that you are Herr Cousins of the English Secret Service. When you left Potsdam, trace was lost of you – perhaps you suspected that you were being followed, and took steps to put those trailing you off the scent. I do not know, and it is of no concern of mine—'

Cousins could have informed her that he had gone to Gottfried's establishment, and, in accordance with the strict rule of Sir Leonard Wallace that a Secret Service man visiting a branch of the firm of *Lalére et Cie* must on all occasions, whether on duty or not or convinced of freedom from surveillance, take the utmost precautions, had travelled in no less than three different taxicabs, over circuitous routes, and had visited several shops during his progress, always emerging by a different door from that by which he had entered. He felt a great wave of relief now at the recollection of his caution. 'Watch, however, was kept on your hotel,' went on the girl, 'and much concern caused by your non-appearance. Before taking any steps against you, Marlene desired to be quite certain that she was right, and she was much troubled by your disappearance.'

He eyed her thoughtfully.

'May I know,' he asked, 'who you are, and why you tell me this?'

She shrugged her shoulders.

'It does not matter much who I am,' she returned, 'but perhaps you will be more convinced that I mean you no harm if I tell you that Colonel Schönewald is much upset at the treatment that has been meted out to Baroness von Reudath and Herr Foster. He knows that Herr Foster and the baroness are deeply in love with each other, and considers that, if you are indeed Herr Cousins of the English service, you will no doubt be eager to help them. In that case, though he can do nothing, he is desirous of thwarting Marlene in her efforts to have you apprehended. Today, anticipating that you might return here, he succeeded in withdrawing the men who were watching this hotel for you, but he cannot keep them away for long lest suspicion fall on himself. He asked me to telephone and, if you came back, to make an appointment with you, and warn you. I have done as he desired.'

'What interest have you in the affair?'

'The same as his. I feel as he does, you see,' she added simply. 'I am his fiancée. My name is Hilda Zeiss.'

CHAPTER EIGHTEEN

The Failure of Hanni

Cousins rubbed his chin reflectively. The situation called for a good deal of thought. On the face of it she must be telling the truth. There could be no reason for her to come and inform him of Marlene Heckler's activities except the one she had given; that is, to warn him. He felt a glow of gratitude to her and to Colonel Schönewald. It did not take him long to realise the risk they were running. They must be very certain of his identity, otherwise they would not have dared to have been so open with him. Had it chanced that Marlene Heckler had made a mistake the consequences to them of admitting so much to a genuine Otto Bräun would have been disastrous.

'Presuming that you are correct,' he remarked, 'with what object has this warning been conveyed to me?'

'I have told you,' she replied quickly. 'Leave this hotel at once and, if you can, get away from Germany. Once in England you can bring pressure to bear for the release of Herr Foster from the mental home in which he is confined. Alas! Neither you nor anyone else can help the poor baroness. She is doomed. Today commenced her trial for treason. It is being held secretly, and is expected to last for three days. Colonel Schönewald does not know actually of what her treason is supposed to consist, but he says there is no hope for her – she is certain to be condemned to death.'

Tears rose quickly to her eyes as she spoke. Cousins felt tempted to tell her that the trial was over, and that the baroness had been sentenced to be beheaded early the following morning, but he refrained.

'If I happened to be the Herr Cousins of whom you have spoken, Fraulein Zeiss,' he observed earnestly, 'I would always feel most deeply grateful to you and the Herr Colonel for the risks you have run to warn me. I would also take your advice.'

She smiled and rose.

'I understand,' she murmured, 'and I am very glad. Now, Herr Cousins – I mean, Herr Bräun –' she smiled again '– I must go. I am not very brave, and all the time I am here, I am very much in a state of fear for myself.' She held out her hand and Cousins took it warmly.

'There seem,' he murmured, 'to be several very noble ladies in Germany.'

He let her out, deciding that it would be safer for her if she left the hotel without his seeing her to her car. When she had gone he stood for a moment or two in deep thought, then quickly he opened his suitcase, took out certain articles, including a revolver, which he might need, and laid them ready on the bed. After that he stripped off the clothing he was wearing, removed the padding, and rapidly attired himself in another suit, becoming once again his own slim self. His own extraordinarily creased and mobile countenance was now visible, too. Rapidly he darkened his skin, taking care to rub the stain well up his arms and down under his collar. This done he wound a muffler round his neck, placed a pair of horn-rimmed glasses on his nose, and a soft hat on his head, after which he surveyed himself in the mirror. He saw a studious though somewhat wizened Indian gazing earnestly at him, and was satisfied. The change of disguise would pass muster for the time being, he decided. People looking for a fat man with a fierce moustache and bristly hair would hardly glance twice at an inoffensive-looking Indian student. The articles he had laid out on the bed were one by one tucked away in his pockets. He had taken care to leave nothing that might suggest that he had altered his disguise. The suit of clothing he had discarded was hung in the wardrobe, the padding was stuffed well up the chimney. He chuckled a little to himself at thought of what would happen if it remained undiscovered until the weather became cold in the autumn or winter and the then occupier of the room had a fire lit.

A glance at his watch showed him that it was ten minutes to nine. He would just have time to join Sir Leonard. With great caution he opened the door and glanced out. A chambermaid was walking away from him some distance along the corridor. There was nobody else about. He slipped out, shut the door, and hurried to the stairs, avoiding the lift purposely. He reached the lounge unobtrusively, and was glad to note that it was crowded. Nobody took any particular notice of him – Indians in Berlin are not uncommon. Walking casually to the entrance he received a shock. A car drew up outside, and from it descended Marlene Heckler, Colonel Schönewald, and two Nazi troopers. Cousins stepped quickly behind a pillar, and they passed within a few feet of him.

He noticed that the young Colonel looked a little perturbed and worried, and guessed the reason. He was wondering if the man to whom he had sent the warning had yet had time to get away.

'Just did it,' murmured Cousins to himself, 'thanks to you, Schönewald.'

A minute later he was outside the hotel sauntering in aimless fashion towards a large closed car drawn up to the kerb a little distance away. Several times he paused to look in the shop windows, thus making sure that he was not being watched or followed. He came abreast of the car and standing well within view of the man in the interior, whistled softly an air which British Secret Service men the world over make use of to indicate themselves to each other. Almost immediately the motor moved slowly and silently away. It disappeared round a corner, and Cousins continued his apparently purposeless stroll. He reached the turning and entered a narrow bystreet almost completely deserted. The car was waiting for him a few yards away, the door partially open. He walked along, took one quick, comprehensive look round, and skipped nimbly inside. At once the powerful saloon glided away. Purposely it was driven round side streets, doubled on its tracks, and underwent other manoeuvres to safeguard it from possible pursuit. Satisfied at length that all was well, the driver headed in the direction of Potsdam. Neither Sir Leonard nor his companion spoke until Berlin had been left behind; then the chief eyed his companion thoughtfully.

'Well?' he queried.

Cousins told him all that had occurred, and Sir Leonard listened with a frown on his forehead.

'Worse than I thought,' he commented at the end of the recital. 'I should like to know how Marlene Heckler found out who you really are. I have always heard she was particularly astute and dangerous – she has certainly given us a proof of her shrewdness. One can understand now why such precautions are taken to guard the baroness, and keep all unauthorised persons away from Wannsee Prison.'

'I rather fancy the hue and cry for Keller and Minck,' observed Cousins, 'is likely to be keener than we anticipated, sir.'

Wallace nodded.

'Much keener,' he agreed. 'It is comforting to know that we got rid of those disguises so quickly.'

He spoke as though it were sheer chance that had caused them to revert to the characters they had previously portrayed. Cousins smiled.

The two were silent most of the way to Potsdam. Sir Leonard who, all the time, appeared extremely thoughtful, once looked at his companion to remark:

'I have been trying to discover if it is possible that Schönewald and Hilda Zeiss could have had some ulterior motive in arranging to warn you. I am quite satisfied, however, that their intentions were honest. No matter which way one studies the situation, their object appears convincingly altruistic. The knowledge that they are deeply in sympathy with the baroness may be very useful to us before we are through with this business. In fact, I have a feeling that it will be. You did very well to alter your disguise with such promptitude, Jerry. If you hadn't, you would be in or on your way to a German prison by now. Possibly I would have been with you.' Cousins eyed him reproachfully, but said nothing. 'Ah, well!' added Sir Leonard with a sigh, 'even if we have another danger to avoid, we do know it exists, which is something. I only hope Marlene Heckler doesn't get on your – or rather our – track before we rescue the baroness.'

'Do you think there is a possibility she may, sir?' Sir Leonard shrugged his shoulders.

'A woman who was clever enough to see through your very excellent disguise is capable of a good deal. It all depends upon what she thinks you were watching the baroness for. If, as I suppose, she considers it was for the purpose of making an attempt to obtain from her the information she possesses, she will probably think you have been properly baulked now. On the other hand, like Schönewald, she may have an idea that you are desirous of helping Foster and the baroness. In that case, I shouldn't be surprised to find her turning up in the neighbourhood of the prison sometime tonight. If so, she must not see you. Eyes that saw through the more elaborate disguise will not have much difficulty in penetrating your present one – even at night.'

The car turned down a mere track between the trees not far from the prison. There it drew up, and the lights were extinguished. Leaving Cousins and the driver there, and warning the former to be keenly on the alert, an order which he well knew was quite unnecessary, Sir Leonard walked away in the direction of the palace that had shed its ancient glories to become a political gaol. It had grown quite dark by that time, but when opposite the grim entrance gate, he found there was sufficient illumination thrown on them from a great lamp suspended above to enable him to see all who entered or left. He took up his station in the midst of a dense mass of shrubbery, and waited.

He had just looked at his watch to find its luminous dial indicating twenty minutes to eleven, when the wicket gate opened with a clatter of chains and the squeak of rusty hinges. A woman appeared and the door immediately closed again behind her. For a moment or two she stood looking about her indecisively; then set off down the road in the direction of the town. Sir Leonard stepped cautiously from cover, and followed her without a sound, keeping always to the deeper darkness. He allowed her to get some distance from the prison before overhauling her. A little flash lamp, very much of the shape and size of a fountain pen, was now in his hand, and when within a few yards of her he switched it on. A brilliant ray of light stabbed the darkness; was almost at once extinguished. A little choking cry of fear came from the woman, while a bitter sense of disappointment pervaded the whole being of the Englishman. She was Hanni. The Baroness von Reudath had not escaped.

'It is all right,' he encouraged her. 'It is I – the man who spoke to you last night. What has happened?'

'How you startled me I – I thought – oh! I do not know what I thought.' She paused, then with a little sob, added: 'You see, I have failed. I did all I could, but it was useless. They would not even let me see her tonight. I spent nearly half an hour pleading with the governor, but it was hopeless. They were guarding her in a manner most extraordinary – just as though they were expecting an attempt to be made to rescue her.' Her voice faltered, and again came a sob. 'She – she is to be executed in – in the morning – she and Fraulein Reinwald.'

'I know,' returned Wallace gravely.

He guessed she was staring at him; attempting to pierce the darkness in an effort to see his face.

'How do you know that? Who are you?' she whispered.

'I have means of knowing these things, but do not fret, fraulein; you have done your best, I am sure! We shall now have to take other measures. Come! I have a car hidden among the trees.'

They reached the car. Cousins was immediately by Sir Leonard's side, enquiring hopefully whether he had the baroness with him. He spoke in German, and his chief replied to him in that language. The little Secret Service man's disappointment was very great when he learnt of the non-success that had attended Hanni's venture. Wallace stood for a long time thinking over a desperate scheme, which he now knew was the only hope left. Nobody interrupted him. The driver sat at the wheel like a graven image, Hanni sank to the running board of the car, and buried her face in her hands, Cousins stood by, alert, eager, ready to enter at once into a discussion concerning their future arrangements, but making no attempt to speak to the man he was confident would yet save the baroness and Dora if it were humanly possible. He could just dimly discern the motionless figure before him. Sir Leonard stood in a favourite attitude, his artificial hand, as ever, in his jacket pocket, his right caressing his chin. At length he became suddenly galvanised into life.

'There is no time to lose,' he declared sharply. 'We must get back to Berlin.'

'What are we going to do now, sir?' ventured Cousins.

Hanni looked up eagerly, waiting almost breathlessly for the reply. More than ever she wondered who this man was who was treated with such respect by the other. The driver, no less eagerly, abandoned his statuesque pose, and turned his eyes on the shadowy figure of the famous Chief of the British Secret Service.

'There is only one thing left to do,' remarked Sir Leonard in English, and Hanni gasped. 'You and I, Jerry, are going to interview von Strom. It is he who will rescue the baroness and Fraulein Reinwald.'

Cousins stiffened, stood as though he thought his chief had

become suddenly bereft of his senses, then he laughed quietly to himself.

'Poetic justice!' he murmured. '"Far from her peril free she strode, Saved by him who had flouted her."'

Hanni sprang to her feet; grasped Sir Leonard convulsively by the arm.

'You are English,' she cried in her own language. 'Now indeed I have great hope. You are perhaps friends of Herr Foster. But it is useless to go to His Excellency. He will not listen to you. He is without pity and mercy. You will only suffer if you do that.'

'You leave it to us, Hanni,' was his reply. 'I do not fancy he will have very much choice.'

He bade her enter the car, Cousins followed and, after giving the driver instructions, Sir Leonard sprang in. A few seconds later they were speeding back to Berlin. A powerful car passed them a mile or so from Potsdam, and in the fleeting glimpse of its passengers he was able to obtain from the headlights of his own vehicle, thought to recognise Marlene Heckler and Major Wilhelm. He frowned a little but said nothing. Hanni was dropped near the Brandenburg Gate, and told to be there again at three in the morning. She was to wait until four; then, if nobody came for her, to return home. Wallace heard her utter a fervent prayer for his success as the car glided on its way. It stopped close to the Esplanade Hotel, and he descended. He had rapidly outlined his plans to Cousins, as a result of which the little man went on to the garage, there to wait in concealment until Sir Leonard joined him again. The latter approached the hotel very unobtrusively. He did not anticipate that he, like his assistant, had come under suspicion, but he had no intention of taking any chances. He succeeded in reaching his room unobserved; entered, his hand immediately seeking the automatic in his pocket. There was no cause for alarm. It was vacant, and showed no signs to his keen eyes that it had undergone a search.

He locked and bolted the door, then, from its place of concealment, drew out his make-up box and various articles, including crêpe hair and a wig. These were packed into a neat parcel, which was strapped to his person beneath his coat. A bulge was caused, but it was not too noticeable. Locking his suitcase again, he glanced once more round the room, still anxious to make certain that there had been no intruders during his absence. Satisfied, he went out cautiously, descending by the service stairs, and thus succeeding in avoiding observation. There were a good many waiters and other members of the staff about below, and he was forced to remain hidden for some time before he was able to emerge from the hotel without being seen. When eventually he left the building, he hurried by a circuitous route to the garage where Cousins awaited him, taking steps on the way to ascertain that he was not being shadowed. It was not that he had any expectation of anything of that nature, but too much depended now on his complete freedom of person and action to allow him to take the slightest risk.

He reached the garage. As he expected, it was deserted. It was a private place shared by three men, of whom Gottfried was one, and had the advantage of being secluded while actually in the very midst of one of Berlin's business districts. The car which had taken him and Cousins to Potsdam had not been Gottfried's, but one hired from the garage proprietor. There was always a possibility that it might have come under observation by someone connected with the authorities, and the number noted. If anything had gone wrong Gottfried therefore could not have been involved. Sir Leonard was always most particular to keep members of the firm of *Lalère et Cie* from being concerned in anything that might bring them or the business house that cloaked their real activities under suspicion of being in any way connected with the British Secret Service.

He found Cousins and the driver in a small room that the latter rented above the garage in which the car had been locked. They greeted him with sighs expressive of their satisfaction at seeing him again. He partook of the refreshment his host had thoughtfully provided, and went more fully into his plans.

'I have decided to dispense with the car, Reichmann,' he declared. 'It would be more of an encumbrance than a help on the job we are about to undertake. When we do use a car, the Supreme Marshal himself will have to provide one of his.'

The member of the association of guides looked disappointed. His face fell woefully.

'Then you will not need me, sir?' he murmured.

Sir Leonard smiled.

'On the contrary, I certainly shall need you.' Reichmann expressed his relief. 'We will go now to von Strom's house. Somehow or other, despite the strong guard with which we know he surrounds himself, we are going to get inside, and have a private chat with our friend. It is no use attempting to plan our entry now. Circumstances will have to show us the way. I hope also that we will be fortunate enough to catch him before he goes to bed. It might be awkward if we don't. I have been thinking over the position, and it has occurred to me that there is too much risk connected with my previous intention of forcing him at the point of a revolver, to accompany us to Potsdam and order the release of the prisoners. I don't think he lacks courage, and he might defy us when he is surrounded by his men, as he would be once inside the

Wannsee Prison. I have brought the necessary materials, therefore, to enable me to impersonate him. I'll be the Marshal of State for the time being, but we'll take him along with us gagged and bound, and hidden from sight, in order that there will be no danger of an alarm being raised while we are on the job.'

Cousins whistled long and thoughtfully, the guide Reichmann stared at Sir Leonard with wide-open mouth as though stupefied.

'Good Lord!' ejaculated the former. 'What a scheme!'

'It's the only possible way of saving the two women as far as I can see,' returned Wallace in calm, matter-of-fact tones. Had any stranger entered the room at that moment he would have imagined that the Chief of the British Secret Service was talking of a matter of little moment instead of a daring venture that would require the utmost nerve and resource. 'Of course,' went on the chief, 'impersonating von Strom in the midst of a crowd of men who see him regularly, and are probably well acquainted with every gesture, every feature, and every shade of inflection in his voice is going to be a ticklish business. This, on the face of it, must appear as sheer lunacy. But none of the other ideas that have occurred to me hold out such hopes of success, and we shall have the living model to copy. It will be up to you, Cousins, to see that there is no flaw. I can't say I am altogether looking forward to the ordeal. You haven't thought of a better plan, I suppose?'

Cousins shook his head.

'No, sir – nothing that has the same promise of success as that. But where do I come in? I can hardly accompany you as an Indian student.'

Sir Leonard smiled.

'No; you can't do that. We must see if we can find Nazi uniforms for you and Reichmann. I may require him to drive the car.'

Cousins laughed joyfully like a schoolboy, delighted at the prospect of a glorious adventure.

'How shall we take von Strom with us, sir,' he asked, 'and yet keep him concealed.'

'There are such things as luggage compartments on most cars nowadays,' returned Sir Leonard. 'I hope there is one attached to the motor we use and that it is roomy and airy. I should not like His Excellency to be cramped or suffocated.'

CHAPTER NINETEEN

The Marshal Receives Unwelcome Visitors

They found a belated taxicab and drove to the Konigs-Plats. There they dismissed it, walking the rest of the way to von Strom's residence. The nearer they drew to his great mansion the more cautious became their progress. The square in which it stood was practically deserted, but from the seclusion of a thick group of trees they could see the numerous sentries marching up and down before the great iron railings or standing on guard at the gates. Lamp standards every few yards threw a radiance of light on the scene which in one way was helpful, but otherwise disconcerting. To enter such a place secretly seemed well-nigh impossible, but the word 'impossible' has no place in Sir Leonard's vocabulary. He studied the building in silence for some time. A small gate at the extreme left of the railings attracted most of his attention. It stood open, and a sentry was stationed to one side of it. A few yards from it was a large chestnut tree. He decided that their entry should be made at that point. Whispering instructions to his followers, he made a wide detour, crossing the square some distance away, and avoiding the light as much as possible. In single file, and treading without a sound, they gradually approached the tree until they stood behind it.

Sir Leonard gazed reflectively at the lamp throwing its powerful illumination on the gate and the sentry box. If he could cause it to fail the neighbourhood would be thrown into darkness, and make it fairly easy for them to enter the courtyard. A shot would have the desired effect, but a shot would bring the guard to the spot in double quick time, and put a complete end to their hopes. No; it was out of the question to extinguish the light. By some means or other the sentry's attention must be diverted. He bent down and, to his satisfaction, found several small stones at the base of the tree. He picked up two or three, bidding his companions do the same. They then proceeded to throw them at regular intervals some yards beyond the sentry.

As the first fell lightly to the ground, the man grew rigidly on the alert. Glancing round the tree, Sir Leonard saw that he was staring in the direction from which the sound had come. Another and another stone followed; then came the rattle of a rifle as it was shouldered. The sentry, as Wallace had hoped, marched to the place whence the noise appeared to come. Directly his back was turned, the three sped like shadows across the intervening space, and succeeded in passing through the gate. They reached the deeper darkness surrounding a linden tree; stood there with every sense acutely on the alert, hardly daring to breathe. But no alarm was raised; they had entered without being seen. Reichmann, who was unused to such ventures, gave vent to a great sigh of relief, which was immediately stifled by Cousin's hand.

'Be quiet!' whispered the little man. 'This courtyard is patrolled by police. There may be one or two close by.'

He had hardly spoken when they heard the measured tramp of feet, and two shadowy forms passed by a few yards away. They waited until the sound had died in the distance; then, running on tiptoe, and with Sir Leonard leading the way, they reached a side entrance of the building, and stood safely under the portico. The chief had noticed that this was the only one in darkness, the other doors, visible from the square, all being illuminated. So far everything had gone well. It now remained for them to enter the house. Obeying instructions, Cousins produced from somewhere on his person, a case of finely-tempered steel instruments. Selecting one of these, he quickly had the door unlocked, but it would not move.

'Bolted!' he muttered tersely.

Bolts, however, were not impossible obstacles to men who had, of necessity, become expert at opening all sorts and conditions of doors and windows. Once the bolts were located, Cousins worked silently and skilfully, using a long, slender instrument with a gripping, curved end. The operation took some time and when Sir Leonard heard a clock in the distance strike one, he whispered to his assistant to hurry. At length the job was done and muttering a fervent hope to himself that no burglar alarm was connected, Cousins slowly and silently pushed open the door. It was at that moment that they heard the sound of approaching footsteps. Another police patrol was coming. Sir Leonard drew his automatic ready, if discovered, to take the aggressive, but the man went by, greatly to his relief. He had no wish to risk an encounter with any of the guard if such could be avoided. A moment later the three of them were inside the house. The door was shut, locked, and bolted again, and, in place of his case of steel implements, Cousins now held a revolver in his hand. Reichmann was unarmed, and was instructed to keep close behind the chief, the little Secret Service man bringing up the rear.

His faculty of being able to see quite well in the dark now stood Sir Leonard in good stead, for he was reluctant to use his torch. He had led the way unerringly along a narrow passage, which presently broadened out into a wide corridor. While in the square, he had noted light issuing from two windows on the first floor. It was his object to reach the room or rooms in which the electricity burnt, hopeful that inside he would find His Excellency at work. They passed several rooms, all in darkness, before emerging into a large, lofty hall adjoining the main door. The light from outside illumined the place, showing them a broad staircase ascending to the upper regions. Without hesitation and in the same order as before, they went up. The corridor above was in darkness, but after traversing several passages, they came to a corner where light was dimly diffused from a lamp, apparently some distance away. Sir Leonard glanced cautiously round; almost immediately drew back. He had found himself looking along a gallery lighted by a single electric globe half way along. Sitting in a chair close to a shut door, and almost directly under the lamp, was a man in Nazi uniform. He appeared to be dozing. The Chief of the British Secret Service was not disconcerted. On the contrary he felt quite a glow of satisfaction. The presence of the man in the chair suggested that von Strom was up and working in the room outside which the orderly was sitting. He stole another look. The Nazi's head was bent forward, his eyes closed. He was not a very vigilant attendant, which was all to the good. If he could be approached without alarming him, it might be possible to overcome him without causing a disturbance. It was a pity they would be forced to encumber themselves with an additional prisoner, but it could not be helped. Sir Leonard retreated a few yards, and, putting his automatic in his pocket, asked Cousins for his revolver.

'Your Nazi uniform is along that corridor,' he whispered to Reichmann. 'Mr Cousins and I are going to get it for you. Remain here until we come back.'

The guide eyed him in puzzled fashion, but nodded. Sir Leonard whispered to Cousins to follow him and be ready to prevent the Nazi from falling noisily to the floor when rendered unconscious. The chief regretted the necessity that would force him to stun the man, but did not care to risk pointing a revolver at him and ordering him to be silent. The fellow would quite likely dare being shot to raise the alarm. Creeping round the corner, and keeping close to the wall, the pair gradually approached the unsuspecting man, who still dozed on. They were within a few paces of him, when he suddenly stirred and looked up. For a fraction of a second his eyes encountered those of Sir Leonard. He appeared momentarily stupefied; then his mouth opened to cry out. The butt end of the revolver wielded with scientific precision, descended on his head with a soft but sickening thud. Without a sound he sagged forward, Cousins catching his body and preventing it from sliding to the floor. He supported it in his arms, while he and his chief listened intently to make certain that no alarm had been caused in the room.

Satisfied that all was well, Wallace sent Cousins back to fetch Reichmann, he himself keeping a hold on the senseless figure in the chair. The little man quickly returned with the other, and they were directed to carry the Nazi to the end of the corridor. Round the corner Sir Leonard ordered them to strip the man of his uniform.

'He is about your size, Reichmann,' he whispered, 'which is fortunate. Later we shall have to disguise you. It won't do for you to be recognised, or not only will your usefulness in Berlin be gone, but you will probably lose your life as well. I don't know quite what we are going to do about a uniform for you, Cousins. I doubt if there is a Nazi on the staff here so small. You're a problem. However, quite a minor one.' He smiled.

The unconscious man was quickly divested of his clothing. Reichmann discarded his own outer garments and donned the uniform. It proved an excellent fit. When that was done, Cousins was sent to search for materials with which to bind and gag the Nazi. He was gone for several minutes, and Sir Leonard began to grow anxious lest von Strom who, he firmly believed, was in the room, should emerge or summon the orderly. However, the little Secret Service man came back at length armed with a tablecloth and several napkins. He had discovered the dining room from where he had abstracted the articles. The German was gagged and bound with scientific thoroughness, after which, he was carried along the corridor, and placed in a room almost opposite the apartment in which they presumed von Strom to be at work. Cousins had glanced in during his search to find it an office apparently used by clerks of the household. Deserted at that hour, of course, it would do as a temporary prison for the orderly. Reichmann's clothing was also placed inside, and the door closed. The guide was then told to sit in the German's chair, and keep watch.

Sir Leonard bent down and endeavoured to look through the

keyhole of the Marshal's room, but the key was in the way, and he could see nothing. He stood with his automatic in his hand – the revolver had been handed back to its owner – while Cousins softly turned the handle. At a word from his chief, the little man suddenly swung the door open, and stepped aside. Sir Leonard entered at once. He found himself in a large room furnished, not elaborately but quite comfortably, as a library. In the centre of the apartment was a large desk, almost covered with books and documents. Behind it sat a man. The Supreme Marshal of State!

He looked up in startled fashion at Sir Leonard's entry and, as it dawned on him, that here was a complete stranger, sprang to his feet. The sight of the automatic held steadily pointed at him, caused him to pale a little, but he showed no sign of fear. For a moment the two stared straight at each other, but those cold, steel grey eyes of Sir Leonard's were too much for von Strom. His gaze flickered and fell. Then abruptly he recovered from his surprise.

'Who are you, sir,' he demanded in harsh, angry tones, 'and how did you come here?'

'That hardly matters,' drawled Sir Leonard. 'I am here, and it is quite sufficient to concern you for the present. Sit down, and keep your hands above the desk.'

Von Strom took no notice of the order. He remained standing, his eyes flashing fiercely.

'You will suffer severely for this,' he stormed. 'Do you think you can enter in a manner so threatening the private apartment of the Supreme Marshal of Germany, and escape without severe punishment?'

'I have no time to bandy unnecessary words with you,' retorted the Englishman. 'As you see, I have the advantage of you. If this little weapon happens to go off, the Chancellor will be forced to look for a new Marshal. That will be sad for you, will it not? Though doubtless of great benefit to Germany. However, I do not intend to shoot you unless you force me to take such a drastic course. Sit down!'

'Do you think I fear that stupid weapon?' snarled the other.

'Yes,' was the calm retort. 'You would hardly be human if you did not. Few of us wish to die, least of all you, bloated with power and ambition.'

'You fool!' snapped the Marshal. 'Within call are a hundred men who, at a word from me, would tear you to pieces. What is to prevent my summoning them?'

'This,' replied Wallace, nodding at the automatic. He slowly approached the desk. 'Sit down,' he repeated sternly. For a while von Strom defied him, but his resolution was not proof against the grim little weapon pointed so unwaveringly at his head, and presently, with an oath, he sank back into his chair. 'Ah! That's better,' commented the disguised Englishman. 'Now we can talk. There is quite a lot to discuss. Keep your hands together on the desk. That's right. Thank you.'

Cousins had entered behind his chief, and, closing the door, remained standing with his back to it, his revolver swinging loosely in his hand. Von Strom, whose attention had hitherto been centred on the florid faced man with the automatic, now seemed to become aware of the second intruder for the first time. He frowned in rank astonishment.

'An Indian!' he ejaculated. 'What is the meaning of this theatrical display?'

'I am glad you can look upon it in such a light,' observed Sir Leonard cheerfully. 'You have certainly come quite near the mark, as far as my friend and I are concerned. But there is no time to waste. I have a lot to do, and quite a lot to say. Today you caused two young women to undergo the humiliation of a farcical trial for treason – I refer to the Baroness von Reudath and Fraulein Reinwald.' Von Strom gasped audibly. He leant forward, and studied the speaker's face intently. 'There are no words expressive of the foul manner in which you have behaved,' continued Sir Leonard sternly. 'The so-called trial had not an atom of justice or mercy in it. From first to last it was evident that the judges and attorneys for both sides had received their orders. They obeyed them only too well. These two poor girls have been condemned to be beheaded at sunrise, and all because *you* were scorned by one of them whom you could not bend to your will.' Von Strom spat out a forcible exclamation and half rose to his feet. 'Sit down!' snapped Sir Leonard, and the automatic was again raised threateningly.

The Marshal sank back, and looked round him with the suggestion of a hunted expression in his eyes. The Englishmen, watching him intently, were rather pleased to note that he had turned a little pale. It seemed that he was not quite so brave as he pretended to be. Perhaps his conscience, if he possessed one, was troubling him a little, perhaps he read nemesis in the cold eyes of the man confronting him.

'Those women are traitresses,' he grunted, 'and, as such, deserve the fate that is about to overtake them.'

'They are not traitresses,' retorted Sir Leonard. 'Whether or not the baroness contemplated betraying the secrets you confided in her for your own vicious purposes, is neither here nor there. She is not a German, though the law may have dubbed her as one on her marriage to the Baron von Reudath. She is an Austrian, and I happen to know gave a vow to you of secrecy, only on your giving your word that your military plans were non-aggressive. You deluded her. Anyone with any knowledge would have known that they could not possibly be.'

Von Strom was now white to the lips. His mouth kept opening and shutting convulsively as though he were endeavouring to speak, but could not, while his eyes appeared to be very nearly protruding from his head, as he stared at the stern, calm man before him.

'What do you know?' he muttered hoarsely at length.

'Everything,' was the reply, 'and before many hours have passed, my knowledge will be public property.'

'Who are you?' gasped the other, and a sound very much like a groan broke from his pallid lips.

'It does not matter in the least who I am. I have come here to demand justice, and justice I am going to obtain. The baroness must be released. Dora Reinwald, who is entirely innocent, must be released. The Englishman, Foster, whose great crime in your eyes was that he dared to love a woman whom you desired, must be released. Why, you cur, do you think you can use your power unchallenged to perpetrate gross, hideous crimes, that call to heaven for vengeance? I do not pretend to be heaven's instrument of punishment, but, at least, I am here to give you the opportunity of righting the wrongs you have already done, and of preventing a bloody crime that, if carried out, will ring down the ages as one of the worst acts in history. You have paper before you, pen and ink. Sign at once, an unconditional order for the release of the Baroness von Reudath, Fraulein Reinwald, and Herr Foster, and a safe conduct for them to leave Germany.'

'And what of you,' sneered the other, 'you and your black companion? Do you not want a safe conduct also?'

'We desire nothing from you for ourselves. All we require are the documents I have mentioned.'

Abruptly the Marshal was on his feet, his face livid with rage, his whole body trembling violently with the passion of his anger.

'God in heaven!' he screamed. 'Who are you to force yourself into my presence and dictate to me? Am I safeguarded by traitors that such things can be. Someone will suffer for their slackness, and you, you swine hounds, will undergo the punishment that Sophie von Reudath is about to suffer. You would demand an order for release and a safe conduct, would you?' He laughed harshly. 'Fools, madmen, you have walked into the lion's den and from it, you will never escape.' Leaning forward, he added between clenched teeth 'And you shall tell me who you are, the extent of your information, and from where it was obtained.'

'Quite a pretty display of temper,' commented Sir Leonard coolly, 'but useless. Write those orders!'

The Marshal stormed in more violent fashion than before. A string of bloodthirsty and blasphemous denunciations poured from his lips, which was in no wise restrained by sight of Sir Leonard's automatic approaching closer to his head. He was beside himself, in a rage far too great to take account of the danger in which he stood. Wallace began to fear that his shouts would be heard, and bring people to the room bent on finding out what was wrong. He gestured to Cousins who promptly stepped up to von Strom, swinging his revolver by the barrel. Sir Leonard interrupted the flow of invective sternly.

'I give you one more chance,' he snapped. 'Write those orders for release and safe conducts at once—'

'Or you will murder me!' snarled the other. 'Try it, and see what happens to you and your Indian friend. There is an electric alarm bell in the floor, and my foot is on it. I am just about to press it.'

'You're a liar!' retorted Sir Leonard deliberately. 'There is no bell push in the floor. A friend of mine who knows your residence well, described this room to me. The alarm bell is rung by that rope hanging by the fireplace behind you. Your chances of pulling it are not very great.'

Another great cry of rage broke from von Strom. He swung round and made a desperate dash for the silken cord, but Cousins was too quick for him. The butt of the little Secret Service agent's revolver descended on his head with sickening force. He grunted and went down as though he had been poleaxed. Cousins eyed his recumbent form with the air of an expert who had performed his task skilfully and well.

'"Down to the ground the tyrant sank",' he quoted, '"His eyes fast closed in death—" Well, not exactly in death,' he interrupted himself, 'but he will be as good as dead for some time.'

'It was fortunate Gottfried knew this room,' commented Sir Leonard, 'and had described it to me. His tale of the alarm bell in the floor might otherwise have bluffed us sufficiently to enable him to reach the cord. Turn him over Cousins, and drag him right under the light. I'll get on with the make-up right away.'

Cousins did as he was bidden.

'You won't have to alter your figure much, sir,' he observed. 'The padding you are wearing for the general naval officer makes you just about the same build as von Strom, and your height is not noticeably different.'

Sir Leonard placed his make-up box with the other articles he had brought with him on the desk and, aided by Cousins, commenced at once on his preparations, working with the most meticulous care, and studying every line and feature of the face of the unconscious Marshal, he gradually transformed himself into a marvellously complete double of the man. When he had finished, he stretched himself at full length beside the other, and while Cousins held a mirror over them, compared the two faces with painstaking thoroughness, making a slight alteration here and there. Satisfied at length, he rose to his feet, and he and his assistant proceeded to strip the Marshal of his outer clothing. Sir Leonard took off his own and donned the other. When that was done, he made another careful examination of himself. Cousins' bright eyes twinkled with delight.

'It is the finest thing you have ever done, sir,' he declared. 'It is amazing. There is not a flaw anywhere.'

'Now for the voice,' observed Wallace. 'I let him talk and shout more than I should otherwise have done in order to be able to study it and catch every shade of inflection.'

He rattled off a series of commands. Cousins listened with admiration shining from his eyes.

'Perfect!' he declared, when Sir Leonard stopped, and looked at him enquiringly. 'You have caught the voice in every particular. It is great. Not a soul will ever dream that you are not the great man himself. I bet you'd take in his wife, sir.'

'I have no wish to make the experiment,' returned Sir Leonard drily. 'Now will you make up Reichmann to resemble the fellow whose place he has taken? After that you'd better remove that stain, and we'll think of a disguise for you.'

There were many points of resemblance between Reichmann and the orderly, which made it fairly easy for Cousins. Quarter of an hour later his task was finished. He found a bathroom and with the aid of grease followed by warm water, removed the stain from his face and arms. When he had finished, he contemplated the towel he had used.

'Someone will wonder what has happened to this in the morning,' he murmured, and rejoined Sir Leonard.

The latter was a little puzzled at first regarding Cousins' disguise. Several ideas were mooted and dropped – the lack of a uniform causing most of them to be ruled out. A search had failed to bring to light anything, either of a fit or type, to transform the little man into a Nazi storm trooper, or a member of a similar body. Neither of them felt like looking for what they required in any of the bedrooms for fear of disturbing any of the people sleeping in the house.

'You're a great problem, Cousins,' frowned Sir Leonard.

'Well, sir,' commenced the little man, 'it is well known that Euclid—'

The chief interrupted him by laughing softly.

'Marlene Heckler,' he remarked, 'is convinced that you are in Berlin. Therefore it does not matter much if you are so long as you get out safely. You shall remain yourself, Jerry. If she sees you with me, she will have the astonishing experience of observing the Supreme Marshal of Germany in friendly association with a member of the British Secret Service.'

Cousins stared at him a moment, then he also laughed.

'Splendid!' he ejaculated. 'Perhaps she will think I have touched your hard and flinty heart regarding the fate of the condemned women.'

'Now we're ready, not the least difficult part of our job remains. I'll go down myself and shout for a car. In the meantime you had better gag and bind von Strom; then carry him, and afterwards the orderly, down to the hail and place them out of sight. How we're going to get them into the car without being spotted, I don't quite know – yet take steps to see that the way is fairly clear, but there is such an infernal amount of light round the front door. I can hardly use any other.'

'You leave it to me, sir,' remarked Cousins. 'I have an idea.'

Sir Leonard smiled, and departed thoroughly satisfied. He had great confidence in his famous assistant. Cousins' fertility of imagination was probably the chief reason why the little man was still alive and on the active list.

CHAPTER TWENTY

To be Executed at Sunrise

The numerous members of the police force as well as storm troopers who were on guard in the courtyard of the Supreme Marshal's residence were somewhat astonished when the main door of the building was thrown open soon after three in the morning and His Excellency stepped forth. He did not seem to be in a very pleasant mood, judging from the irate manner in which he summoned an officer.

'Order a car to come round immediately,' he snapped, when the young man ran up.

Commands could now be heard from all parts of the courtyard, and several detachments of men were marched to the front door, apparently to act as bodyguard. Their commanders must have felt a trifle indignant at the curt manner in which they were ordered away again, but it taught them that His Excellency had no wish for any formality, desired in fact to be alone. Thereafter the police and troops remained at a safe distance. He looked a morose figure as he stood at the top of the steps, the light shining down full upon him. His left hand was stuck in his jacket pocket. Once or twice he stamped his foot impatiently. A little over five minutes went by, then a large black saloon car glided up to the door. There was a man sitting by the side of the driver, another standing on the running board. The latter sprang down and opened the door.

'I do not require an escort or a guard,' snapped the false Marshal. 'My orderly will accompany me, also a friend. You can go.'

The two additional men saluted and marched away. Sir Leonard glanced at the rear of the car and was somewhat mortified to find that it merely contained a luggage grid. He would have sent it away and ordered one with a proper box compartment only he did not know anything about the cars connected with the Marshal of State's household, and was rather fearful of making a *faux pas*.

'Ah!' sighed a relieved voice in his ear. 'I was afraid it might have a box, which would have made things a little awkward.' Sir Leonard turned to find Cousins standing by his side. 'Will you send up the driver to help carry out two trunks, sir? They are to be strapped on the back.'

The chief nodded. The trunks contained von Strom and his orderly, and he felt inclined to smile. The driver was given his instructions, and presently he and Reichmann emerged from the house carrying a long uniform case. This they carefully strapped to the back of the car.

'His Excellency is in that,' murmured Cousins, 'the orderly is in the other. I am afraid he is rather uncomfortable. There is plenty of air, however, and we punctured several holes in each case.

I thought of the notion when I came upon a box room during my peregrinations while looking for a bathroom.'

'Good for you, Jerry,' whispered Wallace. 'It has certainly solved our greatest difficulty. No doubt the onlookers are wondering where His Excellency is going at this time of the morning with baggage, but it doesn't matter whether they're puzzled or not, so long as they don't tumble to the truth.'

Cousins stood by his side while the second case, a shorter but broader trunk, was being strapped on. Gradually his face creased into one of those inimitable smiles which never failed to cause observers of them to smile also. It was as though the extraordinary wrinkles were each puckered in a grin of its own denoting relief from the disguise which had masked it for so long. As a matter of fact, Cousins was delighting in a unique experience. There they were, Sir Leonard and he, men whose names were anathema in official circles in Germany, standing on the steps of the Supreme Marshal's residence, the one posing actually as His Excellency, the other, without disguise, basking under the protection of his colleague. To make the situation more entertaining, His Excellency himself, neatly packed in a trunk, was ignominiously strapped to the back of his own car where he would remain until Sir Leonard had rescued the women he had determined should die.

As soon as both boxes were securely fastened to the luggage grid, Sir Leonard stepped into the car, followed by Cousins. Reichmann closed the door, and sprang in by the side of the driver, giving him instructions to take them to the Wannsee Prison at Potsdam, first going by way of the Brandenburg Gate, and picking up a woman who would be waiting there. The car glided away and the rattle of rifles was heard from all sides as the men presented arms.

Both Sir Leonard and Cousins gave vent to sighs expressive of their satisfaction and relief as they passed between the great main gates, which had been opened. The little man chuckled.

'I wonder what they are all thinking,' he observed, referring to the guard. 'This must strike them as peculiar behaviour.'

'No doubt,' agreed Sir Leonard, 'but what right have they to think or criticise?'

The car reached the Brandenburg Gate about half past three. Hanni was soon discovered. She had been waiting in a fever of impatience, dread, and hope, and it was a tremendous relief to her when a large black motor drew up within a few yards. Her mind had been too much worried at the time to notice particularly the car that had carried her from Potsdam. She had no idea, therefore, that this was not the same. When, however, a man descended from the front attired in the uniform of a Nazi storm trooper, she received rather a bad shock. Shrinking back as he approached her, she demanded in a quivering voice to know what he wanted. Reichmann was compelled to whisper for fear the driver might hear.

'The Englishmen are in the car,' he explained. 'I am disguised like this because there is a very desperate and daring scheme on foot. You have nothing to fear, fraulein.'

Nevertheless, Hanni entered the car rather doubtfully. Her doubts were certainly not allayed when a light was switched on to enable her to find her seat. She gasped, and her eyes seemed as though they were about to dart from her head as they alighted on the man sitting comfortably in one of the corners opposite her.

'Your Excellency!' she exclaimed.

He bowed.

'At your service, fraulein,' he remarked, and the voice was that,

in every particular, of the man she had grown to hate. By then
the car was on its way again. There was no possibility, therefore,
of Hanni being able to spring out, but she was convinced that
somehow she had fallen into a trap. In consequence, from hope
and eagerness, she was suddenly plunged into rank despair. The
glimpse she had caught of the second man had done nothing to
lesson her anxiety. He did not correspond in any way with either
of those with whom she had travelled from Potsdam as far as she
could tell. No interior light had been switched on at all in the first
car but from time to time she had caught sight of her companions
in the sudden glare caused by the headlights of a motor travelling
in the opposite direction. She decided that the Englishmen had
been trapped, that it had been discovered she was to meet them,
and that all hope of the lives of the baroness and Dora Reinwald
being saved was gone. The Supreme Marshal was probably on his
way to see the execution and, having discovered the part she had
been trying to play in the rescue of her mistress, had determined to
take her along and force her to witness her death. It was the kind
of horrible, vicious thing he would do. A great sob broke from her
and suddenly she burst into a storm of violent weeping.

'Do not upset yourself, fraulein,' Cousins remarked gently, 'all
will be well.'

She recognised the voice, and again hope surged through her.
She bent forward, found his hands and clasped them.

'You are the Englishman!' she cried.

'One of them,' returned Cousins.

'Then it is not a trap? We go to help the baroness?'

'Of course.'

'But what of your companion – the man who planned
everything? Where is he?'

'Not very far from you,' he returned.

There was a pause; then timidly she asked:

'Why is His Excellency here? I do not understand.'

'I go to order the release of the Baroness von Reudath and Fraulein Reinwald,' Sir Leonard explained in his cleverly assumed voice, 'and bring them away from the prison.'

Hanni gasped audibly. This was something beyond her.

Dawn was just beginning to break when the car reached the gates of the Wannsee Prison. Wallace gave a little sigh of satisfaction. They had arrived in plenty of time. The insistent sounding of the horn brought out a sergeant who, on finding that the Supreme Marshal himself had arrived, immediately gave orders for the gates to be opened, while word was sent to the governor. The car passed in between files of men standing at the salute. A cry of dismay broke involuntarily from Cousins' lips as the significance of the scene in the courtyard occurred to his mind. Sir Leonard uttered an exclamation of anger. Curtly bidding Cousins and Hanni stay where they were, he sprang out while the vehicle was still moving.

Drawn up on all four sides of the square were men standing grimly at attention. Striding rapidly forward, Wallace broke through the ranks nearest to him. His eyes immediately fell on the scaffold erected in the centre, the block at which a female figure in white was kneeling, the executioner in his fantastic garb, the other female figure standing between two guards. He took little note of the three men and a woman hurrying towards him. Everything depended on his disguise, on his power of imitating von Strom's voice now.

'Stop!' he thundered. 'The execution is cancelled. Release that woman!'

Two men ran up the steps of the scaffold. The figure kneeling there was unstrapped, helped to her feet. Apparently too overcome to walk, she was carried down and placed on the ground. Sir Leonard raised his hand to his forehead, wiped away the beads of perspiration that had collected there. He then turned to confront the people who had hurried up to him. The supreme moment of his ordeal had arrived. The governor of the prison, Major Wilhelm, Colonel Schönewald and Marlene Heckler stood before him. Of them all he feared the woman most. She had seen through Cousins' disguise, would she recognise that he was not von Strom? There was one great flaw in his otherwise perfect masquerade and, at that moment, he was deeply conscious of it. His and the Supreme Marshal's eyes were of a different colour. He did not think the men would notice, but Marlene Heckler very possibly might. Luckily the light was still too dim for any of them to be able to see clearly. Deliberately he turned away from the woman, directly facing the governor. He looked in a fiendish rage. None of the four standing anxiously before him ever remembered to have seen His Excellency look more angry.

'What is the meaning of this?' he thundered harshly. 'Why were you proceeding with the execution before sunrise?'

The governor, a very frightened man, stared at him, and seemed, for the moment, to be unable to speak.

'It – it was your own order, Your Excellency,' he faltered at length. 'You sent Major Wilhelm and Fraulein Heckler with the written command that the executions were to be advanced to dawn.'

That was an unexpected *contretemps*. Sir Leonard was taken aback but showed not the slightest sign of surprise or hesitation.

'Did you not receive my second message?' he demanded in tones as angry as before.

'No, Your Excellency,' the other assured him earnestly. 'No other message has arrived.'

'Bah!' snarled the sham Marshal. 'What nonsense is this? Do you mean to tell me that an order of mine has not been obeyed? I gave instructions that the executions were to be postponed, and that I myself was coming here. God in heaven! Am I served by a parcel of fools or traitors or what?'

The governor pathetically strove to convince him that no message had been received. In this he was supported by Major Wilhelm and Fraulein Heckler, who had been with him most of the night. Sir Leonard gathered that von Strom had sent Wilhelm and Marlene with the order that the executions were to be advanced to dawn, and that they were to stay themselves, see them carried out, and at once carry the intelligence to him. Wallace did not know what Schönewald was doing there and, of course, could not ask. He noticed that the young Nazi's face was pale and drawn. It was obvious that he had been assisting in an event that was utterly hateful to him. The pretender waved them all aside, and strode forward to the scaffold. The Baroness von Reudath, who had been the one chosen to suffer first, and whom he had been just in time to save, sat now on a chair that had been procured for her. She appeared dazed, her face was as white as a sheet, but she looked up at him bravely. Dora Reinwald, still standing between her guards, was as pale, but her face was as serene as ever, her great eyes full of defiance.

'Has the great Marshal of State actually relented?' she asked mockingly. 'Are we really to be left with our heads?'

'You are, fraulein,' he rejoined, and turned to the baroness. 'Later on I will endeavour to express my sorrow for the ordeal you have been forced to undergo. At present it is my desire to take you from here as soon as possible. Do you think you are fit enough to travel?'

The wondering, amazed relief that now shone in the eyes of both brought a lump to Sir Leonard's throat. He turned to a guard, and bade him fetch the woman Hanni.

'I am quite all right,' Sophie assured him. 'I am only anxious to leave this horrible place as soon as possible.'

Hanni arrived and, throwing herself on her feet before her mistress, clasped her in her arms, laughing and crying at the same time as she strove to express her happiness. At the order of Sir Leonard the two ladies, who had so barely escaped a terrible fate, were escorted to the car, which they entered. Cousins continued to keep well in the background, but immediately assisted Hanni in administering to them, refusing to answer the questions which Dora asked him. Sophie was still too dazed to bother about anything but the wonderful fact that she had miraculously escaped a hideous death.

Sir Leonard was eager to be away, but did not wish to show undue haste for fear that doubt might even now be roused. He noticed that Marlene Heckler seemed to be showing a great anxiety to address him, but adroitly managed to avoid her. He still retained his pretence of anger, which caused the men to make themselves as inconspicuous as possible. Fraulein Heckler at length succeeded in forcing herself on his attention. He looked at her through narrowed eyes; then turned abruptly; began to pace to and fro.

'What do you want?' he demanded, as she kept step by his side.

Her first words proved to him that she was on more confidential terms with von Strom than he had suspected.

'Why have you done this, Excellency?' she asked. 'When I persuaded you to give orders for the two to be executed at an earlier hour than sunrise for fear that that little Englishman was organising an attempt at rescue, you agreed with great alacrity. You seemed then anxious that the baroness and her companion should die as soon as possible. What has made you alter your mind? Are you indeed setting them free or have you another scheme in your mind?'

'What right have you to question me regarding my intentions?' he demanded harshly. 'You go too far, Fraulein Heckler.'

'But,' she cried in dismay, 'you have never objected before. Have I not always served you well and faithfully?'

'You have. That, however, does not give you the right to be impertinent. I have changed my mind regarding the Baroness von Reudath, and that is the end of it.'

She was silent for some seconds, and he noticed from the corner of his eyes that she continually cast concerned and puzzled glances at him.

'Has the little Englishman been caught yet?' she asked at last.

The supposed von Strom laughed stridently.

'You were very sure that he was an Englishman, were you not?' he asked.

'Very sure!' she retorted confidently. 'I have seen Herr Cousins so many times. Nevertheless, I should not have recognised him – his disguise was so excellent – if I had not been able to lip read. When he sat at the Cafe at Potsdam after I had followed him there, and studied him through the curtain, I saw his lips move. He was whispering poetry to himself and in English. I happen to know that Herr Cousins has a proclivity for quotations and poetry.'

'That is a poor sort of proof of his identity,' commented the pseudo-Marshal sarcastically. Nevertheless, he felt an added respect for the girl by his side. 'However,' went on Sir Leonard, 'you happen to have been right in your surmise. The man is Herr Cousins.'

'He has then been found and arrested?' she asked eagerly.

'Arrested!' he snarled. 'It seems more as if I were the one under arrest. The man Cousins has come with me to Potsdam. He is in my car as my guest. What do you think of that, Fraulein Heckler?'

For some moments she appeared stupefied with amazement.

'In your car! Your guest!' she repeated presently. 'Do you mean, Excellency, that he it is who has forced you to release the baroness and the other woman? He has discovered something of your great plans and—'

'Now you have learnt what you want to know,' he snapped, 'perhaps you are happy and will leave me in peace.'

'But is there nothing to be done. Surely—'

'Leave me, Fraulein Heckler. Perhaps it would be as well if you paid your respects to Herr Cousins. I understand he is quite anxious to meet you. He knew you had seen through his disguise and was apparently quite amused at your efforts to trail him, or have him trailed.'

She bit her lip, and frowned angrily.

'I should like to shoot him with my own hand,' she cried.

'Do not try, I beg of you. It might prove too expensive for Germany.'

She walked away. The governor of the prison found courage at last to address him.

'You will sign an order for the release of the two ladies, Excellency?' he asked.

That was a poser. His handwriting would immediately betray him, but Sir Leonard was not at a loss. He waved his hand casually.

'That will be sent from the Reichstag in the course of the morning. In the meantime you can have the scaffold dismantled.

The Baroness von Reudath and her companion will not be executed.'

Sir Leonard walked to the car. Marlene Heckler had preceded him, and was engaged in talking in biting fashion to Cousins. She was extremely annoyed that her discovery of his identity had ended in a manner so tame. The little secret agent was amused. Again and again his face puckered into its scores of happy creases. He was quite certain that he had never been in a more ironically funny position in his career before, and was enjoying every moment of it. Marlene turned away from him, and came face-to-face with Sir Leonard. He was looking up at Colonel Schönewald, who stood by at the moment, and the strengthening light was full on his face. She gasped, stepped suddenly back to be brought up by the car.

'Grey eyes!' she muttered, a look of extreme astonishment on her face. 'They should be—' A great cry broke from her. 'You are not—'

She was interrupted by the unmistakable feel of a revolver barrel stuck forcibly in her back.

'Not another word,' hissed the voice of Cousins behind her, 'otherwise this will kill you before you can utter the foolish remark that was on your lips. Kindly run and enter the car.'

Fraulein Heckler was a wise woman. She also probably thought that it was quite impossible for the man she had discovered to be an impostor to get away from Germany and take with him the people he had rescued. She, therefore, entered the car. There were already four people in the tonneau, but Cousins told Hanni to get out, and forced Marlene to sit by his side, taking care to remind her every now and again by the feel of the revolver that it would be injudicious on her part to contemplate giving the alarm. Colonel

Schönewald was the only person near enough to have heard or witnessed what had occurred. Sir Leonard looked at him to find that a puzzled expression on his face, caused by Marlene Heckler's cry, was now giving way to one of understanding. He resolved on a gamble.

'I believe you have guessed the situation, Colonel Schönewald,' he remarked in a low voice.

'I believe I have – up to a point,' came the reply in tones as moderate.

'I also believe that you would rather almost anything happen than that those two innocent ladies were brutally executed. Now I am holding in my pocket an automatic. I am an excellent shot and it would be easy enough to kill you. I do not wish to do that, and candidly I do not think it would be of much use if I did. Can I ask you to give your word to say nothing in order that the two ladies may escape the fate to which they have been sentenced.'

'The reasons you have advanced are hardly adequate enough,' murmured Schönewald, 'to cause a German officer to forget his duty. Are there no others?'

Sir Leonard nodded at the two cases strapped to the back of the car.

'I have a trunk full of reasons there,' he declared dryly, 'If anything happened to the contents, Germany would suffer a severe loss.'

Schönewald's eyes stared in fascinated fashion at the box indicated.

'Do you mean to say—' he began.

'I do,' interrupted Sir Leonard, 'and I shall not hesitate to act if you do not give me the promise I require. I do not intend to allow myself to be baulked now.'

Schönewald clicked his heels together and gave the stiff little bow of the Prussian officer.

'My car is here, Your Excellency,' he declared. 'Yours is rather crowded. I will esteem it an honour if I may be allowed to offer you accommodation in mine. You have my word that I will say nothing.'

Sir Leonard smiled.

CHAPTER TWENTY-ONE

A Trunk of Priceless Value

Sir Leonard gave orders to Reichmann, then walked with the Nazi officer to a touring car standing near the guardroom. Hanni was called, and told to take her seat next to the driver. Schönewald and Wallace sat side by side in the back. The gates were opened. Commands were barked as the two motors left the courtyard, the troops sprang to the salute, which Sir Leonard gravely returned. A few seconds later Wannsee Prison was left behind. They were a mile or more away before anything was said. Schönewald then looked at his companion.

'I don't know who you are,' he observed in English, 'but I presume that, as the other man, Cousins, is a member of the British Secret Service, you also are of that corps. I don't think I have ever seen a more amazing disguise. It is a great tribute to Fraulein Heckler that she saw through it.'

'Ah! Those eyes,' sighed Wallace in his own voice. 'I was afraid they might give me away.'

'I should never have noticed. Marlene is a wonderful woman.'

'She is. Would you mind telling your driver to stop? I want to have a chat with her and with the others.'

Schönewald obliged. The second car, following fifty yards or so behind, pulled up. Inviting Schönewald to accompany him, Sir Leonard walked to it and opened the door.

'I am sorry we have had to kidnap you in this manner, Fraulein Heckler,' he remarked in German, 'but I am afraid your own perspicacity is responsible. However, you will be released as soon as we reach the frontier. I am afraid I cannot allow you or Colonel Schönewald to go before then.'

'You will be stopped long before you get to the frontier,' she retorted.

'I do not think so,' he replied easily. 'You see, we have the real Marshal with us, and it would be a great pity if any hasty action caused harm to overtake him.'

'You have His Excellency with you!' she repeated in dumbfounded tones. 'Where is he?'

'In one of the trunks you probably noticed strapped on behind.'

She cried out in great consternation. 'Let him out!' she pleaded. 'Oh, let him out! He will die.'

'I do not think so. Still, we'll have a look to see how he is getting on. I am afraid he must find his position rather cramped and uncomfortable, but that cannot be helped.'

She was tremendously upset by the revelation. She stormed and threatened; then turned to cajolery and pleading, but Sir Leonard shook his head alike to all.

'You will gather,' he remarked, 'that any foolish action on your part may well be fatal for the cause of Germany. I advise you to make no attempt to raise the alarm, therefore.'

'But can't you see it will take a long time to reach the frontier. You cannot possibly keep him cooped up in his ignominious position until you get there.'

'I am afraid there is no help for it. We will do the best we can for him.'

'Who are you?' she demanded.

He smiled.

'Keep your voice low, please. The driver happens to be His Excellency's own man. It would be as well if he did not hear. You have penetrated Herr Cousin's disguise, fraulein. Now it is up to you to discover who I am – if you can.'

The baroness and Dora Reinwald had not once removed their eyes from his face since he had appeared at the door of the car. They were almost overwhelmed by the knowledge of what this man and his companion had dared for them. The fact that he was not the Supreme Marshal whom he had actually overcome, kidnapped, and impersonated in order to save them from execution, filled them with an amazed wonder, and a gratitude beyond expression. They had by this time recovered a little from the effects of their terrible ordeal, but it had left its mark on them, and it was obvious that it would require time and attention to efface from their minds the memory of their nightmare experience. Sir Leonard cut short their faltering attempts to thank him, enquired anxiously how they were feeling, and insisted on their both drinking a good proportion of the brandy he had thoughtfully provided. The colour began to steal back into their cheeks after that.

While Sir Leonard stood on the alert, his automatic in his hand, Cousins and Reichmann opened the cases at the back in order to ascertain how von Strom and his orderly were faring. The cars had drawn up well to the side of the road among the trees.

As the hour was little past five, the road was practically deserted; nevertheless, Cousins was urged to hurry. He turned to Wallace one of his fascinating grins on his face.

'They are both conscious,' he announced, 'and apparently very little the worse for wear. If their eyes could kill, though, I'd be a dead man now. "Eyes that sleep, that dream, that love; Eyes that hate, that curse, that kill; Eyes that speed the owner's will; Eyes that—"'

'All right, Jerry,' interrupted Sir Leonard. 'That is enough about eyes. It is time we got on.'

The baroness looked anxiously at him.

'What have they done with Herr Foster?' she asked. 'Is there any hope of your being able to help him also?'

He smiled encouragingly at her.

'We are going to get him now, Baroness,' he assured her. 'In a little more than half an hour I hope that he will be free and with us.'

Their passengers still arranged in the same manner, the two cars rapidly covered the distance to Neu-Babelsberg. Dr Hagenow's private mental asylum stood in a secluded spot on the verge of the park, surrounded by high walls, in which a pair of wrought-iron gates, presided over by a burly-looking fellow who might have been an ex-pugilist, prevented ingress or egress except to a large mansion situated in beautiful grounds. Schönewald made no objection to accompanying Sir Leonard within. Once the custodian had been roused, the sight of His Excellency himself caused that worthy to open the gates at once without hesitation. The car was driven through, went on up the drive, and came to a standstill before the imposing front doors. The saloon had remained outside the walls under the watchful eyes of Cousins and Reichmann. Hanni had stopped with it. The supposed arrival of the Supreme Marshal threw the sleeping place into a state of excitement and bustle. The night staff, still on duty, called Dr Hagenow, who, on being informed of the identity of his august visitor, almost went into a state of panic. Schönewald watched the flurry with an enigmatical smile on his face. Sir Leonard felt that it would be interesting to be able to read his thoughts. Dr Hagenow burst into the room into which his visitors had been shown, mumbling apologies, and endeavouring to get some order into the garments he had obviously donned in a great hurry. Wallace cut his excuses short.

'Bring Herr Foster, the Englishman, to me at once,' he ordered curtly. 'I am taking him away.'

'Taking him away, Excellency!' repeated the doctor stupidly.

'I said taking him away. Is there any reason why I should not?'

'No, no, of course not, Excellency. I will see that he is brought at once.'

'Do!' Hagenow hurried away. Sir Leonard looked at his companion. Suddenly he held out his hand. 'Thanks, Schönewald,' he said simply in his natural voice.

The Nazi officer looked puzzled; nevertheless, he grasped the other's hand warmly.

'Why are you thanking me?' he asked in English.

'There are a score of ways in which you could have turned the tables on me since we entered this place. Yet you have refrained. I am alone here, armed with only an automatic. It would have been quite an easy matter for you to have given the alarm, and afterwards captured the others outside.'

'I gave my word,' Schönewald reminded him somewhat stiffly. 'I was more or less on parole. You trusted me, and that is all there is to it.'

'Exactly! But there are quite a number of German officers I would not have trusted – Major Wilhelm for instance.'

The other smiled.

'It seems to me,' he remarked, 'that it is my turn to thank you. I am quite convinced, all the same, that you would not have entered here as you have unless you were quite certain that all would be well. A man with your amazing resource and courage does not take stupid risks.'

Sir Leonard laughed.

'We seem to be becoming a kind of mutual admiration society,' he declared. 'There is one thing worries me, however. Von Strom is not a man of reason. Marlene Heckler will tell him that you were concerned, even though against your will, in our escape from Wannsee; she may make it appear that you were too easily coerced. I am afraid that the result may not be pleasant for you.'

Schönewald shrugged his shoulders.

'That cannot be helped,' he returned. 'To be perfectly candid, there are things happening in Germany today which I cannot stomach. I only know vaguely, of course, that von Strom is building up certain schemes of a military nature. No doubt you and Cousins were after those schemes. Whether you found out what they are all about or not, I do not know. I am afraid I do not care, because, in any case, it means that the Chancellor has broken faith with other countries. Perhaps my upbringing in England has made me feel like this. I do not know. The trial and proposed execution of the Baroness von Reudath and Fraulein Reinwald was the last straw, as far as I was concerned. It was all too beastly for words. I was sent to the prison this morning to take full command of the extra men drafted in. All the time I was searching for some means of preventing or, at least, postponing the execution. When the baroness ascended the scaffold, I could bear it no longer. As she knelt at the block, I was about to interfere, order my men to mutiny, in fact, anything, to hold up the ghastly business. Whether they would have obeyed my orders or not is a debatable point. It is unlikely, the governor would have overruled me. You arrived on the scene just in time, so I actually have quite a lot for which to be grateful to you. But I am finished. Hilda Zeiss, who is my fiancée, and I have decided to leave this country and settle down in the United States. We both have ample means, and have already made arrangements for its transference to America. You see, therefore, that whether I am disgraced or not it does not matter a great deal. The result will be the same.'

Sir Leonard slowly nodded his head.

'I do not blame you,' he commented. 'I sincerely hope you and Fraulein Zeiss will find peace and happiness in the United States, which reminds me that I owe her my thanks for the manner in which she warned Cousins of Marlene Heckler's discovery.'

'We were hoping that he was engaged in some sort of attempt to save the baroness. It turned out that we were right – thank God!' he added fervently.

Foster, looking pale and worn, as though he had spent an anxious vigil without sleep, entered the room followed by Dr Hagenow. He eyed the man he thought was the Supreme Marshal of Germany with a look of the utmost contempt, nodded curtly to Schönewald.

'Well,' he drawled, 'what is the new scheme? Something with boiling oil in it this time, or do you think you have given me enough mental torture to satisfy you? I don't care what you do to me, but tell me how the Baroness von Reudath is?'

'The baroness well is,' returned Wallace gutturally and in very bad English. 'Soon you will her see.'

Schönewald suppressed a smile, but Foster gazed at the man he believed to be von Strom with eyes in which hope was struggling desperately with distrust. At that moment he certainly did not look a very intelligent young man.

'Is this a trick?' he cried hoarsely.

'No trick there is,' declared Wallace sternly, though a close observer would have seen a twinkle in his eyes. 'I wish only that you and the Baroness von Reudath out of this country go mit quickness.'

Schönewald did more to remove the lingering doubts in the young man's mind than Sir Leonard, short of declaring his identity, could have done just then.

'You can take my word for it, Foster,' remarked the Nazi officer, 'that within a few hours you will be the other side of the frontier and the baroness will be with you. The longer you delay here with your questions the longer you will have to wait before you see her.'

Foster's eyes lit up with an expression of beatific happiness now.

'God!' he ejaculated. 'I don't know what to say, Schönewald. It is all so amazing that I—' he paused, at a loss for words. 'Let us go!' he added eagerly.

They were escorted to the car with great pomp and ceremony. Practically the whole staff had assembled to see His Excellency, and to give him a rousing send-off. Before stepping into the car, Sir Leonard looked sternly at Dr Hagenow.

'A word of advice to you, Herr Doctor,' he said. 'The profession of medicine is something very noble. A man practising it should always keep that thought in his mind; he should never allow himself to be influenced by sordid, unworthy considerations even at risk of offending those in high places. The true disciple of Aesculapius would refuse to prostitute his skill at any behest.'

He entered the car leaving the medical man standing on the

steps looking dismayed and stupefied. As the car glided swiftly down the drive, Schönewald laughed softly.

'You have given him something to think about,' he murmured in English. 'I hope he will benefit by your advice.'

'He will probably make good resolutions until he knows that he has been deceived,' returned Sir Leonard in the same language and in his natural voice. 'The wigging he will receive from the real von Strom later on will no doubt keep his mind otherwise occupied.'

Foster was sitting on the other side of Schönewald and had heard everything. The sound of the chief's voice caused him to start violently. For the moment he was taken entirely off his guard.

'Good God!' he ejaculated, 'Sir Leonard Wallace!'

Schönewald gasped, and looked quickly at the man who had so cleverly impersonated von Strom.

'Sir Leonard Wallace!' he echoed in astonishment; whistled softly to himself.

Wallace had frowned at Foster's indiscretion. He glanced at him now a trifle scornfully, to find him biting his lip, looking utterly ashamed of himself.

'Foster,' he observed, 'you're a fool.'

'I know, sir,' was the reply, uttered in abject tones. 'I have known it for a long time.'

Sir Leonard laughed at that.

'Ah, well,' he remarked kindly, 'I'll forgive you. You have been through a lot, and accomplished a lot. And it was my intention to tell our friend Schönewald who I am before leaving him.'

'So!' exclaimed the Nazi colonel, 'I am in the presence of the famous head of the British Secret Service! I am honoured to meet you, sir, but I may tell you that if it was known in this country who you are, your life would not be worth a snap of the fingers.'

'I am quite well aware of that,' nodded Sir Leonard, adding with a smile: 'I hope your promise includes keeping my identity secret.'

Schönewald shrugged his shoulders.

'"In for a penny, in for a pound," as you English would say. I shall not give you away as you know.' He turned and smiled a trifle quizzically at Foster. 'So you were connected with the British Secret Service after all? If I may be permitted to say so, you hoodwinked us all rather neatly. There is not much of the fool about you, Foster.'

The car glided between the gates, the pugilistic-looking custodian bowing himself almost to the ground. Outside, Sir Leonard beckoned on the saloon, which immediately followed. In that order they travelled for two or three miles; then, when well in the park, the order was given to stop.

'I know that you must be exceedingly anxious to be reunited with the baroness,' observed Wallace to Foster, 'and to hear all she has to tell you. I can't allow you any more than ten minutes, I'm afraid. Still I don't suppose that will matter since you have your lives before you. Wait here!'

He left the car and walking to the other, invited the baroness to step out. For a moment she and Foster confronted each other; then with a cry of utter happiness, and quite forgetful of the onlookers, she was in his arms. Sir Leonard turned away.

'That's that,' he murmured in a tone of great satisfaction.

Sophie and Bernard presently wandered away among the trees, anxious like all lovers to spend their precious moments alone and free from observation. Wallace contemplated the great expanse of green turf stretching away before him, and slowly a smile appeared on his face.

'Why not?' he muttered to himself. 'It would save a lot of

trouble.' He beckoned to Schönewald who joined him at once. 'I have a notion,' he observed, 'that I can save myself and my party a great deal of trouble and von Strom some hours of discomfort. I am going to leave you here ostensibly under the charge of Cousins, in order that Fraulein Heckler's suspicions may not be roused against you, but relying still, of course, on your word. I myself shall drive His Excellency's car to the airport. I have heard that there are several new air liners there that have recently been completed for service. I shall invite myself to a trip in one and order it to come here. Then I shall borrow it and fly to England, leaving you, Marlene Heckler, and the two chauffeurs to release von Strom and his orderly. Except that you may quite unreasonably fall into disgrace for not making a desperate bid to checkmate me, a bid which would only have ended in your death, I don't think any harm will come to you. I should like your opinion on that point though.' Schönewald shrugged his shoulders.

'I shall be disgraced without a doubt,' he replied, 'but I am pretty certain nothing worse will happen to me. To all intents and purposes I have only been made a prisoner. Fraulein Heckler did not hear our conversation after she had been forced by Cousins to get into the car. Since then, as far as she is aware, I have been intimidated by your gun in the same manner as Cousins has compelled her to keep quiet.'

Sir Leonard smiled.

'Under the circumstances,' he remarked drily, 'it would be as well if you took that revolver out of your holster and handed it over to me. Don't let her see you though.'

They walked behind the second car, where Schönewald gave up his weapon.

'I hope you do not think I am playing a traitor's part, sir,' he observed a trifle anxiously, 'in not putting up resistance of some sort or making an effort to detain you. But, as I have said, this present Germany is not my country. It is alien to me – von Strom's methods go utterly against the grain – and I have resolved to become an American citizen. If I were a party to the recapture and death of the Baroness von Reudath I should always feel myself a murderer.'

'I understand,' nodded Sir Leonard. 'I admire you for the course you are taking. It shows courage and idealism of a high order.'

'Do you really mean to say you are intending to commandeer an air liner?'

'I am. In my present character it should be quite a simple matter.'

'My hat!' murmured Schönewald very fervently, and in a manner decidedly English.

Sophie and her lover came strolling back. She was looking delightfully happy, though the dark rings under her beautiful eyes still remained as evidence of the terrible ordeal she had undergone. Foster was white-faced, and grim. She had told him of the manner in which Sir Leonard had snatched her and Dora Reinwald from death. He walked straight up to his chief.

'I can't begin to express to you how I feel, sir,' he stammered, overcome by his emotion, 'but—'

'Don't try,' interrupted Sir Leonard, who hated what he described as emotional scenes of gratitude. 'I know how you feel, so we'll leave it at that. I am sorry Baroness,' he added, turning to the girl, 'that it is impossible to save any of your belongings or collect our money. I am afraid they will all be confiscated, but if I try Fate any more highly today, she may turn on me. We've been marvellously lucky so far.'

Marching Schönewald before him for the sake of appearances, and followed by the baroness and Foster, Wallace went up to von Strom's black saloon, and opened the door. Marlene Heckler frowned at him, but said nothing. Dora Reinwald, who was lying back in a corner, her great eyes half closed, as though she were extremely weary, managed to smile at him. In a sense the reaction affected her more acutely than the baroness. By an extreme effort of will she had maintained a mocking, defiant demeanour from the time of her arrest until the last dreadful moments. Even when she stood by the scaffold in momentary expectation of seeing her beloved employer's head fall severed from her body, knowing that she was directly afterwards to suffer the same cruel fate, she had appeared the personification of scorn.

'And all lived happily ever after,' she murmured.

'You are not out the wood yet,' snapped Marlene Heckler.

'My dear,' drawled Dora, 'we are not even in it.'

Germany's celebrated woman secret agent turned impatiently from her, receiving an unpleasant reminder of Cousins' alertness, when her body came sharply into contact with his revolver.

'I require this car,' pronounced Sir Leonard, 'so I must ask you all to get out and enter the other; at least Fraulein Heckler and Colonel Schönewald, will enter the other! Perhaps the baroness and Fraulein Reinwald would like to rest under the trees for a while. Take this revolver, Foster,' he handed Schönewald's weapon to his assistant, 'and help Cousins to keep watch. You, Reichmann,' he whispered in English to the disguised guide, when they were momentarily alone, 'keep your eyes open, and be ready to go to the aid of Mr Cousins if there is any trouble.'

The transference to Schönewald's touring car was adroitly managed without its being made apparent to either of the drivers that the colonel and Marlene Heckler were under restraint. They may have wondered at the queer happenings of that glorious June morning, probably did, but everything had been conducted so well that they certainly had no inkling of the truth. When the two Germans were seated with Cousins and Foster opposite them, Wallace leant towards them.

'I am taking the trunks with me,' he observed in a lowered voice. 'That will save you from giving yourselves headaches trying to hatch a plot to rescue His Excellency. If, when I return, I find you have made the slightest attempt to raise the alarm, I may be tempted to rid Germany of him after all. I shall not be gone long.'

'Where are you going?' demanded Marlene.

'You will know soon enough. Remember to conduct yourself with circumspection while I am away.'

Her eyes flashed viciously; her whole body was trembling with the violence of her anger.

'You will pay for this,' she ground out between her clenched teeth. 'Oh, you will pay to the very uttermost.'

He bowed mockingly.

'Maybe with a post-dated cheque, fraulein,' he returned suddenly; 'not otherwise.'

He stood for a moment watching Hanni ministering to her mistress and Dora, who were now lying gratefully under a tree. A little pleased smile parted his lips; then, instructing the chauffeur to drive him to the Templehof aerodrome he entered the car, and was driven away.

CHAPTER TWENTY-TWO

The Borrowed Aeroplane

There were few members of the personnel visible when the black saloon arrived at Berlin's great airport. Directly it was known, however, that the Supreme Marshal himself had paid a surprise visit, great activity prevailed. In a remarkable short period of time the scene became intensely animated. Mechanics and other officials appeared, and paraded with military precision in front of the hangars. Sir Leonard explained that he wished to make an inspection, and perhaps take a little trip in one of the new air liners.

He was escorted round the aerodrome and received eloquent proof of the fact that, although on the surface everything and everybody had a civilian appearance, beneath was an undoubted and significant suggestion of military efficiency. The men acted like well-drilled and disciplined soldiers; machines were run out for his inspection in a manner that was no whit inferior to the well-trained effectiveness of the British RAF. The officer in charge quite innocently divulged certain facts concerning the secret constructions of some of the new machines that Sir Leonard found decidedly interesting. Almost every one could very cleverly and in a short space of time be converted into a warplane. He spent over half an hour, taking great care all the time not to betray his ignorance, inspecting the cunningly concealed mechanism on some for the dropping of bombs, the equally well-hidden fixtures for machine guns on others. Eventually, when he had selected a large four-engine machine on which to take his proposed trip, he decided mentally that his visit to the Templehof aerodrome had been worthwhile in more ways than one.

The aeroplane chosen, his greatest difficulty was to avoid being accompanied by an escort. Sir Leonard's adroit management, however, enabled him to depart with a single pilot and without raising the slightest suspicion against himself, though his decision undoubtedly caused a certain amount of surprise. Before leaving the aerodrome, he gave the driver of the car instructions to proceed to the Supreme Marshal's residence, declaring that he himself would return with Colonel Schönewald, and impressing on him the order that the trunks at the back were not to be moved or touched until he or Colonel Schönewald arrived. He explained to the commandant that he would alight in the park at Babelsberg where he had left his attendants. The necessary orders were given to the pilot.

The huge machine took off beautifully, the personnel of the aerodrome standing stiffly to the salute. Sir Leonard sat in one of the well-upholstered seats in the saloon, and laughed softly to himself. It had all been so deliciously easy. The final coup had been actually the simplest part of the enterprise, thanks to the entire absence of suspicion in the minds of the aerodrome officials. There remained the actual capture of the machine and the flight to England.

It was not long before Babelsberg was reached. As they descended, Sir Leonard looked down anxiously, his eyes searching for signs that people were being attracted by the unusual sight of a large air liner alighting in the park. Apparently, however, it was still too early for inhabitants of that neighbourhood to be abroad. With the exception of his own party, which he and the pilot had quickly sighted, there did not appear to be anybody about.

The man in control made a perfect landing, bringing the great machine to a halt a few yards from Colonel Schönewald's car. Wallace stepped out, and was just in time to catch the look of hope in Marlene Heckler's face before it changed to an expression of intense mortification. Apparently she had thought for the moment that by some means, the tables had been turned; that von Strom had succeeded in escaping from his ignominious position, had come to rescue her and Schönewald, and recapture the baroness. But those steel-grey eyes soon undeceived her. She groaned aloud. Sir Leonard smiled, and bowed ironically.

'Sorry to disappoint you, fraulein,' he drawled. Then his manner and voice became sharp, incisive. 'There is no time to waste,' he snapped. 'Cousins, search the pilot for weapons, and disarm him if necessary. Foster, do the same to the driver of this car. Colonel Schönewald and Fraulein Heckler, I beg you to remain exactly as you are. I have you covered, and I should hate any indiscreet movement on your part to cause an unfortunate accident. Baroness, Fraulein Reinwald, and you, Hanni, enter the aeroplane. Be as quick as you can!'

The three women obeyed almost in a state of stupor. The arrival of the machine had filled each heart with foreboding and dismay, which had given place to a wonderful sense of relief. There seemed no end to the resource of this amazing Englishman. It was little wonder, therefore, that the two women, who had undergone so much, and the maid who had suffered very nearly as acutely, should feel rather stupefied by his arrival in one of Germany's very latest air liners, and order them to enter.

The gloves were now off with a vengeance. The driver of Schönewald's car and the pilot of the aeroplane were probably the most astonished men in Germany at that moment. For some time they could only sit and gasp, the one at Cousins, the gaze of the other alternating ludicrously between Foster and the man he had believed to be the Supreme Marshal of Germany. The thought that Marlene Heckler might be armed prompted Wallace to recall Hanni from the aeroplane and order her to search the woman. It was well he did so. Marlene carried a deadly little automatic in her handbag; there was nothing concealed on her person. The pilot was commanded to descend from the air liner. He was unarmed, but several weapons and ammunition, of which Cousins took possession, were found in a locker in the large and admirably fitted cockpit.

'I am borrowing this plane and you,' Sir Leonard told the airman, 'to take my friends and me to England. You have gathered by now that I am not the Supreme Marshal. Any attempt on your part to draw unwelcome attention to us or frustrate my designs will only end unfortunately – for you. Both of these gentlemen,' he indicated Foster and Cousins, 'have pilots' certificates and are capable of assuming control. I am taking you with us principally to bring back the machine from England. You will see, therefore, that any attempt to trick us will merely result in your being superseded. No harm will come to you so long as you do what you are told.'

The man was far too amazed to do anything else but stare with wide-open, startled eyes at the speaker. He was ordered to climb back into the aeroplane, Cousins accompanied him, and took the seat at his side, holding his revolver pointed suggestively and in businesslike manner at him. Sir Leonard was not satisfied, however. He felt they were too much at the pilot's mercy. It would be so easy for the man to crash the plane while taking off. He would be quite likely to risk a bullet or his own death in the accident to frustrate the attempt at escape from Germany of people who, though he was unaware of the real facts, were obviously 'wanted'. The Chief of the British Secret Service called Foster to him.

'Do you think you can take control of that bus?' he asked in his own language.

Foster grinned.

'I have never handled anything like her, sir,' he announced cheerfully, 'but I'm willing to try.'

Sir Leonard sighed.

'It seems to me you will be the lesser of two evils,' he commented dryly. 'Go ahead, and take charge. Tell Cousins to remove his man into the saloon. Once you get her into the air, you should be all right. For heaven's sake don't crash us taking off; that's all I ask. Make sure there is plenty of petrol.'

Foster went confidently about his job. He appeared to have little doubt of his ability to manage the huge machine. In a few moments the four engines were running smoothly and, after a careful inspection, he was able to announce the good news that there was plenty of petrol and oil to take them comfortably to England. Sir Leonard had managed to convey unnoticed instruction to Reichmann to go quietly away, remove his disguise, and find his way, as best he could, back to Berlin. He waited until the guide had disappeared, and had had time to place himself in a position of safety, where he would be secure from any possibility of the car containing Schönewald and Marlene Heckler coming upon him, then turned to the two.

'You are at liberty to depart now,' he declared in German. 'I regret that circumstances compelled me to hold you prisoners.'

'You will regret more than that,' cried Marlene, her eyes flashing fiercely. 'You will regret many things.'

'You have said something of the same nature before,' he retorted. 'Come, come, fraulein! This sort of thing is all in our job. Why should you resent being outwitted. I would not have been vindictive if you had beaten us. Be a sport!'

'You talk as though we were playing a game,' she snapped. 'It is not a question of sport.'

'On the contrary it is. We have been playing a game – a big game perhaps; nevertheless, a game – and I have won. Perhaps we may someday be opponents in another.'

'That time you will not win. What have you done to His Excellency?'

'I sent the car back to his residence. He will be waiting – still in his trunk – for Colonel Schönewald to free him. Here are the keys, Colonel.' He tossed them to the Nazi officer. 'You had better get back as soon as possible. The day is growing very warm, and he will not be happy.'

She cried out in great anger. Schönewald, who was nearer to Sir Leonard, regarded him sternly, but the eyelid which Marlene could not see, dropped in a rapid wink.

'If you think you can escape,' growled the young man, 'you are a fool. Within half an hour squadrons of airplanes will be up to cut you off. Their orders will be to bring you down irrespective of the fact that you have a German airman on board.'

'How kind that will be,' commented Sir Leonard.

'Kindness does not come into the matter,' retorted Schönewald, purposely ignoring the sarcasm.

'Fly north-west – Denmark,' his lips framed in English.

Wallace nodded almost imperceptibly. He understood the warning. Schönewald would do his best to see that the pursuing or obstructing aeroplanes would block the way to the Netherlands, the route which the escaping Englishman would be expected to take.

'There certainly seems to be little of the milk of human kindness in Germany,' drawled the Chief of the British Secret Service.

Schönewald snapped an order to his driver. In a few minutes the touring car had passed rapidly out of sight. Sir Leonard entered the aeroplane to find the pilot sitting moodily by the side of Cousins. The expression of chagrin in his eyes caused the chief to reflect that he had been wise in ordering Foster, despite his inexperience, to take control. The baroness, Dora, and Hanni looked thoroughly happy. They, at least, were convinced that their troubles were over.

There were a few breathless seconds as the great air liner took off. She lurched in drunken fashion as she left the ground and commenced to climb, whilst flying in a semi-stalled condition. It seemed that she was about to crash, as she missed the top of a tree by inches. A moment later, however, she was soaring into the sky beautifully. Foster had quickly remedied the initial faults caused by his lack of experience in piloting a large, four-engine machine. Sir

Leonard and Cousins looked at each other, and smiled their relief.

"'She spread her wings in glorious pride,'" quoted the latter. "'And straight to Heaven seem'd to glide.' Now for England, home and – er – safety.'

'Thank God for England, and – and for you two wonderful men,' came earnestly from the baroness.

'I am terribly sorry,' remarked Sir Leonard hurriedly, 'that I have nothing to offer you ladies to eat. You must be famished.'

The baroness stared at him, then laughed softly.

'Fancy thinking of food at a moment like this!' she exclaimed.

'We had coffee and rolls offered us,' put in Dora calmly, 'before we were led out to have our heads chopped off. Neither of us indulged, though.'

'Don't, Dora!' cried Sophie, and shuddered. 'I am trying to forget.'

Wallace joined Foster in the cockpit, and gave him instructions to fly high and set a north-easterly course. That young man was rapidly becoming at home and was thoroughly enjoying himself.

'It's as easy as flying a Puss Moth, sir,' he confided.

'I'm glad you think so,' smiled Sir Leonard. 'I hope you get us down as well as you got us up.'

Travelling at a height of ten thousand feet and at a speed of close on a hundred and fifty miles an hour, the magnificent aeroplane made stimulating progress towards Denmark. Sir Leonard entered the small, perfectly fitted lavatory, and leisurely removed his disguise. When he emerged his real self for the first time since leaving England, though still, of course, wearing von Strom's clothing, Hanni greeted his appearance with a cry of alarm. It took her some time to realise that he was the man who had been so wonderfully disguised as the Supreme Marshal. Dora Reinwald had fallen asleep, the Baroness von Reudath had joined her lover in the cockpit. Thither Wallace went, and she gave a little gasp as she recognised him.

'You have become yourself,' she exclaimed. 'I am glad. You were so absolutely the Supreme Marshal before that, every time I looked at you my heart jumped painfully with fear.'

'I don't think fear would ever enter that gallant heart of yours, Baroness,' he responded. 'But how is it you know me?'

'You were pointed out to me in London,' she told him. 'Oh, Sir Leonard, how can I ever thank you for—'

'Please don't try,' he implored hastily, adding, in a desperate effort to get away from an embarrassing subject: 'I wonder what that town is down there.'

'Haven't the vaguest idea, sir,' remarked Foster cheerfully, 'but it won't be long before we touch the south-east corner of Denmark. There's the sea on the horizon to our left.'

Visibility was extremely good and, flying at such a height, their range of vision was immense. After shading his eyes, and looking keenly in the direction indicated, Sir Leonard agreed that his assistant was right. It was at that moment that he became aware of three aeroplanes flying in formation a couple of thousand feet below, but apparently ascending rapidly towards them. He decided at once that their object was to cut off the air liner. Schönewald's efforts on their behalf had not altogether succeeded. The squadron had probably been sent from Hamburg, and Hamburg, therefore, must have been warned. The very visibility which had enabled them to glimpse the sea had also permitted the watchers to spot the escaping air liner. His lips came together in a tight line, but, when he spoke, his voice was calm, almost casual.

'There is going to be a little excitement,' he remarked, indicating the rapidly approaching squadron below them on the port side. 'You'll have to get every ounce of speed you can out of this bus, Foster, even if you run us out of petrol in the effort.'

The baroness paled as the significance of his remark and the three aeroplanes dawned on her. Foster grinned happily, his eyes dancing with excitement. He, apparently, was quite convinced of their ability to escape from the German airmen. The needle of the indicator rose until it was pointing at two hundred miles an hour. The aeroplane vibrated tremendously, and all within were being unmercifully shaken. Sensing that something was wrong, Cousins and his captive glanced out of one of the port windows; became at once immensely interested as they saw the three planes, now, beyond doubt, flying rapidly to cut them off. Hanni crouched in her seat in terror. Flying held no joys for her. Dora was shaken into wakefulness, and staggered to the cockpit. Sir Leonard felt her behind him, and looked round. At sight of his face she started.

'Who are you,' she queried in astonishment, 'and where did you get on?'

'My name is Wallace – Sir Leonard Wallace at your service, fraulein,' he smiled.

'Oh!' she exclaimed, and added in her usual calm drawl, 'How you have changed! Are we going to have a battle or something?'

'Not if I can help it,' was the reply. 'They'll be right ahead of us in two or three minutes,' he went on to Foster. 'When I give the word, go into a nosedive.'

The German aeroplanes rapidly came on, their course taking them in a line that was calculated to bring them directly in front of the air liner. Presently they were so close that the fugitives could see their pilots, looking, in their flying helmets and huge goggles, like grotesque creatures from another world. They also saw the machine guns with the men sitting grimly behind each. Cousin's captive paled. He realised at that moment that he was to be offered up as a sacrifice by command of the German authorities in order that the others might be destroyed.

'Are we to do any shooting, sir?' asked Cousins.

'No; of course not,' snapped Wallace then, 'Hold tight, everybody! Now, Foster!'

At the moment that the German squadron reached the same level, and were little more than fifty yards away, the command came to be immediately obeyed. The huge machine nosedived, descending sickeningly, like a rocket, beneath the others. In a few seconds it was a couple of thousand feet below them, and Sir Leonard ordered his young pilot to flatten out and go ahead. All the time his eyes were searching anxiously for other aeroplanes bent on the same mission as the squadron they had eluded, but to his relief, there were none. The nosedive had shaken the passengers considerably. Dora, who had retreated to the saloon at a word from Sir Leonard, had been torn from her grip and had fallen, bringing down the German pilot. Sophie would have slipped from her seat had not Wallace gripped her. Hanni had managed to retain her seat, but her face had turned green and she clasped a hand now tightly over her abdomen.

A desperate chase ensued, but the giant air liner, admirably controlled by Foster, succeeded in holding her own, the squadron, now frantically pursuing her, being unable to gain on her sufficiently to catch her up and disable her before she crossed the frontier. There was a general sigh of relief, even the German signifying his satisfaction, when Sir Leonard declared that they were over the border. A minute later Cousins, who had been keeping an anxious watch, strode into the cockpit to announce that the pursuing squadron had turned back.

The remainder of the journey was uneventful. Sir Leonard was rather exercised in his mind concerning the spot in England at which to land. To bring the machine to rest in a military aerodrome was out of the question – such an act would be likely to cause too many complications. To land in a civil airport would be almost as inconvenient; in addition it would give rise to endless conjectures, curiosity, and embarrassment. However, the problem was solved for him. They were approaching the coast of Essex when the petrol began to give out. Wallace sought for and found a long stretch of turf that looked safe and convenient. He ordered Foster to land there. The machine glided down beautifully. The acting pilot could not be said to have made a perfect landing. He bumped rather badly two or three times before the wheels were firmly on the ground. For one moment of suspense they all felt the great aeroplane was going over on her nose, but she righted herself, and came to rest within a few feet of a cattle pond.

'Well, that's that,' exulted Foster. 'I've brought you back in style.'

'There is style and style,' commented Cousins caustically. 'You're a lucky young devil, Bernard.'

'Lucky be hanged. You wouldn't have handled her with such skill.'

'Not if you call your performance skill. Personally I rather fancy she handled herself in spite of you.'

He had departed in search of a village and a car to convey them to London before the indignant young man could think of an apt retort. Sophie looked up at Sir Leonard with shining eyes as they stood by the side of the gigantic machine. He guessed what was coming, and hastily interposed.

'Please don't,' he pleaded. 'It isn't necessary. There is only one thing I long for now.'

'What is that?' she asked softly.

'Twelve hours of uninterrupted, solid, profound sleep,' he told her, raising his hand to his mouth to suppress a yawn.

CHAPTER TWENTY-THREE

Blessed Are The Matchmakers!

Cousins returned in half an hour seated in a car driven by a phlegmatic individual, who did not seem particularly surprised at sight of the huge air liner standing in the meadow.

The three ladies and Sir Leonard Wallace crowded in, Foster being left to look after the aeroplane and the German pilot. In the neighbouring village the chief telephoned to the Foreign Office, getting a clear line through to the Secretary of State himself. The latter was in a condition of intense excitement. He had received the very important documents sent by Gottfried from Paris. There had already been a Cabinet meeting. Sir Leonard asked that the Ambassador in Berlin should be immediately communicated with and told that he could now raise the question of the detention of Miss Meredith and Foster. The Minister was vastly interested, demanded to know details, but Sir Leonard told him they must wait. The message, however, was to be sent to the Ambassador at once with instructions to send Miss Meredith home. The Foreign Secretary promised to see that that was done. Wallace then described rapidly the borrowing of the German air liner. He impressed upon his hearer the necessity of its landing being kept as secret as possible and a supply of petrol sent to enable it to return to Germany without delay. This time the astonished statesman forbore to ask questions which he knew would not be answered until Sir Leonard chose. He declared that he would immediately communicate with the Air Minister. Wallace left the telephone satisfied that his work was completed.

Rosemary Meredith arrived by aeroplane from Berlin next day in time to be present at the hastily arranged wedding of Sophie von Reudath to Bernard Foster. Sir Leonard had pulled the necessary strings that made a marriage at such short notice possible. It was a delightfully happy affair but of necessity very quiet. Apart from the bridegroom and the bride, the only people present were Sir Leonard and Lady Wallace, Major and Mrs Brien, Rosemary Meredith, Dora Reinwald, Cousins and Mrs Manvers-Buller. The latter declared herself thrilled and certainly looked it. Sir Leonard gave the bride away, Cousins was Foster's best man. A reception was held at the Wallace home in Piccadilly after which the gloriously happy couple left for their honeymoon in Scotland. Foster had been given a month's leave of absence. When they had departed, Sir Leonard went to Downing Street to meet the Cabinet, and give his full report.

He and Lady Wallace were present at another wedding a fortnight later. Colonel Schönewald and Hilda Zeiss arrived in London very secretly from Berlin, and were married by special licence, matters once again being expedited through the influence of the Chief of the British Secret Service. Schönewald had, as had been expected, fallen into disgrace. His actual part in the escape of Sophie von Reudath and her rescuers from Germany was not suspected, but he was blamed by the Supreme Marshal for letting them get away, even though it was apparent he had had no choice in the matter. Schönewald and his wife were deeply grateful for Sir Leonard's care on their behalf. They are now living happily in Los Angeles, and frequently communicate with the man for whom they both have such tremendous respect and whom they regard as their dearest friend. They seem to think that their happiness is due in a great measure to him.

'You used to say I was a matchmaker,' Lady Wallace remarked to her husband one morning at breakfast after reading a glowing, blissful letter from Frau – now Mrs Schönewald, 'but you're just as bad – or good, whichever way one chooses to regard it.'

'Don't blame me for the Schönewald affair,' protested Sir Leonard. 'I only helped there, Molly, you know.'

'What about Sophie and Bernard Foster,' accused his wife with a smile. 'You certainly were responsible for bringing them together, Leonard.'

'Yes; I admit that,' he nodded. 'Ah, well! Blessed are the matchmakers, for theirs is the pleasure of making others happy – sometimes.'